THE THIRST

A PARANORMAL VAMPYR ROMANCE

REMY CAVILICH

The Thirst: A Paranormal Vampyr Romance

This book is dedicated to the feeling I get when I write the last page in a story,
When my mind is at peace and my characters are quiet.
When every word is finally out of my mind and on the page before me.
But mostly, this book is dedicated to the hope that one day, my kids will stop asking me what I'm writing and my husband will find a new friend to converse with when I am trying to tell a story.

Just kidding, I love them all.

Most of the time. But not at deadline time.

CHAPTER 1

~LUCIEN~

Darkness.

It's always the first thing I notice when I wake; before I even open my eyes. Always the silent, brooding darkness. It envelops me in a cold, bone-chilling hug as I realize, once again, I am alone.

Slowly, my eyelids peel themselves back unwillingly as my blood-red irises adjust to the faint glow of light from across the room. The solitary candle flickers in the slight breeze that I can't seem to find the source of, though I've tried many times. Must be a draft of air somewhere, a crack in the old walls of this victorian monstrosity.

Whoever's idea it was to rent me this huge house, this vast, unending, empty reminder of my desolation, really did have a dark sense of humor. And such a cliche. Of all the places to house a vampyr like myself, did they have to shove me in the cheap leftover props from a B-rated horror movie?

My eyes had adjusted well to the dim interior of the old parlor; I felt the faint tug of little-used muscles pulling at my stone countenance in the vague reminiscent shadow of what passed for a smile. *How long had it been since I truly smiled?*

Surely forever.

The butler I'd had since I was a boy must have left the candle for me in some small gesture of kindness. The smart man had obviously learned by now that I could see just fine in the dark without light, as I'd had to find my way to him with no assistance many times in our long past, but Jasper kept treating me like I was…

Like I was still human.

Ah, there's something I try not to dwell on—my sordid past as a human. And I had made a terrible one, for sure. Awkward, reserved, unsure. Always looking over my shoulder, no matter where I went, afraid of my own mortality. What a sick twist of fate that I would one day become what I was, and turn into an entirely different being, both in body and in mind. My very soul, if I still had one, had become warped over so many years of watching men who were just like who I used to be, tearing each other apart as the generations came and went.

I had let life pass in front of me as I became accustomed to being a creature of the night, content to watch the world burn, as they say, while I sat in my high tower, never aging, never changing, but always watching. The few humans I'd interacted with since I'd turned had known I was unnatural. Their very instinct warned them to flee from me, and so they did—most without a second glance.

It would be nice if someone would choose to stay, for once. I'd long ago given up on having any sort of happiness or love in life. It was ridiculous to expect anyone normal to fall for a creature of the night, one nobody believed existed. After all, if a woman ever knew the true me, she'd die from shock, or have herself committed to an insane asylum.

Sure, I'd frequented hookers and ladies of the night in my heyday, preferring the company of the women who came with no strings attached and wanted nothing from me. They relieved my more primal urges, and I fed on some of them on occasion while they were passed out from their highs. The high-priced Italian hookers had always shown up on some designer drug or another, and it would be a lie to say it wasn't enjoyable to feed on the secondary buzz.

But drugs were never my thing, and it got old, fast. Soon, I wasn't sure if I was still visiting the same women, or their daughters. The satisfaction from these antics having waned, I withdrew to the solitude of a bachelor's life. I remained there until the day I'd stumbled across a newspaper from America, announcing a Vampire Museum being built in the states by the rich husband of a half-Romani immigrant. The woman's image had appeared on the front page next to the building, and she was stunning, but it wasn't the older couple I was drawn to.

No, it was the image of the woman who stood behind them, wearing a very sharp, professional skirt and blouse that looked like they'd been plucked out of my own centuries-old closet. Her flaxen hair flowed down over her shoulders in the tightest little corkscrew curls, and I'd had to resist the urge to reach out into the picture and brush them from her face. Somehow, I just knew they'd bounce in a light breeze as she laughed, holding her skirt down to prevent embarrassment.

Her full lips were coated in a lipstick so dark the red was almost black, and her eyes…

Her eyes were golden in the sunlight, which was impossible. It must have been those decorative lenses I'd seen people wearing for Halloween in the states. But she intrigued me, more than I cared to admit. And though I'd been running from it for years, I had some unfinished business in the States to attend to, so Jasper and I had packed up and come across the ocean without so much as a question about my erratic change in routine.

The same routine I'd stuck to for hundreds of years. Never changed, never altered. I'd been known to throw a fit if a single minute in my schedule was unaccounted for or misused. But I just uprooted us at the snap of a finger, and the quiet, unassuming man who'd been with me practically since birth had reacted as if it was normal for us.

As if on cue, he appeared at my doorway, his footsteps signaling his arrival just moments before I heard the old creaking of the mahogany door straining against the brass hinges.

"Ah, Young Master, you're awake. How was your rest?"

I shook my head at his ridiculous choice of words. "Just because I've been frozen in time at twenty-nine doesn't mean I'm young. I don't know why you insist on that title when I'm centuries old, Jasper."

His hesitant smile broke the somber atmosphere, and he handed me the daily newspaper that I'd missed, of course, being asleep during the day. "Your paper, sir. And my apologies for the title; if you'd like, I could stop using it."

I truly did smile at that one, my skin stretching taut as my lips curled up involuntarily at his lie. Of course, I'd asked him before to stop calling me 'Young Master', but the man had simply ceased for a few days before reverting to his old habits.

You truly can't teach an old dog new tricks.

"You and I both know you won't be able to help yourself, so there's no use in me asking. But that's beside the point." I glanced down to the newspaper, hoping the Times had decided to run another article on this stupid Vampire Museum. To my dismay, they had not, but of course, I hadn't expected to see my beauty on the cover again. After all, she hadn't been the center of the article. She'd simply been in the background, probably someone's assistant.

But I would find her. And soon.

"Do you plan to go to the ribbon-cutting ceremony at the museum, sir? It should be cloudy that day, so dark will fall earlier."

I scoffed at the idea that I would burst into flames or dust at the simple touch of sunlight. Obviously, the old legends had to come from some sort of truth, and they were half-right. If the sunlight hit my bare skin for an extended period of time, I would start to burn. Badly. For a lesser vampyr, that would usually be fatal. But I was one of the oldest living vampyrs left on Earth.

Living? Was that really what I was? Living? Was I alive, in the sense that I needed sustenance to survive? Or in the sense that my mind and my lungs still worked? That I needed my heart to beat, or that I needed to breathe in the air around me still, even as a member of the illustrious undead?

Shaking my head to rid myself of the wayward thoughts, I turned my focus back to the newspaper in my hands. "Yes, I do plan to go to that ceremony. I was thinking of dressing in period clothing, to blend in."

To his credit, Jasper didn't even so much as snicker as he turned towards the windows, pulling the curtains back with a quick flick of his wrist. "I think that would be...*interesting*. Do you want to blend in, or do you want them to put you on display?"

Now I really *did* smile. It wasn't as painful this time, and I hesitated as I pondered my sudden change in mood. Why had I suddenly found myself so lighthearted, so...free? My moods had always been morose, bleak, and full of self-hatred. Now, I was...*excited? Anxious?*

Something must be wrong with me, I am sure of it. There is no way a single human could affect such an advanced, well-traveled vampyr like myself. It would be absolutely comical to think all this had been brought on by a woman who I hadn't ever met.

CHAPTER 2

~IZZY~

I really should change those blinds, I thought to myself as I eyed the torn, ragged, sun-bleached slats hanging from the rail above the sliding glass door. Outside the glass that I'd forgotten to clean sat an absolutely gorgeous view of the beach, where my parents vacationed every summer. Their sweeping two-story summer home was a sight to behold on its own, but the stucco walls and clay roof tiles paled in comparison to the white sands that were basically our backyard.

A light knock on my bedroom door pulled me from my thoughts. The familiar pattern belonged to our housekeeper, Rosalinda. Before I could care for myself, Rosa had been my nanny, taking young me under her wing as if I were just another of her own children. These days, I took care of myself, as most twenty-eight-year-old women were wont to do; and Rosa had become our maid when I'd outgrown a nanny. No matter her job title, though, Rosa always had a shoulder for me to cry on when things got rough.

Too bad it hadn't been my own mother's shoulder I'd leaned on.

Shaking my head, I rose from my usual spot at the desk, heading to open the door for my old friend.

"Good morning, *mija*. I see you're already awake." Rosa's accent was thick from her time in her homeland, but I had picked up her special blend of Spanglish over the years and understood every word.

I smiled at my only friend in this lonely existence I called a life. "Rosa, what a pleasant surprise. I didn't know you were coming with us this year."

She cast her eyes at the floor, fidgeting nervously in place as she avoided my gaze. "Well, *mija*, since they're occupied with some personal issues, I decided to stay with you this summer. *Mi familia* will be okay without me for a summer. Besides," she said, looking up suddenly, "I've always wanted to see the white beaches of Florida."

"Well, you'll get your chance. Do you know if my parents will be back today? I have an important gallery opening tonight at the Museum, and I was hoping they'd find the time to attend."

Rosa's lips turned down in a scowl as she fumed, her next words laced with anger on my behalf.

"No, the Mister and Missus will not be home this evening. They left for the country club some hours ago."

Of course they wouldn't be around. They never want to see me unless I'm to be displayed like their greatest trophy. I turned to the window, a single tear escaping from between my lashes as I blinked furiously, trying to maintain my composure. This would hardly be the first time my parents had missed a huge event in my life. I'd been lucky to have my drivers, or I'd probably have walked home from many recitals and awards over the years. So many times, a younger, naive me had scanned the crowd of proud parents, hoping that maybe this time, they'd come to see me.

But they never did, and I'd had Rosa and my drivers to witness the soul-shattering disappointment and wipe my tears.

After a while, I'd stopped feeling. I just *was;* nothing more. Emotions got in the way; they made you weak. It was the only lesson my parents had taught me, though they'd never intended to.

"Would you like to come to the gallery opening, Rosa? As the only Stanton in residence, I believe it's within my power to give you the night off. And I could use a friendly face in the crowd. I *hate* mingling."

A shudder ran through my body at the idea of talking to strangers. I much preferred to be in the background; conversation had never been my strong suit, much to my parents' dismay. Part of me suspected that my introverted nature was part of why they pulled away from me so young. My personality was like night to their day, reserved to their outgoing. Like oil and water, we didn't mix well.

Maybe I was adopted, and they couldn't bring themselves to reveal the scandal. It would certainly explain a lot.

*I*t was no secret that I never interacted with other people if I didn't have to. I much preferred the solitude of my own company and that of my animals.

"What should I wear?" Rosa asked. Gesturing at her work-stained cleaning sweats, she added, "I don't think this will fit in with *tu gente.*"

Wrinkling my nose at the thought of the rich clientele looking down their noses at my dear friend, I nodded in agreement. "I think you'd be fine to wear a plain black dress. Maybe the one you wore to my graduation?"

Rosa nodded. "Si, *mija.*"

"I think that would work just fine. You could ride with me, but I have to be in early to help the curator set up."

Rosa's smiles were usually contagious, but I had settled into my resting bitch face; it was stuck like glue, hiding my inner turmoil from the world. Still, my eyes softened as I took in Rosa's genuine excitement.

"Oh, thank you, but I should be fine. The driver can come back for me, and I'll meet you there."

My eyes drifted off, the pain in my head rising. Another anxiety session was coming fast, and it was going straight through the roof. *Damn you; now you're going to take this moment away from me too?*

"I think I should get ready, Rosa." I rubbed at my temples, sighing in frustration, and Rosa took that as her cue to leave. She was familiar with the signs of my oncoming anxiety, and she disappeared out into the hallway without another word.

I found myself alone once more. Just how I liked it. But deep down, buried under years of disappointment, rage, and sadness, was the little flickering of hope that someday I'd meet someone I could be myself around. Someone I could sleep next to without my crippling anxiety kicking into overdrive. Someone who loved me, not just because it had been their job or because of what I could offer, but for *me.*

Flawed pieces and all.

The Museum Curator was an absolute mess, from his slightly askew tie to his ruffled ascot. He ran his hands through his hair for the umpteenth time as he sighed.

"I just don't understand why one of our biggest benefactors would pull out last-minute. This is an absolute *disaster*, Miss Stanton. One we cannot afford on opening night for the Vampire Wing." His eyes scanned the crowd mingling about on the floor below his vantage point in the second-floor, glass-walled office. He turned on me, his eyes wild and panicked as his night suddenly got much, much worse. "Lady Daniels is here. Just when I thought it couldn't get any worse. How am I supposed to tell our owner I lost the biggest account of the night?"

I shook my head, knowing *exactly* where this was headed. I didn't like it one bit, either, but I knew it would fall to me to fix the problem that stared us in the face like a looming storm on the horizon.

"What are you thinking, Curator Chandless?"

He eyed my Victorian-era steampunk outfit warily, no doubt wondering just how weird his assistant truly was.

If only he knew.

"I was thinking maybe you could schmooze the other benefactors, maybe encourage them to open their wallets a little further." His lecherous gaze slid down to rest on my protruding chest. *Damn this corset top.* "With your wonderful costume—"

"Not a costume, sir."

"—and your beauty, you probably won't have to work too hard to squeeze another five million out of a couple of these rich snobs."

Is he for real? "I'm sorry, sir, for a moment, I thought you said five million dollars."

Mr. Chandless cleared his throat, trying to rid his voice of the high-pitched squeak brought on by panic. "Ahem, yes, I *did* say five million dollars. US currency, I'm afraid. Dr. Whitman pulled out last minute due to some personal matters—which I can only begin to guess at—and we cannot afford to lose that large of a chunk of money on opening night. So either help me fill the gap, or find a new employer. If we don't fix this, both of us will be out of a job."

I chose tactfully not to comment on the fact that *I* had not screwed anything up. Neither had the boss, for that matter; however, the responsibility to find the lost revenue would fall solely on his shoulders, and then on to mine by proxy. My expression remained neutral as I tugged nervously at my corset, the feel of the smooth metal eyelets beneath my fingertips helping to calm me as I began to protest.

"What would you have me do, sir? I am not knowledgeable with any of our clientele; I'm more familiar with the money than the people."

Mr. Chandless clapped excitedly, assuming I'd followed his line of thought in the same direction he had. *A bold assumption, considering I was still lost.*

"Ah, see, that's the rub. You know money. And having two parents who are socialites, you must know some of the rich people coming tonight to the opening gala. It should be easy for you to schmooze them, dropping hints that we hadn't quite made the goal yet, and working them to fill the gap for us."

I threw my hands up, stomping on my mental brakes so fast I swore smoke would leak out my ears. "Hold up - when I took this job, I told you I don't socialize well. I'm not like my parents-"

"Well," he said, staring me down intimidatingly, "you're just gonna have to learn quickly and wing it. I'll handle the big bosses, and you make fast work of separating these people from their money."

He rushed out the door without another word, pausing only to eye his reflection and adjust his tie in a wall mirror before heading down the staircase to greet the museum's founder. I tried to swallow the bile rising in my throat at the idea of socializing with these absolute strangers, knowing I couldn't afford to be sick right now.

This job was the only thing keeping me from being dependent on my parents' money for survival; until my career took off -if it ever would- I needed to save all I could to prepare to leave this godforsaken place behind.

I'd never run from responsibility before, and I was damn sure not going to start now. I just hoped I could get through tonight without losing my lunch all over some rich woman's Versace dress.

Squaring my shoulders, I lifted my head and plastered a one-million-watt smile on my ruby red lips, following the same path my boss had blazed just moments before. If I don't get a raise for this, I swear to God…

On the main floor, people wearing my month's salary around their necks and wrists mingled as only the rich can do: oozing contempt for the help, hurling veiled insults at others, and gossiping in corners—all while sparkling like the sun in the darkness of the dimmed gallery. My black lace ensemble seemed so dull compared to the golds and silvers and whites of the evening, but I'd wanted to celebrate the opening in true gothic fashion. After all, it was just as much my baby as it was the owners'. I'd traveled to other museums across the globe to help procure some of the ancient writings and artwork that were now displayed in cabinets of thick, bulletproof glass or hanging on the walls in a carefully guarded gallery room.

So much time I'd spent in this building as they'd constructed it, insisting on specific Victorian details to give the building the authentic gothic atmosphere this collection deserved. My efforts had gone mostly unnoticed, mostly because Mr. Chandless had been content to take all the credit for the things I'd done that were praise-worthy. *Men, in my experience, were usually like that.*

After greeting what seemed like a thousand random strangers, I could feel my heart hammering against my chest, social anxiety in full-blown panic mode as I struggled to regain control of my breathing.

Why am I like this? I'd been to thousands of social events, I'd talked to millions of people over the phone and in person, mostly strangers. But in a room of people who won't remember my name ten minutes from now, I can't keep calm. I felt sick to my stomach.

Reaching for a glass of red wine from the nearest waiter passing by, I slowly approached the back door marked *Employees Only.* Behind it lay a small hallway that sent me spiraling into a bout of claustrophobia as I rushed towards the freedom of the last door between myself and fresh air. As I burst into the back alley behind the museum, I breathed a sigh of relief, doubling over as black spots danced at the edge of my vision.

Oh, for the love of all that's holy, if I pass out—

One look at the grimy brick path beneath my feet told me I *absolutely did not* want to end up lying on the ground, unconscious. Forcing deep breaths into my lungs, I reached inside my corset and removed a small metal container. The fancy engravings caught the light from the streetlamp above as I rotated the box, flipping it open. I pulled a hand-rolled joint from the box and replaced it in my corset, adjusting it discreetly before patting myself down for a lighter.

Shit.

"Where did I put that stupid thing," I muttered, feeling around frantically for the damned lighter. Just as I was about to give up, my fingertips brushed against the familiar cold steel of my grandfather's Zippo. I brought the lighter up to the thin white stick dangling loosely from my lips, already collecting a stain from my lipstick. I took a drag off the smoke, closing my eyes as I folded my arms across my chest.

As if I could hold myself together with the empty gesture.

After finishing off the smoke, I turned to thrust myself unwillingly back into this hell I'd been dragged into. *Time to mingle.* The thought made me wince as the hallway closed in behind me once again, the metal clang of the heavy door hitting its frame reminding me ominously of a jail cell closing.

The irony is truly remarkable.

CHAPTER 3

~LUCIEN~

The sleek black car pulled up to the side of the brightly lit building, the tinted windows doing their job as they obscured me from the view of people straining to see who had arrived. My driver rapped his meaty knuckles against the divider glass, rolling it down without waiting for a reply from his boss. Me.

How typical. These young men today have no manners.

"You gon' be gettin' out 'ere, master?"

His deep, gravelly voice grated against my normally calm nerves, making me question my own sanity for even accepting this invitation. Of *course* my last living relative would decide to build a "Museum of Vampires". The irony is actually quite laughable, when I can be bothered with it.

The lawyer's letter landed on my desk about six months ago, mixed in with a pile of junk mail and bills. I'd contacted the sender, unsure if they'd just mailed the official-looking envelope to the wrong guy. After all, it was addressed to *Luke Sabatini,* not my proper name, Lucien Sabatini II. Inside the letter was a single sheet of paper, with a note attached to it. The letter was a results test from one of those intriguing genealogy websites, with my name listed as a possible relative. Below my name was my brother's daughter Renata, listed as a possible relative, and a DNA match to what must have been her offspring. The note contained two sentences:

Your name popped up during a search for our missing relatives, with a mailing address and not much else. We would appreciate a few moments of your time to speak about our possible relation.

When I'd finally decided to call—more out of curiosity than anything else—I'd been surprised to find a well-educated, outspoken woman by the name of Padmi on the other end of the line. She'd been given up for adoption at birth, and she'd been eager to trace her lineage when she came of age. Padmi had managed to track me down using old property liens and tax paperwork. She had been convinced that maybe some property had been handed down in a trust or an estate, thus the reason for the unchanged name, but I found myself admitting the truth was much more complicated.

I'd flown to the States, and we'd linked her parentage backward to my brother, Ulrich. He was born in 1785, and he'd had his daughter Renata in 1803, the same year I was born. Her son, Maximus, my great-nephew, fathered two children out of wedlock before he died in 1908. One of those illegitimate children had been Padmi's grandmother, Maxine, and she'd settled here, having ten children.

Her only surviving child was Padmi's mother, Elizabeth. She had married a Romani immigrant. Of course, luck wasn't a thing that ran in their family, and she'd died in childbirth, following her husband, who'd been taken months before.

Padmi had bounced around in the system, as all her relatives were dead, but not for long. An Indian couple had adopted her and raised her, but she'd always wanted to know who she was. So, she'd put her DNA and what she had been able to find out about her birth parents into the website, and she'd found me.

I took a liking to her instantly, and though I didn't tell her my secret, I came close. Perhaps too close. And to my surprise, after five months with little to no contact, she'd sent me a letter of invitation to a grand opening of a museum she'd founded.

The Victorian Vampire Museum. *Fucking spectacular.*

I felt compelled to accept the invitation, but I hadn't been sold on the whole idea until she'd sent me the newspaper edition that I'd spotted my flaxen-haired beauty in. A shudder ran down my spine as I closed my eyes for a moment, imagining her all over again. Her long, blonde curls blowing in the breeze. Her full, pouting lips, begging to be kissed.

I sound like a cheesy Edwardian poet. Poe must have rubbed off on me more than I thought.

"Sir?"

The single word yanked me out of my own headspace and dropped me back into this hellish reality that was my never-ending life. I glanced over at the handle of the car door, reaching out to grab its smooth surface. With a single nod to the driver, I stepped out, pulling my overcoat tighter around me in an unconscious gesture of distrust.

I felt like the quintessential Bram Stroker cliche—*damn that man*—and it felt oddly satisfying, considering the atmosphere. Everywhere I looked were rich, entitled pricks schmoozing to have their name put on the side of this enormous building. From their bodies to their personalities, everything about them was fake. I had no intentions to make the rounds, so to speak. I would stop in, tell my great-great-great-niece hello and congratulations, and politely excuse myself.

There were better ways to spend my night.

I wove through the crowd, moving smoothly from room to room, gallery after gallery of endless vampyr history and artwork passing by in a blur. I had finally spotted my relation across the room, but before I could move another inch, I heard the most beautiful sound in the world.

"Like I was saying, Sir Conan, while we appreciate your charitable donation, you've been passed up in the rankings for the honorary dedication by your ex-wife and another anonymous benefactor."

Her voice was as sweet as a songbird on the first day of

spring, her beautiful blonde hair hanging loosely over her shoulder as she leaned into a man who was much older than herself, his eyes plastered to her full chest. I watched as she laughed at his response, but I had stopped listening to him. I had eyes and ears for only her, *mio bellissimo amore. The woman from the newspaper photo.*

The black tulle of her skirt swished around her ankles as she moved to detangle herself from the handsy, drunk benefactor. I watched her lean against the pillar beside her, those long, slender fingers caressing the stone carvings lovingly, as if she'd designed them herself. Her luscious lips were smiling; though I could tell from experience, it was forced.

I myself was a master at the art of falsifying human interactions.

Her body was stunning, curving in all the right places, her skin tinged with a healthy glow and a nice, natural tan, something I missed quiet often as a vampyr. The only thing between me and looking sickeningly pale was my Italian blended heritage. I'd been avoiding the sun for so long, I forgot what it was like to be warmed by its rays without turning into a hot mess. But if I could remember what it felt like, I imagined it would feel something like what I felt simply by being around this wonderful angel before me.

"Well, why don't you and I discuss increasing my donation, somewhere a little more *private*?" Sir Conan pleaded with her to go off with him, and I could tell she was starting to grow uncomfortable.

Without a second thought, I watched as my body acted independently, reaching a hand towards her in greeting as I maneuvered myself between my angel and this leech. I heard myself speak, but I was no longer in control. I'd lost my mind.

"I'm sorry, miss, but I couldn't help but overhear you're looking for benefactors for the museum? Allow me to introduce myself." I took one of her small hands in my own, pulling her to the safety of the other side of the room before speaking again. To my delight, Sir Conan the Inebriated didn't follow us.

I turned back to the beautiful, albeit stunned woman before me. "Lucien Sabatini, at your service, *cara mia.*"

She blinked in disbelief, unable to believe her luck, I suppose. I'd pay to know what was going through her head as she worked to form a response.

~Izzy~

The man standing in front of me was absolutely stunning. His refined demeanor somehow seemed right at home in the dark interior of the gallery, a pair of crimson, brooding eyes staring down into my own from his stoic face. My mind didn't linger over his strange eye color, focusing instead on his prominent jawline and tall stature, which only added to his classical appeal. Standing by him made me feel almost insignificant as I stared up at his face, admiring the way his long hair hung in a low ponytail at the nape of his neck. It reminded me of a dandy from the 19th century, and I had to force myself not to focus too long on his toned, lean figure and ethereal good looks. If a man could still be considered beautiful, he was the definition of it. I swallowed my anxiety from the incident with Sir Conan, grateful for the gentleman who'd saved me from being pawed by a British millionaire.

Lucien. It sounds so…dangerous.

"A beautiful woman such as yourself must have an equally beautiful name. May I know it?" His lips turned up into a smile as he studied me carefully, my hand still cradled gently in his own. A shiver went down my spine as he ran his fingers absently over my knuckles, my knees feeling oddly like Jell-O. My mouth was drier than the Sahara, and I struggled to remember the process of breathing.

It's an automatic process, you dipshit. Get it together, I reminded myself—no time to swoon over hot, rich men. I had a job to do. I couldn't dwell on his particular manner of speech or the way those arms of his might feel around me. *Jesus, I'm losing it.*

"Lizzania Stanton, assistant curator of the museum." I could feel the shift in my body from panicked victim to efficient schmoozer, the transition happening almost effortlessly once I had my libido *somewhat* under control. "This project is my personal baby, and it's a wonderful thing to see all my hard work culminated in a sizable collection like this one."

I watched one perfectly sculpted eyebrow raise at the mention of my work, as if he'd forgotten where he was. "This is *your work?*" His lips curled up in a smile, revealing perfectly straight, white teeth that somehow seemed...unnatural. They were too straight, too uniform, too white. Too perfect.

"Yes. I helped pull the museum together under the direction of Mrs. Daniels herself. Some of our pieces have come from as far away as Transylvania and as close as our very own backyards. I traveled to many museums and private collectors to solicit this wonderful collection you see before you." I knew I sounded a bit conceited, but I couldn't help but be proud of what we had here. What *I* had here. Too bad only the curator knew how much work I'd poured into this project, and he wasn't about to share credit.

The statuesque man before me rubbed his jaw absently as he glanced around, taking in the paintings around us. His intriguing eyes locked onto a cabinet in the corner, holding a collection I'd had to work particularly hard to obtain.

It had been nearly impossible to separate it from its owner, who had looked as if he'd been running from death for years. He'd told me he wasn't accepting offers, but when I said it would be immortalized in a museum, he was all too happy to name his price.

His price nearly bowled me over, but I'd gotten used to the rich elite throwing money around for whatever struck their fancy. So, I swallowed my apprehension at the gross frivolity and reckless abandon with which they parted with their money and handed over the blank check my boss had given me to use for this exact thing.

In the cabinet Mr. Sabatini had been drawn to sat three significant pieces which were flanked by other very noteworthy mentions. Seeing an opportunity, I tried to reel him in like a fish in the hopes that I could encourage him to help cover the gap I still hadn't quite bridged yet.

"Ah, I see you noticed my crowning jewel of the entire collection. The original copy of *Dracula,* courtesy of a true collector." At my mention of the book that defined vampire subculture, he groaned, his eyes rolling as if in mockery. Ignoring his odd reaction, I plowed on. "The same collector also parted with his copy of *The Giaour,* one of the first-ever references to vampires in literature, from 1813. It's the only first edition left in the world. And the last focal piece here is—"

"*The Vampyre*. First edition. And I believe this one was owned by John William Polidori himself. Lord Ruthven was a favorite character of mine. I very much romanticized his brooding personality and reckless attitude as a boy."

This man must be off his rocker. These people lived hundreds of years ago, and these books weren't exactly something fitting for a young child. I figured maybe he was a little eccentric. Most rich folks had some weird quirks, but then again, when you had the money to throw at a problem and make it disappear, you could afford to be eccentric and weird.

That was a luxury I'd never been able to afford.

"Ah, yes. According to the previous owner, it *was* Polidori's personal copy of their first printed edition." I swallowed my discomfort, trying my best to display my personal knowledge on the pieces that seemed to intrigue this devilishly handsome stranger. "You seem to know a lot about vampire culture—"

"I would hardly call it a *culture*, young lady." He patronized me as if he was vastly older than myself, which was impossible if one went by his looks. But his mannerisms…well, they were the sort of quirks that made one refer to a person as being 'in the wrong time'; as if he belonged to another era altogether. "More like an exclusive, members-only club of degenerates and reckless idiots. It's more like a curse, really."

He was speaking as if he himself was a vampire in disguise. This guy must be one of those super role-play fang chasers, the kind who treated vampirism as a kink. I had to admit, I understood. I, too, fantasized about being whisked away in the dead of night by my very own horror story creature.

But this was reality, and I kept reminding myself I had a job to do.

"Well, you know, those with the means to support the cause should use them wisely."

"Ah, a paraphrased Austen quote. You're well-read."

I was used to nodding silently as I smiled, accepting compliments, but somehow, it sounded genuine when the compliment came from his mouth. And for once, the first thing I'd been complimented on was my intelligence. Or my love of books. But still, both were better than being told I'm pretty. I would rather they notice me for what I've done, not what I look like.

It wasn't an achievement to be beautiful.

"Jane Austen was a wonderful writer. And she's vastly underappreciated, in my opinion. But that's beside the point. You see, the weak fail to follow through on their promises, and so we've lost a large benefactor tonight. His name would have hung on the walls of this museum, but he pulled his check at the eleventh hour, and without his generous support, we come up short on the whole affair. So you see, a man such as yourself could be an immense help-"

"So you want money." His voice was flat, lacking all the emotion from before, which pulled at my heartstrings a bit. I knew what it was like only to be wanted for the material things you had to offer. And I'd just compared him to a virtual wallet.

"I-I didn't mean to offend." *Shit. Way to go, idiot, insult the rich man.* I'd be lucky if he didn't announce my stupidity to the entire group of charitable benefactors.

Just when I thought it couldn't get any worse, I noticed my boss heading towards me, his gait so fast he almost ran right into me. And behind him? Mrs. Daniels, the owner, founder, and the source of my livelihood.

Just as I realized my situation had gone from bad to worse, Mr. Chandless opened his mouth to speak, leering at my chest the whole time. It was evident from his slurred speech that he had already imbibed a little too much.

"Ah, Miss Stanton, how are you doing this evening? I'm so glad we found you; Mrs. Daniels was hoping to see that special cabinet of vampire stuff you put together."

"Actually, I just finished showing it off to Mister Sabatini here. He was very knowledgeable about our rare collection, Mrs. Daniels."

Padmi beamed from ear to ear, reaching out to shake the hand of the man. "This is the relative I've been telling you about, Mr. Chandless. Meet Sir Lucien Sabatini, ancestor to the famous Italian architect Francesco Sabatini. I see you've already met my very talented Assistant Curator, Lizzania."

Lucien grinned down at me as if I were a piece of meat for a brief second, and when I blinked, his eyes were back to their normal, unexpressive selves, making me question what I'd really seen. The atmosphere of the museum was getting to me.

"Why yes, I did meet the lovely Miss Stanton. She's been very accommodating in explaining the collection to me. Did you know she worked extensively to gather you the most perfect and riveting pieces of vampire folklore and literature?"

Beside me, I felt Mr. Chandless stiffen, and I realized I'd royally screwed up by telling this stranger my hidden truths. One little slip, and it may have just cost me my job. I felt Rick's hand wrap around my upper arm menacingly, his meaty hands tightening against my bare skin as I struggled not to make a scene. My throat constricted, and my anxiety was through the roof. Suddenly, I couldn't speak.

"Oh, is that so? Well, Rick, why did you never tell me you had such a talented and devoted assistant? You'd better not let go of that one. It's hard to find true dedication."

Padmi Daniels nodded a dismissal at the two of us as she led her cousin towards the private conference rooms.

However, I was rooted to the spot, as Curator Chandless had still held my arm in his vice-like grip.

"I thought we had an understanding that understudies don't get credit. And you go around tonight of all nights, spinning your sob story?" He chuckled maliciously, starting to tug me along as he made his way across the crowded gallery. We passed the conference room where my boss and her family member had just disappeared, and my whole body tensed. I realized as Rick pulled me further past the doors that he had no good intentions, and I'd better separate myself, fast.

CHAPTER 4

~IZZY~

"P-please, Mr. Chandless-"

He yanked my arm practically out of the socket as I struggled weakly, trying to escape his iron grip. "You're not getting off that easily. You and me, we need to have a little chat."

When we reached the bottom of the stairs, I planted my feet firmly against the first step, hoping someone else would notice his alarming behavior and intervene, but most guests had moved into the open gallery to mingle in better lighting. We were all alone on this side of the museum, and Rick knew it.

I'd never seen my boss drunk, and he'd never before done more than stare at my breasts a little too long, maybe commenting on my legs. He'd certainly never been aggressive towards me, but alcohol and stress had a way of turning the best of people into a completely different version of themselves.

"If I have to yank you up these godforsaken stairs the whole way, you'll regret it, Miss Stanton. I suggest you stop acting like a disobedient pup and come along." His teeth were bared in a malicious grin as his arm twisted mine uncomfortably, making me cry out in pain. I'd never know true fear until this very moment, and if I ever got out of this situation, I would make sure to never put myself in a similar one again.

"Hey, that hurts, sir!"

"I told you we're going up these stairs to have a chat. I don't want to hurt you, but you leave me no choice."

Where had this man come from? This can't be my boss!

"Sir, please, I think you've had too much to drink; you're not yourself-"

I recoiled in shock as his free hand connected sharply with the soft skin of my cheek, eliciting a gasp at the pain. I felt the sting of tears forming behind my eyes, and I blinked frantically to fight them back, refusing to let this man see me cry. His voice was a low snarl now, and I could clearly see just how much trouble I was in.

His eyes were glassy; his pupils dilated from the copious amounts of alcohol he'd imbibed. His stale breath smelled like cheap vodka as he leaned closer, his words low and angry. Frantic, I scanned the room again for any sign of help, finding none. *Shit.*

"I've seen the looks you give me in my office. I know you want me, Lizah," he growled, screwing up my name in the process. *Had he even bothered to learn my actual name, or had he been calling me wrong this whole time?* I turned my eyes back to his face, my terror plain as day to his predatory eyes. "I've grown tired of this game, Miss Stanton."

"As have I." From over my shoulder came the voice of salvation, and I had to bite back the urge to fall to the floor in a heap of tears and hysteria. My mind was racing, and my vision was spotty at best. I felt like the whole room was closing in on me as Rick's eyes narrowed, redirecting their piercing gaze to Mr. Sabatini, who must have been standing right behind me.

Rick didn't seem to realize he'd been caught and continued to pull on my arm, a little less aggressively this time. "Why don't you mind your business, sir. The lady and I are just going upstairs for a little chat-"

"You'd better let the lady go, you filthy pig, before I break your arm

off and beat you with it." The words were quiet and calm, as if he were discussing the weather, but I felt an eerie chill settle around the three of us as he stepped beside me, reaching out a single hand to pry Mr. Chandless's fingers away from my arm. When their hands connected, Rick yanked his back like a flash of lightning, his eyes wide and fearful. I watched as he sputtered in place for a moment before taking a few steps up the stairs behind himself, his eyes never leaving Lucien's.

It was almost as if he was afraid to turn his back on the man.

"You seem to get into a lot of trouble with men, *signora."* His words drug my hyperventilating wreck of a self back to the present. I realized Rick had disappeared, and I was just standing there at the end of the stairs, my heels dug in as if still expecting to be drug away. I concentrated hard on relaxing my body as I moved away from the rail, running my fingers through my hair in a feeble attempt to calm my racing heart.

It wasn't working, and I was sure to pass out at this rate.

"Uh, yeah, I guess I have had a bit of an eventful night." *Think, dammit. I've gotta get out of here before I have a breakdown.* "I should thank you for your help, Mr. Sabatini. This is twice now you've rescued me from a tight spot."

He raised one perfectly sculpted eyebrow at my choice of words, his ire plain as day. "Tight spots? That was your boss who assaulted you, was it not?"

I felt my cheeks warm at my embarrassment. If you had told me earlier today that I'd almost be molested by my boss tonight, I'd have laughed you out of the room. But something about him had always been off, and I'd always chalked it up to male chauvinism. Surely, it had been the liquor that had turned him into a monster tonight.

"He was drunk. I'm sure by tomorrow he-"

"He won't *have a job* tomorrow. I'll make sure of that."

Before I could reply to him, I heard a familiar Spanish accent calling out to me from across the room.

"*Mija,* I've been looking all over for you!" Rosalina had

dolled herself up and was quite attractive for her age, her megawatt smile blinding but contagious, as I felt myself smile in genuine happiness at her arrival.

Things were getting awkward fast, and I needed an ally tonight.

"Ah, *tia*, I'm glad you're here. Meet Mr. Lucien Sabatini, Mrs. Daniels' cousin."

He extended his hand out to take hers, but Rosa's smile faltered as her fingers connected with his for a brief moment. "I'm pleased to make your acquaintance, *signora*."

"I'm sorry, Mr. Sabatini, but Izzy and I have some *muy importante* things to discuss."

Rosalina grabbed my hand and practically fled from the room at warp speed, and I cast a glance back at Lucien Sabatini as I was dragged from the room. His piercing crimson eyes stared back at my own, watching me quizzically as I disappeared around the large double doors into the gallery beyond.

"I don't like that man, *mija*. Bad juju. Something's not right about him, I'm telling you."

She'd caught me staring at him again. We'd sat down along the far wall to people-watch while the fundraiser/opening night gala wound down. Rosa usually rode home with me, which meant she stayed till we closed up. And tonight would be a late one, but I knew she wouldn't complain. She was a trooper.

And she worried about me a lot.

"Rosa, he's just a rich guy. And if you've forgotten, he rescued me from being assaulted by Mr. Chandless-"

"I've always known *that* one was a snake." She folded her arms over her ample chest, huffing at my nimble dance around her concern. "But I'm telling you, there's something unnatural about that man. I feel it in my bones."

I shook my head at her superstitious mojo and forced myself to not immediately look back over in the direction of the handsome man I couldn't keep my eyes off of. *Down, girl. He's a rich, elite relation of your boss. Not the sort of guy to go for a girl like you.*

I felt a tingling along my spine, followed by the feeling of being watched. Seconds later, I heard the aggravated huff from Rosa confirming Lucien was, in fact, staring at me.

"He looks at you like he wants to eat you whole, *mija.*"

He can eat me whole any time he wants to. I smiled as I imagined the ways I'd prefer he devour me, forgetting Rosa was still talking.

"Mija," she chided, becoming frustrated at my dismissal of her concerns. "Your boss lady is heading this way."

Sure enough, Mrs. Daniels was heading our way, a frown on her face. She stopped in front of me, all business. "Miss Stanton. I wanted to talk with you for a moment if you don't mind."

She gestured to the conference room she'd been in earlier, and like any good employee, I followed without a word. Once the door closed behind us, she turned her attention to me.

"Miss Stanton, it has come to my attention that Mr. Chandless has acted unacceptably towards you, and I just wanted you to know I terminated him. Also, I wanted to apologize for what you went through tonight. I never want any of my employees to feel afraid for their well-being on the job."

I was still a little upset from the whole ordeal, and I was stunned to find it had already reached the ears of my boss. What was even more shocking was the fact that she'd terminated the man so quickly, without even speaking to me. I wondered how she'd found out, but I was happy to put it behind me if it meant I wouldn't have to relive what I'd almost experienced.

"Ma'am, it was hardly your fault, and he'd been drinking-"

"Drinking or not, he had no reason to act that way towards an employee, especially one as dedicated as you. I want you to take the next week off—paid, my treat. I even have a nice villa available for you to retreat to, get away from the stress of all the work you've put in for me. It's the least I could do."

I usually prided myself on my professionalism, but my

brain chose that moment to short-circuit, and what came out of my mouth was more of a sputtering statement of gratitude than an intelligible response. Mrs. Daniels didn't miss a beat, and she kindly led me out of the conference room, a hand at my back as she assured me I wouldn't need to stay late to close up, promising to send me the transportation details when she got home, telling me to have a nice night.

I stopped at the other side of the gallery to collect Rosa, feeling a familiar set of eyes on my back the whole time. I knew if I turned around, though, that man's brooding eyes and aloof countenance would have me melting into a puddle on the floor. It had been a while since I'd been with a man, and it wasn't like I was some chaste virgin. *I'm nearly thirty. A woman has needs.* And while I'd played the field on both sides of the door in my twenty-eight years alive, I found that most people vastly underestimated me when I warned them I had crippling anxiety and eccentric tendencies.

Most women were looking for a long-term relationship, and most men had a problem with a woman not being exclusive. And I had a problem with people and anxiety. Nobody stuck around long when the woman they dated couldn't function in large groups without having to break out an inhaler and a Xanax or sneak off into the alley to light up a joint. Most people also wanted to be touchy-feely, and I couldn't get past my claustrophobic aversion to being wrapped up in blankets and human limbs and unable to move.

More than once, I'd woken after a one-night stand and injured a sexual partner or paramour in my brain's frantic attempts to flee. Most of them never bothered to call me back, obviously.

Laughing off my libidinous urges, mostly fueled by the two flutes of champagne backwaiters had handed me, I chanced a glance back at the man I would probably never see again as I made to leave this night behind.

But he was no longer there. *What a shame.*

~Lucien~

Her driver was a quick one, with a familiar nose for all the shortcuts in town. Following him had been difficult. But my driver was capable and skilled, part of why I'd hired him. He navigated the congested streets like a pro, weaving in and out of traffic while never losing sight of the car I'd ordered him to tail.

He hadn't asked any questions about that, either, which was an admirable trait in someone who worked for a vampyr. My demands were a bit odd at times, and very vague. Having the discretion to fulfill orders without questioning them was a level of professionalism I could appreciate in my employees.

My driver tailed Miss Stanton's car from a safe distance with the skill of a pro, and I watched from the backseat as her driver led her to a home of substantial size. I raised an eyebrow curiously, eyeing the house as the driver opened the door for the two women inside the car.

The woman she was with tonight had referred to her as her niece, and they seemed uneasy in the room full of wealthy donors, meaning she herself wasn't used to wealth and affluence. So who was she really? And why had I felt as if she'd known what I was? I'd caught her offhand comments about me being *unnatural* that she'd made to the girl.

The same girl who I'd been unable to keep my eyes off of all night.

Something about her drew me in, and though I'd been an emotionless husk for years now, I was a man, and I still had *needs*, whether I was dead or not. Blood still flowed through my body, and my organs still worked for the most part. At least, the ones that mattered did—a fact that both amused and frustrated me.

When the woman I'd quickly become obsessed with stepped out of the car, her skirt hiked up to reveal her long, slender legs, and I felt my hand curl into a fist as my body reacted on a primal level. *It was strange to feel lust for a human after going so long without.* I had been content with myself; humans, especially women, came with many strings and too much baggage.

As the older woman stepped from the car, her eyes shot over to where my driver had parked, far enough down the road for her to be unable to identify the occupants. Still, that didn't stop me from feeling as if she knew I was here; like she could see right through the heavy tint, to my very soul.

Or lack of one, as the case may be.

The women quickly moved towards the house and soon disappeared from my sight. After the first floor's lights came on, my driver cleared his throat, meeting my eyes in the rearview mirror.

"Orders, sir?"

I glanced back to the house, where I could see a curtain pulled back, and I could only assume it was the Spanish *tia* who stood in the shadows, watching us. "We wait."

For what, though, I wasn't quite sure.

After the last light in the house had gone out, and stayed out for almost an hour, I shook my driver awake through the divide. He'd fallen asleep an hour ago, probably from sheer boredom.

"I'm going to pay a visit to my friends, and I won't be long. Keep the car ready.

He couldn't be implicated in a crime if he had no knowledge of it, after all. After he nodded in confirmation, I slipped silently from the backseat of the car, closing the door carefully so as not to make a sound. We had turned the interior light off inside the car to avoid being seen by anyone who might look out their window at five in the morning. It was nearly dawn, which meant I didn't have much time to do what I had planned before I would need to get home. Of course, it wasn't a matter of life or death, *but still.*

I climbed the rock wall in the house's backyard, clearing it in one jump as if I was a professional. My expensive loafers made no sound on the perfectly manicured lawn as I crossed the expansive backyard. Once on the ground-level patio, I carefully examined the sliding glass door. As I'd expected, I found a small alarm box on the inside of the doorframe, and I realized this would be harder than I had anticipated. I looked up at the sky as I ran my fingers through my hair, which had worked its way loose from the tie that had been holding it back.

And then I noticed the open window on the second floor.

I found myself in the room of my intended target: my new obsession, the woman who I couldn't shake from my mind. Why thoughts of her had invaded my mind, I wasn't sure, but I did know that I had never before been driven to break into a woman's house, just to see her. *How embarrassing; I'd become a stalker.*

She was sprawled out across her bed, snoring lightly, her hair trailing lazily across her pillows. Her lips were just barely parted, and her skin seemed to glow in the moonlight from outside. I pulled back the curtains to truly admire her in all her stunning beauty. She'd discarded her black corset dress over a nearby chair and switched it for a thin tank top and silk shorts, which left little to my imagination. Her blankets were twisted up around her long legs, and her torso was only half-covered, leading me to assume her sleep, until now, had been restless.

Frowning, I glanced around her room for the first time since entering it. She lived quite richly, but everything she had seemed to be a handed-down antique, and her clothes, while designer, were well-worn and out of season for today's market.

A thrifty woman from high society. There's a first for everything, I suppose.

She stirred in her bed, extending a single foot over the side of the bed as she smiled in her sleep, snuggling closer to her pillow. I held my breath, watching as a small black book fell from under the pillow. The words "Journal" and "Private" were scrawled in bold across the cover, but I can't restrain myself as I reach out and lift it from the floor, cracking it open to the most recent entry. *From today.*

'I can't believe I'm on vacation. Paid. My bank account doesn't have to suffer, and I get to relax. Too bad there's nobody to relax with. And I wouldn't know how to relax if you smacked me with a script for Xanax. Some days I just wish I could travel, see the world. Or at least more of it than this.

I hate my parents. They don't care, and they wouldn't notice if I left. But they spend the family money faster than they can make it, and if I left, who would handle their basic finances?

Rosa insists I'll find someone perfect someday, but how can I expect perfection when I'm such a mess myself? I wish all her stories about creatures of the night stealing you away if you uncovered your feet were true. I've been waiting thirteen years for that trick to work, with no success. Boy, she'd get a kick out of that.'

I got a chuckle out of that line, the irony not escaping me as I continued to read. I skimmed line after line of anecdotal BS before I got to my own name, in very bold letters, the lines varying slightly, as if she'd traced it over and over.

'Lucien Sabatini, a relative of my owner. What a piece of man-candy. I wonder what he looks like without all those fancy Victorian clothes on?'

I smirked at that one, feeling myself react to her obvious physical attraction. I was not above appreciating a comment, and admiration was the best form of flattery. I was tempted to read on, but I knew time was ticking. I held my breath as I leaned in, inhaling the unique scent that was her perfume and shampoo. She smelled of vanilla and sugar, so sweet to my senses. As I turned to glance at her closet door, I noticed a section of clothes peeking out that caught my eye.

Victorian Gothic. Like my own.

I quickly pulled back the door entirely, revealing clothing so familiar, it was like stepping back into my youth. I sent up a silent prayer of thanks to whatever higher power had decided to gift me such a beautiful specimen to match myself, and closed the closet door, hoping she would bring some of those outfits with her. I could only hope she would forgive me for keeping my presence a secret.

CHAPTER 5

~IZZY~

This has to be a dream. This isn't my bed; these aren't my sheets. Where am I?

Sunlight filtering through a crack in the curtains had woken me. From the bright sun and the angle it entered the room, it had to be late morning. But the light had a tint to it that wasn't quite normal for ten AM. It threw me off, and I edged over to the side of the strange, huge bed, making my way quietly to the window. Cautiously, I peered outside.

We're not in fucking Kansas anymore, Toto. I felt my head spin, realizing I was definitely *not* in Florida. There were sprawling, picturesque mountains dotting the landscape outside the window and the unmistakable shape of a vineyard in the hills beyond the estate courtyard. As I reeled back from the foreign scenery, the curtains fell back into place, casting me into darkness once more. Though I could no longer see, I knew wherever I'd ended up, nothing looked familiar.

The night before came crashing back to me in a rush, and I remembered everything in stunning clarity, my heart calming down slightly. My boss had decided to send me on an all-expenses-paid vacation, and I'd gladly taken her up on the offer, meeting up with a charter pilot at the airport just hours after waking the morning after the opening. My doctor had sent me to the pharmacy with a script for heavy tranquilizers to take, making the flight manageable. That probably explained why I hadn't remembered where I was right away. *I should probably stop taking enough tranqs to knock out an elephant when I fly. Might remember more that way.*

I'd been greeted on my arrival by a butler; I think he'd said his name was J-something. *James, Johnny, Jace…no…Jasper! That was it!*

I wondered when he would come to visit me this morning. He'd promised a meal and a tour when I woke, and even though I'd slept the whole flight, I had been exhausted, crashing almost immediately after hitting the room. Part of that was thanks to the heavy tranquilizers my doctor gave me to deal with pre-flight anxiety. Flying was sometimes part of the job, and I needed all the help I could get when dealing with it.

I heard someone outside my door, and I held my breath, waiting for someone to knock. The knock never came, and for a second, I thought I'd imagined it all. Maybe I was in some sort of heavy sleep cycle, in a dream. What did they call that, lucid dreaming? I tiptoed over to the door, trying not to pass out from lack of oxygen. As the skin of my ear grazed the door, I felt—and heard—the heavy knock from the other side.

I couldn't keep myself from crying out, and I jumped back so fast I fell to the floor, landing soundly on my ass. *That's gonna leave a mark.*

"Miss? Are you awake?"

Obviously. I stayed silent, but just as I thought he'd leave, I saw the doorknob turning. I panicked, and my breathing became erratic, each breath shallower than the last. A stranger was about to break in on me, and I had no way to defend myself.

What a hell of a night.

The door swung open to admit a tall, pale man I'd never seen before, his clothes consisting of an old, faded tee and a pair of basic jeans. He was good-looking but in an unremarkable way, and his presence seemed non-threatening, though I couldn't get my brain to process that information. It was busy trying to black me out at the entrance of this stranger into the strange room I'd been trapped in.

"So you are awake, I see. Are you hungry? You must have a ton of questions." He milled about the room, pulling the first layer of curtains back to let a muted light bathe the room, and I realized it must be nearly night. The light was starting to turn a goldish orange hue, and that could only mean one thing—sunset.

But there was no way I'd slept until the next day. *Was there?*

"Ma'am, if you'd take a moment to get prepared, my Master has asked you to join him for dinner. I took the liberty of unpacking your luggage for you, and you should find your belongings in the dressers and closet. I believe you should find everything else you may need in the bathroom to your left. I will wait outside of your door and escort you down to dinner when you're ready."

"Y-your master? I thought this villa was going to be empty…."

My eyes were drawn involuntarily to the door at the mention of a guard, an *escort*, to this *Dinner With A Mysterious Stranger.* For a brief moment, I debated the possibility of escaping, and the man before me looked down at me as if he knew exactly what was going through my mind. He frowned, crossing his arms as he moved between me and the door.

"Your stay with us will be much more pleasant if you humor my master, ma'am. He is a unique and powerful individual and is not one to be ignored."

I felt an eyebrow raise in defiance at his words of this mysterious master, this man who demanded I prepare for dinner with him. There was no way I'd make it through the meal with my mental stability spiraling. I tried and failed to open my mouth, so many questions dying on my lips like the first flakes of snow on a too-warm surface. The man saw me struggling with my words and offered me a hand up from the floor. Without thinking, I took his outstretched hand, my body on autopilot as I spiraled.

His hand circled my wrist for the briefest of seconds, but I realized his skin was colder than normal. Almost as if he had just walked out of a freezer. It felt wrong, so wrong that I jerked my hand back as soon as my feet were underneath me. He raised a brow but said nothing as he exited my room, the click of the latch sounding behind him. That single sound felt like the iron bars of a jail cell closing in around me, sealing my fate. Resigned, I turned my head to the corner the man had gestured to when talking about getting dressed, and for the first time today, I recognized my own luggage.

I ran over to the familiar item, relieved to know I wasn't completely alone in a foreign place. One look inside the suitcase told me that the butler truly had unpacked for me. Sighing, I turned to the wardrobe against the wall beside the suitcase and opened the heavy oak doors to reveal my clothes. The gothic attire calmed me somewhat, and I shoved the darker choices aside for a light sundress, feeling too warm already.

I decided to throw it on with a pair of ballet flats from the suitcase and brushed my hair with the hairbrush in the front pocket. Whoever my mysterious stranger was, he had made sure my basic needs were provided for, and I guess that was better than nothing.

But who was he, and what did he want?

The gentleman who had waited outside my room had introduced himself when I met him at the door, dressed and tidied up, albeit nervous. Jasper Trudeau, butler to the Master of the House. He'd been kind enough to explain to me that his master had promised to answer all the questions I likely had built up, but I wasn't sure why he couldn't just tell me himself. He seemed nice enough, but how much could I trust him?

The room I'd been left in was on the second floor, and as we descended the stairs, I took note of anything my eyes could see. There was a large set of doors at the other side of the foyer, and I found it oddly charming that the house's interior was authentic Victorian gothic design. From the tall ceilings and the sharp lines with intricate details, the house had a 'setting for an old movie' feel. Almost like I'd seen it before, even though I knew I hadn't. Mr. Trudeau led me to a set of double doors that opened up to reveal a dining room bathed in the setting sun. The room's far wall was lined with an enormous bay window, and I could see the skyline for miles. It looked out over the ocean in the not-too-distant background, and I sighed, wondering what body of water I was currently seeing. I felt my feet move forward, almost as if being pulled by an invisible rope, and I made my way to the table, where a nice little white name card had been sat out, with my *full given name* embossed on the fine stationery.

What the hell…

This was all too much, and I sat down in the seat before me, my mind reeling. Not only did the stranger know my name, but he was playing mind games. *Why?* I absently fingered the white card before me, turning it this way and that as I admired the classy extravagance behind such a frivolous, empty gesture. As I set it back on the tabletop, Mr. Trudeau cleared his throat behind me, drawing my attention. But when I stood and turned, it wasn't the butler's face that I saw staring back at me, wearing a bored expression and a cunning smile that was a double-edged knife to my defenses.

"I did so like you better in the dress from last night, Miss Stanton."

His tall, lean body rested against the frame of the doorway, an arm thrown above to brace himself, one foot crossed in front of the other. His entire demeanor screamed uninterested, but his *eyes*…

His eyes were burning a trail over my body, and I couldn't think. My mind had given out on me, no logical, coherent thoughts forming in it. All I could think about was the sheer irony that my sexy savior from the night before had somehow become my new roommate at this villa.

"I-I don't understand, Mr. Sabatini-"

"Please," he practically whispered, taking slow steps towards me, "call me Lucien. After all, you are my guest."

His hand reached out to grab mine, but I yanked it just out of reach, refusing to believe what I was seeing, what I was *hearing.*

"Your *guest?* I wasn't aware I'd be sharing this villa with anyone else, sir."

He chuckled, moving past me towards the vast window beyond where I could see the sun had set beyond the mountains to the west. There was still light, but it was the muted light of dusk. I felt my throat tighten as he moved away, which was the complete opposite reaction I normally had when someone put space between us. Especially when it was someone I was unsure of.

And I didn't know what to think of Lucien Sabatini.

"Please, don't call me sir. It sounds so *formal.* I'm sure you have plenty of questions for me, but before we begin, why don't you have a seat, and we can have dinner served. I'm sure you're quite famished."

As if to punctuate his observation, my stomach chose that moment to sound off loudly, the noises embarrassing me as I shrunk down into the seat I had occupied moments before.

I observed him as he sat across from me, staring into my eyes with a blank, unreadable expression. I wanted so badly to ask him the million or so questions on my mind, but I couldn't make my lips move. I felt like a hand was closing around my throat, the feeling not a welcome one as I fought to regulate my breathing. Logically, I knew it was just anxiety, but I couldn't help but struggle with the suffocating feeling I was drowning in.

I was frozen in place, and as my throat constricted, I sent up a desperate plea that I had remembered to grab my medications. He watched me through narrowed eyes as I tried to think. *You have coping mechanisms, you moron. Use them.* But I couldn't think of what they were. I couldn't remember how to focus and calm myself; I was an unstable mess, and it wasn't getting any better. I felt my mouth open, but no sound came out.

I may die from a lack of oxygen right now.

Across from me, Lucien studied me intently, not realizing I was slowly fading to black. I gestured meekly with my hands in a feeble attempt to explain my situation, but all I could do was jerk spastically as I felt myself fading out of consciousness. I mentally prepared myself for the feel of my body hitting the ground as it slid from the chair, but it never came, and my eyes closed as I passed out.

~Lucien~

I've killed her. Somehow, I've managed to kill this poor woman from fright. I watched her slip into unconsciousness, managing to get up and run to her side before she tipped sideways out of her chair and hit the floor. Since she was sitting down when she'd passed out, I was forced to sit on the floor to catch her, a very unbecoming place for a man of my stature to be. Still, I couldn't move as I let my eyes roam over her still form.

She'd put on a simple white sundress, with lace detailing at the edges of her skirt and neckline, and a pair of Converse high-tops — definitely a change from the fancy Victorian dress from the night before. Still, she was beautiful, and I pondered the irony that both times she'd met me, she had ended up in my arms.

I am terrible. It won't surprise me if she hates me.

That thought caused me more pain than I would have thought possible. It was as if, by imagining her rejection, I had spoken it into existence, and my hollow chest felt even more empty at the thought of this wonderful creature turning away from me. Especially after all the trouble I'd gone through to get her here, to my true home.

To Italy.

CHAPTER 6

~LUCIEN~

I hope she doesn't stay out for long.

I remained on the floor, holding her as if she were a fragile piece of glass. It had been a century since I'd felt anything for another living being, and I was woefully awkward, holding this perfect human woman in my arms. I'd forgotten how soft their skin was, how nice it was to feel another body against mine, especially that of the female persuasion, and I shamelessly tucked her closer into my chest, relishing this one moment. *Even if she woke and decided to hate me forever, I would have this moment.*

She didn't know the real me, and she never would, sadly. I couldn't risk her already tenuous mental stability. She couldn't handle what I was.

She stirred in my arms, the fleeting moment of bliss gone, leaving me to wonder if I'd actually felt it at all. Emotions were so few and far between, I'd forgotten what they felt like or how to identify them. I frowned down at her as she opened her eyes, and I'm sure I did not paint the prettiest of pictures for her to wake up to.

Her eyelids fluttered open, and her deep amber eyes gazed back at mine with frightening clarity for just a moment. Her body jerked in my arms, and I had to tighten my grip to keep her from falling to the floor. I tried to get her attention, but she wasn't listening, and her calm eyes had turned feral, casting wildly about as if seeking something. I tried snapping my fingers, shaking her gently and calling her name, but nothing worked.

She was in a trance. A very panicked trance. So I did what any normal person would do and called for my butler. Maybe he would know what to do. I certainly was lacking in experience with humans in general and was of no help to her.

"Jasper! Quickly!" I watched the man round the corner in a panic, not used to the sense of urgency in my voice. One glance down at my position on the floor, and he was beside me in an instant.

"What's wrong with her, sir?"

I rolled my eyes. "I was hoping you could tell me that."

Jasper's eyes glazed over slightly as he examined the girl in my lap, snapping his fingers, calling out to her, still with the same results I'd gotten. Suddenly, he stood, fleeing from the room as fast as he'd entered it. I sighed, looking back down at Izzy still laying in my lap, a frightened mess.

I did this to her.

Jasper returned, a purse in hand. Opening it, he retrieved two pill bottles from the interior and passed them to me.

"This one is an anxiety medication, and the other is an antidepressant. She's probably having a severe panic attack. Do you think you can get her to take these?"

I eyed the pill bottles with disdain, rotating the little orange tubes between my fingers as I read the labels. *Do not operate heavy machinery after taking. Do not take on an empty stomach. May cause drowsiness. Jesus, what do they give her, horse tranquilizers?* I wondered why she was on such strong medications—not that I knew anything about medicine. Two hundred years of life as an immortal and medicine had just never caught my eye.

"Maybe. But you'd better get some water." Jasper stood, setting the purse on the table before heading into the kitchen beyond the swinging door. I felt my hands shake as I worked to remove one of each pill from its container, being careful to secure the lids back tight before setting them down. Izzy had stopped struggling, but she was still non-verbal, and her eyes were still a million miles away.

Whatever I'd done, I hoped it wasn't permanent.

Jasper returned with a water bottle and a small red tube, which he set on the tabletop before taking Izzy from my arms. I reluctantly let her go as he directed me to sit in my chair. Without questioning why he felt comfortable giving me orders, I found myself in the chair, and shortly after I settled he was placing her in my arms again.

I had to admit, this was a much more comfortable arrangement, that was for sure. Tilting her head back, I separated her lips with my fingers, trying not to linger on the feel of their soft flesh against my own cold skin. I let both pills slide into her mouth and down the back of her throat, holding the water to her mouth as I let some slide down after the pills. After a minute or two, her eyes focused somewhat, and she reached out for the bottle, leaning up as she struggled with a dry cough.

Maybe the pills had been a little rough going down.

When she'd finally stopped coughing, she downed the whole water bottle, going stiff as she surveyed her surroundings again. I felt her hands against her sides, and then against the outside of my thighs as she realized she was using me as a chair.

Izzy practically fell over herself, trying to untangle her legs from my own, and she backed against the large bay window, her legs functional once again. But instead of the wild panic I had seen moments before, her eyes seemed to be calming down, her breathing evening out little by little.

Whatever was in those medications, they were helping.

"W-where am I?" She took a moment to look around, and I made no move towards her, knowing she was still in a daze.

"You're safe, Miss Stanton, of that I can assure you. Do you remember who I am?"

She slowly looked me over, her eyes trailing along my entire body. I would have been lying if I'd said it didn't affect me, but I held still, letting her brain process things little by little.

"Yes, we met last night, at the museum gala. You helped me," she trailed off, confusion starting to set back in. "But why are you here?"

I dragged my hand down over my face, as frustrated with myself as I'd ever been. "Something about you just…intrigued me, so after learning my lovely cousin, your boss, was planning to send you away after the incident, I offered up my villa as a vacation getaway, and my cousin extended the offer for you to come here, to my villa. I know how strange and crazy that seems, believe me—it confused me, too. But it was like a compulsion I couldn't ignore, and so here we are."

Her eyebrows shot up, but she managed to keep a straight face as she deadpanned, "Your home? I was under the impression the villa was unoccupied. No offense, Mr. Sabatini, but I think it's time I called a cab and went home." She glanced around the room, her eyes settling on her purse at the edge of the table. Her eyes shot accusingly up to mine, and I held my hands out in a gesture of protest.

"I swear we did not go through your purse, except for to retrieve your medications—"

"So you drugged me, too?!" Her breathing was starting to speed up, and I worried she would faint again from her rising panic. I quickly tried to get a handle on the conversation again.

"Ah—no. Well, yes. But we only dosed you with your own medications when you went into a daze—"

She put her face in her hands, hiding from my sight. I could see the faint traces of a blush creep up her neck. "What exactly happened? I remember…it's all a bit fuzzy."

"Well," I muttered, leaning towards her, "you passed out, and then when you came to, you were catatonic, but…frightened. Your mind had shut down, and you wouldn't speak. It's like you couldn't hear us." I stood, taking a single step towards her. I was pleased when she didn't seem to shrink back from me, and I extended a hand again in her direction.

She eyed it, but she still didn't seem sold on the whole situation. "So, how did you get here before me?"

"Private charter jet, courtesy of my company."

Her eyes snapped up to meet mine, my outstretched hand momentarily forgotten. "Expensive."

"Well, it was an eleven-hour trip to Sicily—"

"*Sicily?*" she shrieked, her eyes going wide and the color draining from her face. Izzy paced frantically before the window, glancing back out at the landscape several times as if trying to take in such a massive piece of information. "So, I flew across an entire *ocean* in my *sleep*."

Her shoulders slumped in defeat as she turned her head to look back out the window against her back. I sighed heavily, already frustrated with having to explain. "Yes. But aside from that episode, you're perfectly safe. There is much here to keep you entertained."

She pressed her back against the cold window, her lips pursed into a thin line that did little to hide her distress. Jasper chose that moment to come in, pushing a cart that held our meal for the evening. I silently gestured for her to take a seat across from me, and to my relief, she seemed to relax as I watched her cross the room.

Her eyes watched Jasper as he moved from one side of the table to the other, setting out our meals before us. During our past together, Jasper decided he missed cooking, and he took it upon himself to train up his culinary skills under a professional. The delicious smell of the food coming from the plates was intoxicating, and I watched as Izzy's eyes followed the steaming food. She licked her lips, eliciting a chuckle from my otherwise stoic countenance.

When the meal was in front of us, she looked up from the steaming food, a quizzical expression on her face. "What is this?"

I smiled, happy to sing the praises of my friend's culinary skill. "This, *signora*, is *involtini di pesce spade,* or baked swordfish rolls. We prefer to deep fry them on this coast, though northerners would say they're better baked."

She lifted one from the plate, twisting the skewer back and forth as she examined her food. I tried to suppress a groan as she brought the fish to her lips and somehow made eating erotic. Never before had food been such a lure for me, and I suddenly found myself making the situation even more awkward.

"Ah, so you like it?" I asked as I bit into a roll of my own. She licked her fingers after the first roll, and I felt my hand curl into a fist under the table, my nails cutting into the skin of my palm. I could smell the blood seep around my fingers, but I couldn't help it. This woman was able to turn me upside down, a feeling which I detested. I was *always* in control, and I wouldn't let someone else affect my emotions like this.

"Mmm, it's delicious! The flavor of the meat comes through nicely, and it isn't over-seasoned. Whoever made this is a culinary artist." She moved to pick up another roll, and I cast my eyes down at my plate in an attempt to ignore her. I wasn't as successful as I had hoped, and I glanced up to see her pull a finger slowly out of her mouth.

I felt like a randy young teenager, unable to control my more base urges. I could feel my hand leaving indentations in the soft wooden underside of the table, and I reached for my napkin on the table, using my bleeding hand by accident.

The red blood stood in stark contrast to the white tablecloth, and I heard her gasp as I rolled my eyes at my own stupidity. Now, I would need to feed, and I couldn't risk leaving for a hunt with Miss Stanton under my care.

"Oh no, you're hurt!" She was standing next to me in a flash, kneeling by the table with my hand in hers as if she'd teleported there. I hissed as she examined my palm, trying desperately to yank my hand back from her, but she held onto it, using her napkin to wipe away the blood.

The blood was abnormally dark, since it was not mine, nor was it fresh. Izzy *had* to notice the discoloration, but she said nothing, giving no indication that she'd registered the oddity. Once she'd wiped away the blood, I could see my advanced healing doing its job. She grabbed a fresh napkin from the table and pressed it into my palm as she stood to her full height and made her way across the table to her own seat. She sat back down, picking up her fork to try the risotto as if she hadn't just tended to a wound a second before.

But her eyes were sharper, as if she knew something was not adding up. She'd have to be blind to miss it, but the human mind has a way of tricking us into seeing what we want to see. I hoped hers would as well.

"So, Sicily. Isn't Sicily an island? Does that mean I'm stranded? And you *do* know I have a job to go back to. A family. People who are going to be concerned." Her fingers tapped nervously against the side of her fork, betraying her nerves. "Just in case you were thinking of trying anything shady."

I had to smile at her anxious little tics; they were almost endearing. She didn't seem to notice them, but I saw every single one as she worked through her anxiety in stages. "We have no intention of letting any harm befall you here, Miss Stanton. And as for your job — since I am related to your boss, I'm sure she wouldn't mind you extending your stay with us here if you so choose. Especially since I agreed to stand in as the missing benefactor. I was impressed with your in-depth knowledge of the artifacts I admired." I set my napkin on the table, my wounds already healed.

It took much more than that little scrape to damage my superior immortal body.

"You really do have all the bases covered, don't you? What if I want to leave here in the morning, get a hotel?" Her eyes never left mine, as if she was daring me to tell her she couldn't leave.

The truth was, I had no intention of preventing her from leaving. Though I might not have a soul, I did have a sense of common decency. "I have a friend in town who can help you get anything you might need. As for hotels, it's the busy tourist season. Even I wouldn't pay these prices for a room right now." She didn't *need to know* I had no plans to hold her hostage. I would let her test the waters in her own time.

I might be old and unfeeling, but I still enjoyed a little game of cat and mouse. Maybe this wouldn't be so bad after all.

"So I'm free to go?"

"Miss Stanton, I don't think you'll want to leave this place after you've had the chance to truly enjoy it. There are many things to busy yourself with here in Sicily. My home is your home, and while you are here, you are welcome to anything in it." I drew the last sentence out, letting my lust taint the words in a barely concealed invitation. Her cheeks turned slightly pink, and she looked anywhere but me for a brief second. But then she met my eyes, and I saw my own lust mirrored in her beautiful amber orbs.

A faint smile tugged at the corners of her mouth, and I could tell by the pulse in her throat that her heart rate was increasing. It was nice to know I wasn't the only one affected by the other.

"I am long overdue for a vacation, and I've never been abroad before. I suppose I could stay here. On one condition."

Her smirk was in full swing now, and the calculating look in her eyes chilled me to my core, but my mouth and my brain wouldn't connect, and what came out next was not something I ever thought I'd say to a woman.

"Name your price."

CHAPTER 7

~IZZY~

"Name your price."

Oh, how he would live to regret that phrase. I would make sure of it. Lucien sat there with a smug look on his face, his aloof attitude frustrating me.

"I still don't understand why you brought me here—"

"Neither do I, to be frank—"

"But since I'm here, I want to know why?" I looked back down at my hands and felt my shoulders fall. All the adrenaline coursing through my body had dissipated, leaving me spent. I took a deep breath, releasing it like a slowly leaking tire as I placed my palms down on the table. "If you can't tell me why you brought me here, I can't stay. Should you accept my terms, I will stay as your guest."

His eyes narrowed as I placed my hands on my hips, waiting him out. His hands joined together on the tabletop as he contemplated ways to get out of the question. Finding none, he sighed, running a hand through his hair. I watched carefully as a few stray tendrils of hair fell in front of his alabaster face.

"Well?" I had no idea where this burst of confidence had come from, but I was riding it like a surfer rides the last wave at sunset—to the bitter end.

Lucien stood suddenly, his chair scraping the wood floor

noisily behind him. He stalked over to me, a bored expression on his face, but in his eyes was a look I couldn't quite place. As he closed the distance between us, I braced myself for my body's irrational reaction to the closeness, closing my eyes, but it never came. Cautiously, I peeked from beneath my lashes to find Lucien almost nose to nose with me. My heart stuttered for a brief moment, my breath catching in my throat. I couldn't breathe, I couldn't move, I couldn't look away. His eyes transfixed me, the deep pools of crimson that I was sure were his natural irises.

But how?

Rationality and logic had flown out the window the minute I'd met this man, and I wasn't sure why. I had always been a bit guarded, thanks to my anxiety and nerves. But standing here, face to face with one of the most *unnatural* men I'd met in a long time, I felt...*normal.* As if being around him sucked away all the anxiety in the room. I felt as if I'd known him my whole life, as silly as it sounded.

Get a grip, you lunatic. He's from Italy, and you've been lucky to leave the state you were born in. You've never met this man before.

I wanted to listen to the inner me so badly, but I was emboldened by the false bravado I felt, probably a result of the anger-fueled adrenaline coursing through me at finding out I had been duped.

"Why did you invite me?" I managed to whisper, the sound more reminiscent of a squeak than actual words. Straightening my shoulders, I tried again. "Why bring me here, to Italy, under a false pretense?"

I fought hard not to cringe as he raised his hand to my cheek, caressing the skin along my jaw as he traced the lines of my face. When his second hand came up to join the first, I realized neither of us had spoken, but neither of us had looked away. Hie crimson eyes stared back into my own amber golden ones, a familiar emotion at the edges of his vision that I recognized all too well.

Loneliness. Desolation.

"Something about you called out to me, from the moment I saw you—"

"At the museum last night—"

"No," he whispered, his lips so close to mine I could practically feel his warm breath on mine. "No. Not the museum." His eyes searched mine as if he were looking for something. Closing his eyes for a moment, his hands still held the sides of my face, and a deep sigh escaped him.

"Lucien?"

As his lashes fluttered back up, I felt the weight of his soul as he stared bleakly back at me. He looked defeated, almost, and I couldn't help but feel sorry for him. I knew exactly what that felt like.

"I saw your picture in the paper. When they did the article for the grand opening of the museum."

I thought back to the day we'd met with the newspaper, and I couldn't remember being in any of the shots unless they'd caught me in the background. "I didn't get my picture taken that day—"

"They caught you by accident. You intrigued me…your eyes…" he trailed off, his pupils flicking back and forth between mine, searching me for my secrets. "Your golden eyes were as plain as day in the photo, and I'd never seen a human with eyes like that."

I chuckled slightly at his use of the word human instead of 'person'. *He is definitely odd. But then again, so am I.* "So you came all this way to see your cousin—"

He brought a finger to my lower lip, effectively silencing me as he brushed the pad of his thumb along my lower lip agonizingly slow. "No, *stellina*, my relation being the owner was just a bonus. I came all this way to see *you.* "

If I were any more surprised, I'd have looked like a fish out of water, flopping on the docks in the hot sun. My mouth fell open, eyes wide in astonishment. *He'd come across an ocean because he saw me in a picture? How…odd. Impractical. And yet… strangely satisfying.*

Whisked away by a mysterious stranger in the night. Isn't this what I always wanted?

I swallowed my hesitation, deciding instead to do something the normal, rational Izzy would have never done. I leaned forward quickly, not bothering to close my eyes as I pressed my lips against Lucien's cool ones. A gasp escaped him as I laid my hands on his shoulders, my fingers bunching the fabric beneath my hands. He groaned, wrapping his arms around my lower back as he pulled me closer against him. I shivered in secret delight at the closeness of our bodies.

What was I doing? I'd never been so bold in my entire life? Something about this man struck a chord in me, and it was like flipping a switch. I was sure the medicine had something to do with it as well, of course, but there was no denying something in me was attracted to Lucien. Like a moth to a flame, I couldn't look away.

~Lucien~

She was a thing of beauty. One minute, I had been standing across from her, and the next, I'd closed the distance, face to face with the woman I'd lured across an ocean. I had no explanation to give her for my actions, but her request struck a nerve deep inside me, and it was as if the emotions that I'd locked up for so long had finally broken through the stone wall I'd built to contain them. To hide them from myself. After all, I was a soulless immortal—an unnatural thing of nature.

A vampyr.

When I'd opened my mouth to tell her I didn't have an answer, I felt betrayed by the words that left me. Gone was my stoic display of disinterest, replaced by a growing tightness in my hollow chest. I found myself being honest; the words coming from a place I hadn't known still existed.

"No, *stellina*, my relation being the owner was just a bonus. I came all this way to see *you.*"

Imagine my surprise when the little ball of anxiety before me lunged forward, kissing me like her whole world hadn't just been upended. As if she'd been made for this very moment. Been made for kissing me. Her lips felt like the softest satin against my own, her warmth sending shivers down my spine as I felt her fingers dig into my shoulders.

I groaned at the passion I felt roll over me, the unadulterated lust that flowed through my veins. Vampyrs were very sexual creatures, and I'd gone too long without the feel of a woman in my arms. The blood roared in my ears, drowning out all sound and rational thought as I kissed her back with equal fervor.

My mind was adrift, lost at sea like a boat set loose from its moorings with no compass in sight. I couldn't grab hold of anything to still my mind, and I struggled to get these wild emotions under control as they threatened to overwhelm me. If I kept kissing her, I wouldn't stop until I'd taken her to bed, and I'd probably end up killing her with the way I felt right now. I hadn't fed in days, and my body felt the absence of fresh blood like a man in the desert felt the absence of water.

I pulled back as my senses returned, my eyes so deeply crimson they were nearly black. I knew if I looked down, I'd draw attention to the situation in my pants, another bad idea that would lead nowhere and everywhere at the same time. I kept my eyes trained on Izzy as I studied her flushed expression. *Where the hell had I put my manners today? I'd ravished a respectable lady before even getting to really know her.*

"I'm sorry, I don't usually behave in such a deplorable manner. I assure you I won't let it happen again."

Her next words were a faint mumble, so low I knew I wasn't intended to hear them.

"I wouldn't mind if it happened again."

I raised a brow but gave no other indication I'd heard her. A blush crept up her cheeks, her face warm with a sudden embarrassment as she realized what she'd done. Not that I'd mind, but it had seemed very out of character for a woman who had fainted before me just hours before. I held out my arm in offering, and she graciously accepted it, following as I led her from the room and out onto the verandah overlooking the hills.

I led her to a wicker chair near the edge of the stone patio, the first stars beginning to appear in the sky. Her eyes could have trailed up to view the wonderful display in the early night sky, but instead, she stared at the lapels of my blazer, studying the fabric intently. I briefly laughed as I imagined her heated gaze burning a hole through my clothes.

What a way to go; lit on fire by a smoldering gaze.

"Please, have a seat here. I'll have Jasper bring out some dessert for you."

She looked up at me, her daring stare replaced by a hesitant, cautious glance. She'd lost her gusto, and the adrenaline had left her empty, spent. "Are you coming back?"

I frowned, my eyes narrowing as I felt something within me stirring angrily again. Whatever this was, this feeling in my chest, it was unfamiliar and uncomfortable. I wished for the days when I felt nothing instead of this awkward pressure in my ribcage.

"No, I have some, uh, *other matters* to attend to first. You enjoy the dessert, and let Jasper know if you need anything. He will be around the corner, and he has been ordered to get you whatever you want, within reason."

I disappeared around the corner before she could ask more, my chest feeling as if a bear grip was strangling me. *Why do I feel like this?* This suffocating feeling made the void lessen but replaced it with a building pressure; I would be hard-pressed to pick which one was worse. My feet glided across the wood floor almost silently as I quickly fled to the safety of my room. Once the door had closed behind me, I breathed a sigh of relief.

The distance I had put between Izzy and myself calmed me as I worked through these new…sensations. *Why had I told her about the newspaper photo?* It made me sound so desperate, so weird. *Creepy.*

What was it about this human woman that made me lose

control of my senses? Why did she draw me in like a lighthouse draws the eye of a sailor at night?

I had to know more about her. But I had no desire to feel again. I'd been living this long without feelings; I would certainly be fine without them now. Emotions and feelings just served as a weakness—a reminder of my own humanity, or what little remained of it.

I would do well to remember what happens when my emotions ruled me.

~Izzy~

He left me on the verandah, alone and nervous, a world away from home. Jasper appeared shortly after Lucien's departure, a slice of tiramisu on a small white plate. I smiled at him as he set it in my hands, a slight, sad smile on his own face as he looked me over.

"How are you feeling, miss? You had quite the episode earlier."

I blushed, embarrassed that this man had seen me in one of my worst panic attacks of late. Very rarely did I go full catatonic, but it could happen, and I was always prepared with my meds nearby. Thankfully the guys had thought to give me the Xanax, which helped, but I would have eventually come out of the catatonic state on my own.

"I'm much better now, thank you." I felt my old friend anxiety easing its way back into my brain, and I frowned, puzzled by the sudden reaction. Why had I been so calm around Lucien, but his friendly and possibly life-saving butler set me on edge again?

One of life's random, odd quirks, I suppose. Jasper stood awkwardly to the side, his hands in his pockets.

"Is there anything I can do for you, Miss Stanton?"

My eyes lit up as I realized there *was* something he could do to help me.

"Can you take me on a tour of the property?" After all, I would need to know how to get around the place on my own, as it seemed Lucien had other things to keep him busy. What was the harm in a little tour?

Jasper nodded, his eyes glinting with amusement. Maybe I could learn to be relaxed around him like I was with Lucien. "Sure, I can do that. I think you'll like it here, miss."

I sure hope so, Jasper.

CHAPTER 8

~IZZY~

Jasper had led me around for what seemed like an hour, up and down various hallways in the expansive estate. Every room felt like a clone of the last—bare, dark, and lonely. It didn't appear anyone had decorated this house in a century; the wallpaper peeled in spots, the gentle breeze snuck in between the cracked window frames, tiny gaps in the walls all aided the chilly atmosphere. Though the house itself was warm and temperate, the atmosphere felt like a scene in *Dracula*—a chilling void of life.

Surely there wasn't a lack of funds to point to for the house's condition, but more of a general stance of disinterest towards the maintenance. Jasper took me outside and we toured the well-lit grounds in the dark. The side yard butted up against the beach, and in a small cove within walking distance sat a mid-sized building that mirrored the house's exterior design.

That must also belong to Lucien. I wondered how much of this land he really owned. The man was well-off, and his perimeters didn't seem to be confined and mapped out by any fence. Shame my neighbors weren't as easygoing. I'd give my week's paycheck to be able to build a fence between the evil woman who insisted on being in my business every damn day and my backyard.

I pointed to the matching building sitting right on the water, turning to Jasper beside me. "What's that building? It matches the house, so I assume it belongs to Mr. Sabatini."

Jasper sighed, a frown furrowing his brows as he studied the building we were approaching. "Young Master doesn't like me to go in the boathouse because it's one of his personal escapes. But I don't see why I can't let you peek in and see his greatest treasure."

I knew I was practically salivating, but I couldn't help it. There was no telling what would be behind the walls of this boathouse, and I couldn't hide my excitement. Jasper peeked up at the house, a small, self-satisfied smile on his lips as he slid a key into the lock on the door. The door swung slowly open, the salty smell of the ocean permeating the air around us. I hung back as Jasper stepped into the dark room, disappearing for a moment before a light flickered to life in the old wood building.

Intrigued, I stepped forward, crossing the threshold and coming face to face with a massive sailboat that appeared to be a blatant antique. The wood was hand-painted with the scrawling calligraphy of the shipmaker across the hull, and the body was well cared for. Not a single part of the ship gave any indication of disrepair. Unlike his stately home, Lucien must truly care for this boat. I reached my hand up to feel the smooth wood, my fingers skimming the glossy finish tenderly. My mind, of course, had drifted, and thankfully Jasper had made himself scarce, thus avoiding my increasing anxiety. I was grateful for his absence, though he probably had no idea how much it meant to me.

As I walked along the long hull of the sailboat, I marveled at the sheer size of it. The beast had obviously been modernized without altering the integrity of the craft itself. The attention to detail was astounding; not a single imperfection was visible, and the boat smelled of old leather and the briny ocean water. I inhaled deep, appreciating the beautiful collectible. I'd seen many a collector in my search to stock the museum, but even the biggest boat enthusiasts didn't have a boat as spectacular as this one.

Maybe if I could get over the anxiety of this absurd situation, I could convince Lucien to take me for a sail. I'd been on a sailboat before, but it had been a while since my parents had the money to schmooze with the Yacht Club crowd. I pulled my hand away from the wooden hull, a feeling of sadness washing over me at the loss of connection I'd felt with this inanimate object.

I could hear whispering outside, and I edged my way to the door, staying just out of sight so I could eavesdrop. My heart was hammering in my chest, my breathing rapid as I hesitated at the edge of the door frame, clutching the shelf beside me with all the force I possessed. I was desperate for something to support me, and this was the only thing in the vicinity.

"You know the boathouse is off-limits, Jasper. Why are you down here?"

"Well, Young Master, I figured if you wouldn't come down to visit *The Raven*, someone ought to appreciate her beauty. Sir Stoker would be rolling over in his grave if he knew she sat on the shelf in your boathouse, not even in the water. His prized sailboat, wasting away in the darkness."

"Bram ought to roll in his grave for that atrocious book of his."

I heard a chuckle, but I had lost focus on the words. My mind was running in circles at the strange conversation they'd been having against the boathouse. Lucien and Jasper.

Sir Stoker. Bram. There was no way they meant the same Bram Stoker who wrote Dracula. He'd been dead for over a hundred years. Knowing there was probably an explanation for all this, I listened in again, and suddenly I wished I hadn't. The words I heard next chilled me to the bone.

"You know, these underhanded tricks are unbecoming of a vampyr as old as you are, Jasper. Two hundred-ish years old and still toying with me."

Jasper laughed dryly. "Well, sir, if I didn't toy with you,

what fun would I have? And besides, if you plan to keep the woman around awhile, you might have to entertain her, you know. She's not a paid wh—"

"*Enough, Jasper.* You'd do well to remember to bite your tongue when you're speaking to your employer."

"Of course, sir. But what should I do with the woman? Just take her back to her room?"

"Yes. Wait, no." I heard him sigh as I held my breath, not sure I even remembered how to breathe at that moment. "I don't know, Jasper. What does one do with a human after going so long with no companionship?"

"Uhm, sir, I've been your companion for two hundred years practically, so I wouldn't say—"

"But it's not the *same.* You're a vampyr, like me. We thrive on being alone. And now my body is acting in ways I've not felt in forever, and I don't know what to do with all these *feelings*."

I leaned back into the light of the boathouse interior, thinking to myself. I felt the edges of a panic attack sneaking in, but my meds and all my coping mechanisms were in the estate, sitting on the table where I'd abandoned them earlier. Pinching the inside of my wrists, I replayed the key parts I'd managed to pick up from the conversation I'd overheard.

Vampire. They're vampires. Two hundred years old or older. And he planned to keep me. But I couldn't believe the sheer irony of the situation I found myself in, now that I understood some of it. I had literally been fantasizing for years about being whisked away in the middle of the night by a creature of darkness, and of course, I met one at a museum of his relative's, my boss. Not only were they related, but she'd inadvertently dedicated a whole museum to her great great great something or another. And the icing on the cake was he'd rescued me twice that night and somehow decided I was worthy of bringing home with him.

Because *sure,* what self-respecting woman wouldn't be thrilled to be whisked away by a centuries-old vampyr in the dead of night, who she'd only known for a few hours? One with a heavy and misunderstood infatuation, no less.

I had no idea what I was going to do with this information, but I felt oddly at ease, considering I'd just found out my hosts were ancient immortals who could—and would—suck me dry in an instant for their next meal. Clearing my throat, I straightened my spine and marched right out of the building, interrupting the conversation between the two men.

As soon as I was visible, I was the center of attention. Both pairs of eyes swiveled to meet mine as I felt my brain sputter out and die.

"Ah, Miss Stanton, I see my *butler* here has shown you *The Raven.*" Lucien's eyebrows were disappearing into his hairline, but he did well to conceal his complete shock, which only served to make him seem oddly out-of-sorts. His eyes were dead, but his face screamed pained frustration, and his knuckles were turning white from the force he clenched his fists with. I gasped as I remembered his hand from earlier, and without thinking, my body lurched forward, reaching out in concern for his hand.

His expression froze as I approached. Whether in surprise or pain, I was unable to tell. I reached out with both hands, gently cupping his injured hand.

But when I turned his hand over, it revealed smooth, flawless skin. *Where was the blood? Where were the three crescent-shaped indents he'd left in his hand earlier? Had I just been hallucinating them?*

No, that couldn't be right. My brain insisted I wasn't wrong, but I reached for his other hand, seeing it was also uninjured. Dark spots started appearing in my vision as I glanced to the ground, dropping his hands like they were snakes.

For all intents and purposes, it would have been preferable if they had, in fact, been snakes. I blinked rapidly as I watched Jasper's feet shuffle into view beside my own as he reached out to put a hand on my shoulder, probably in concern. An attempt at comfort from someone I'd thought was human until minutes ago. And all the bravado I'd had behind that wall had gone out the window, disappearing into the night air as I struggled to grasp what I was seeing.

He'd *healed.* I knew I had seen the injury, but he'd acted dismissive when I'd pressed the napkin into his palm earlier.

He knew he wouldn't need it. And if he could heal at a supernatural rate, then it was equally possible he could be a vampire. I felt my throat growing tight, and as Jasper's hand closed in on my shoulder, it was as if time stood still, seconds moving like minutes, stretched out endlessly with the sole intent to cause me distress and agony.

"Are you alright, miss?"

When Jasper's hand touched my shoulder, I flinched away. My brain said to calm down, but as usual, my body was in overdrive panic mode, and I nearly fell over from the shock. My eyes were wild, and I knew I must look a rare sight, my arms flailing as I started to topple sideways from the force of my own reaction.

Lucien seemed to snap out of his trance, reaching out to save me from falling in the damp grass. I was secretly glad he hadn't let me fall, but my heart was beating wildly, every sense on high alert as I sat paralyzed in his grasp. I didn't think he would hurt me any more than I thought Jasper would, but my body started slipping away, and I feared I would fall into another panic attack episode.

"Define *alright.*" I clenched my fists at my sides, trying desperately not to meet Lucien's gaze. I could feel his eyes on me, boring into my very soul, as if he could learn everything about me by a simple glance. His chuckle at my response rumbled through his chest and sent a little thrill racing up the arm of mine pressed up against his torso. I shivered, finally bringing my eyes up to meet his cautiously.

A big mistake.

~Lucien~

Her eyes darkened when they met mine, infecting my mind with a single glance. Izzy's gorgeous golden orbs stared deep into my own, and yet she didn't dare move. I knew what she'd seen, though I was hoping she'd been out of it enough to brush it off.

How could I forget I'd cut myself earlier? Of course a human would notice things like that. Stupid oversight on my part, one that could cost me. Still, I couldn't look away, and I watched her eyes go out of focus as she let her body slip back into panic mode.

"Jasper, would you be so kind as to fetch Miss Stanton's medications from the house? And her purse, please?"

Jasper said nothing, but he hastened back to the house on my order. *Wise man.* Glancing back down at Izzy, I tried my best to smile tenderly without baring my fangs. Internally, I was screaming at myself, certain I must look like a ridiculous land shark with these jerky, unnatural displays of emotion.

"Please, Miss Stanton, I'm not going to hurt you. Deep breaths. I don't bite."

What a poor—*and ironic*—choice of words.

Izzy began laughing uncontrollably, her body shaking as she balanced precariously on the fence between a panic attack and hysterical disbelief. Tears formed in the corners of her eyes as she locked eyes with me, focusing back on my own. She opened her mouth to speak, and for once, it was I who was stunned speechless.

"It's funny you say that, being a vampire and all."

I felt like the next breath I managed to choke down burned me from the inside out. I swallowed thickly against the dryness in my throat, and managed to somehow squeak out a very unbecoming reply, the sound strangled and incredulous.

"W-what?" *Smooth, Lucien. Real smooth.*

"You know, a vampire, v-a-m-p-i-r-e. Like at my museum." She seemed eerily detached, as if she'd lost her ability to feel fear. I'd half expected her to bolt but she stayed in my arms, calmer than I'd ever seen her.

"I don't...under...stand..." My vocabulary was failing me by the second, and it took all I had in me to manage the few words I was presenting to her. *How could she know what I was? Surely that wasn't her immediate jump from my healed hands?*

"Well, your hands aren't injured anymore." She glanced down to my chest, avoiding my eyes as she muttered the next part. "And I kind of overheard you and Jasper talking."

"You *what?*" I was blown away by the fact that I'd been so offset by this beautiful woman that I'd missed her presence in the doorway of the boathouse. "So you heard every word?"

She laughed, her voice ringing out as she found amusement in the arms of a deadly predator. *Why wasn't she afraid? Why doesn't she run?*

"I heard enough."

I stood her up on her feet, noticing Jasper running back down the hill to interrupt us. "Jasper is back with your medications if you need them."

"Eh, I think I'm...alright?" She frowned as she looked up and down at herself, realizing she wasn't having a panic attack. "Yeah, I'm fine, for a change."

"Good," I sighed. "Because I have wanted to do this since the moment I laid eyes on you."

Before I could lose my nerve as much as I'd lost my mind, I leaned forward and covered her lips with my own in a tender kiss.

CHAPTER 9

~IZZY~

The moment our lips connected, my body was on high alert. Unlike when I had brazenly kissed him earlier, he took his time with me, his mouth moving across mine like a gentle caress. His hands trailed up and down my arms, raising goosebumps as a little thrill shot down my spine, straight to my core. His touch and kiss were slow, taking their time to assault my senses, and I was eating it up.

Desperately.

I felt Lucien take a step closer to me, and alarm bells went off in my brain like fireworks on the fourth of July. I knew I should heed them and end this before it began, but I couldn't bring myself to stop this runaway train of emotions and *lust.*

Because if I was honest, it was definitely lust I was feeling. It wasn't possible to love someone at first sight. That kind of stuff was for fairytales. Nevermind the fact that I had literally been transplanted into a fantastical nightmare story, complete with deadly creatures and a kidnapping. *If ever before had there been a good reason to doubt everything I took for granted as fact, this would be it.*

His hands slid around my shoulders, dragging me up against him. I couldn't bring myself to pull away, and it seemed he was equally as inclined to end this moment between us. As much as every moral fiber of my being screamed at me to flee, a part of me screamed out that this was *Lucien Sabatini, a gentleman*. I couldn't help but roll my eyes internally as I wondered what exactly that moniker was supposed to mean to me. My brain was so fried from all this anxiety that it wasn't operating as it should.

Yeah, that's gotta be it.

When his lips left mine, I gasped for breath, sucking air in like I'd never tasted it before. I leaned into his embrace, arched against his body as his mouth trailed soft kisses down my jaw, coming around to nibble on my earlobe. I gasped as a low moan broke free from deep within me as he deftly turned me from solid matter to a pooling liquid. Panting, I reached up a hand to his shoulder, grabbing his hair ribbon and pulling it loose.

His beautiful black hair cascaded down around his shoulders, framing his face as his lips found the sweet spot on my neck, right at the jugular. I felt my whole body go tense as he opened his mouth further, expecting him to bite me.

This is how I go out. He's going to turn me into dinner.

I guess as far as death goes, there could be worse ways to go out. I mean, I'd practically invited him to make me a snack. I couldn't move, couldn't breathe; every nerve ending in my body, every skin cell that covered me, was suspended in time as pure fear and anxiety leeched all my will to live. I was unable to do anything but sit there and stare at this apex predator standing before me, his crimson eyes surveying his food source for the night.

I watched him lean in towards my neck again, sucking in what I was sure would be my last breath. I wrapped my arms around his shoulders, embracing this sweet end that fate has stuck me with. How wasteful that I'd never gotten to do more things in Italy before being offed. Such a shame that my vacation was ending before it began. And poor Rosa, she would be left wondering what happened to me.

Just as I felt the tip of his tongue against the thin skin protecting my jugular, Lucien froze, his hands rising from my waist to my shoulders to separate our bodies. He shoved me backward gently, a look of abject horror on his face. His eyes seemed tortured as he stared intently at me, like I had become a poisonous plant.

Well, so much for a quick death.

~Lucien~

I stared at Izzy for what felt like forever, my whole body shaking with outrage at what I'd almost done. Had Jasper not cleared his throat behind me, I'd have probably taken her in more ways than one right here on the dewy grass.

She's not a fucking midnight snack, you insensitive piece of shit.

How could I be so stupid? So reckless? So *rude?* I had been seconds away from biting down and probably draining her dry on my boathouse deck. And she'd just held onto me, cradled in my arms as if it was normal for a vampyr to want to snack on her. As if she'd resigned herself to death.

She'd given up, embraced death as she stared it in the eyes. I was Death, and she'd welcomed me, thinking her end was imminent. She hadn't panicked, she hadn't fought, she hadn't tried to run. And that was dangerous when you were staying with a 200-year-old vampyr with an unquenchable thirst.

She'd smelled so good, standing there, and I'd just kissed her, my body blocking out all rational thought and delivering a proper kiss to this shy, anxious beauty. I felt my primal instincts take over, and she didn't panic when I'd nuzzled her as I searched out her pulsing jugular just below the tender skin. She'd arched into me as I clung to her, fearing she would flee before I had the chance to appreciate the way she fit against me properly.

When I'd opened my mouth, I couldn't help but taste her with the tip of my tongue. She'd frozen in place, her whole body still as a stone, and I hadn't paid it any mind at first. It was when her arms circled me that my mind finally broke through to my body and revolted against my lack of control.

I'd been powerless to stop myself until she acted so unnaturally for a human.

She'd been begging me to bite her, with her body molded against mine, willing and accepting of what was about to happen. *How could I be so reckless?* I'd almost ended things before they'd begun.

Was the Thirst rebelling against my more human emotions?

The Thirst was what drove all vampyrs. It was their base instincts—feed and fuck. Lust and hunger were the only two feelings we had. I'd forgotten how powerful it could be, how overwhelming, especially when one was hungry.

And sexually frustrated.

I held my hands in front of my face, staring at them as if they didn't belong to my body. How could I have let this almost happen?

"You should probably go back to the house. It would be best if you weren't alone with me. Jasper will escort you to your room. I apologize for my appalling behavior tonight, Miss Stanton. I promised you a safe atmosphere, and yet you're in more danger now than you would have been with your weasel of a boss, Mr. Chandley—"

"Chandless."

"Whatever. The point is, you're not safe with me right now. I'm…I'm sorry, I must go."

I turned, locking eyes with an outraged Jasper. Sighing, I made my way back up to the villa, which now looked more empty and ominous than ever. Perhaps it had always looked that way, or perhaps it appeared so because I longed to fill a void I hadn't realized existed in myself before last night.

Could this be what it felt like to be lonely? I couldn't remember, as terrible as it sounds. But if I had to describe it, the feeling was akin to floating in a solo raft down a river with no paddle. The sheer hopelessness played against the empty void, and I realized I was not too fond of this feeling. I wanted to turn around so badly, to go back and pick up where I left off, but I knew that was just the Thirst talking.

I needed to pay a visit to the blood bank and up my shipments if I was going to fight off the heightened urges around my lovely house guest.

~Izzy~

"I don't understand, Jasper. Did I do something wrong?"

Jasper had turned to watch his master's back retreating towards the house in the distance, and I hadn't moved from the spot Lucien had left me in—hungry for more. I had never been the kind of girl who enjoyed doing the horizontal bump the first day, but he stirred something in me that I hadn't paid any mind to in a long time. Since my last failed relationship...

Jasper turned to face me once Lucien had made it to the house, but his face still wore that same expression of disdain and frustration that he'd turned on his boss.

"You shouldn't just stand there as if you have no fear about any of this. You're human, and it's normal to be scared. It's not normal to roll over and offer yourself as a sacrifice. You realize he could have killed you in a split second?"

He sighed, running a hand through his hair and down the back of his neck, rubbing at the tension building between his shoulders. I stood still, realizing I didn't know much about either of these men here. And now I was stuck sharing a house with them while I was supposed to be relaxing. *Who could relax around two superhuman vampires? Why wasn't I panicking? Jasper was right; I should be.*

"I got caught up, I guess. I didn't exactly expect to be turned into a snack on my first night."

Jasper's eyes rolled to the sky as he crossed his arms. "Well, in any case, maybe we should get you back to your room for the evening. Or would you like to do something? I could have the driver take you around for some sights?"

"I could use some fresh air, but I would like to change first."

He nodded, pulling out a shiny, top-of-the-line phone from

his jacket pocket. A few clicks later, he replaced it, heading towards the house. I assumed I was supposed to follow, so I did, of course.

"The driver is ready when you are, Miss Stanton. You head on up to your room and let me know when you're ready to leave, and I'll have him pull around."

"How am I supposed to let you know I'm ready?"

He held out his phone, open to a new contact page. I assumed he wanted me to enter my information, so I did. Jasper seemed to genuinely care about my self-preservation, even if I had not given two shits about it just moments before. I felt my phone vibrate in my purse as he texted me, giving us an open line of communication.

"You just text me." He said not another word before he walked back the way we had come, and I was left to climb the stairs alone. I stared up to the next floor, the darkness heavy and ominous in the absence of the butler. I now knew what kinds of creatures lurked in these halls, and a fresh wave of panic washed over me at the most inopportune moment.

Why aren't these damn Xanax working anymore?

I stepped onto the first stair, the metal railing cold and smooth under my fingers. I willed my feet to move, knowing I had to get to my room and get ready if I planned to get out of this house for a little while. And it was painfully obvious I needed to clear my head.

When I got to the top, the surrounding area started looking familiar, and I managed to make it back to my room without wandering off too far. Once inside, I swapped my light sundress for a pair of leggings and a tunic dress with a hood. Comfortable and warm, the best way to be. Tying off a pair of sneakers and tying my hair back in a low ponytail were the finishing touches to the outfit, and I had only wasted fifteen minutes max.

While I was changing, I'd realized I had managed to keep Lucien's hair ribbon that I'd pulled off earlier. I resolved to take it to him before I left for the evening to see some sights. Maybe he'd want to join me or have some recommendations for me to check out. After all, he was a local. Surely it couldn't hurt to stop by, offer him the ribbon, and thank him again for the use of his villa. Jasper had mentioned Lucien's room was somewhere down the hall from mine. I texted Jasper to have the car ready and slipped my phone in my pocket as I left my room.

In the hallway, my grip tightened around the silk ribbon, sliding the slick fabric back and forth between my fingers as I walked away from my room. At the first door, I glanced around and realized there were a few more rooms on this floor than I'd originally thought. But if the only people staying here were truly the two vampire men and myself, then at least I'd not be disturbing anyone else by accidentally walking into their rooms.

Making my way down the hall, I headed for the next room as my ears picked up a peculiar sound. I stopped at the closest door, hearing a strange groan coming from the door just down the hall from mine.

Stop. Full Stop. You KNOW what happens to the dumb blondes who follow the sound in horror movies.

But I couldn't stop myself, walking further down the hall until I found myself directly in front of the most ornate door in the house. Its' mahogany wood stood in stark contrast to the light paneling, and the door wasn't quite closed all the way. I still heard the strange noise, and it sounded slightly familiar, as if I'd heard it somewhere before. *Maybe he had a headache. Dealing with me tended to do that to people, or so I'd heard.* Still, I had to return this ribbon, and I was sure Lucien would appreciate having it back.

I reached up to knock on the door, but it swung open before my knuckles rapped on the wood. When the door revealed the room, I dropped the hair ribbon on the floor, both horrifically embarrassed, and secretly intrigued at the scene before me.

Lucien was standing in his room, stark naked except for a towel he had tossed over his shoulders to catch the droplets from his damp hair. He must have just climbed from the shower, and I doubted he knew I was there, as his back was to me. For one excruciatingly long second, he stood there, one hand toweling his hair dry, the other in front of him, and then the perfectly sculpted man turned to face me, replacing the wonderful view I'd had of his ass with an even better one.

His eyes widened as he realized he had an audience, his hand frozen around his impressive package, mid-stroke. I realized finally where I'd heard that sound before, and I felt the heat rise in my cheeks from my embarrassment. But another heat had started to build inside me, a heat that pooled deep in my very core. A heat I hadn't felt in a long time.

Arousal.

Somehow, I managed to drag my eyes off his nether regions, following his sleek, well-toned abs up to his chest, and then finally coming to rest on his face. His crimson eyes had darkened nearly to black. I shuddered, a soft whimper leaving my lips before I managed to turn and run.

God, I hope that car is ready. I don't think I can look that man in the face again.

This was already turning out to be a hell of a vacation.

CHAPTER 10

~LUCIEN~

I listened to her rush down the stairs, my wet hair still dripping onto the towel around my shoulders. She'd seen me in a terribly compromising position, and I'd probably managed to scare her away with my primal, disgusting single-handed self-pleasure.

What the actual fuck was I thinking? I wasn't some newbie who couldn't control himself. I was an Elite, a centuries-old vampyr with training and abilities and *control.*

Except for tonight, apparently. The poor woman had been here for a day, and she'd already been exposed to my lack of decorum and my shameless self-love.

Too bad she hadn't stayed to help me with it.

Fuming at my own libido and stupid innuendos, I tried to force my brain to redirect. Unfortunately for me, I couldn't get it to cooperate, and there was no way I was walking out there with such an *obvious* issue rearing its head…*literally.*

I had to make this right, but first, I had to deal with my *condition.* I headed back into the bathroom, resigned to the idea of a cold shower. A *very cold shower.*

~Izzy~

I sat in the car, a very confused Jasper standing beside the back door. I hadn't explained anything, hadn't said a word when I'd come rushing down the stairs at breakneck speed, almost bowling him over in the process. I was still trying to process what I'd just seen, and the image was too fresh in my mind for me to shake.

His body was like a perfectly sculpted statue of Adonis, chiseled in all the right places, made of the rarest alabaster stone. I imagined his hands on me again, trailing down to touch me like he touched himself—

What the fuck? Where had that line of thought come from?

I had to get out of here and *fast*. I was on vacation, not on an orgy retreat. I needed to get my head out of the gutters and back into taking time for *me*. I needed to relax, and tonight had me on edge. My heartbeat was pounding in my chest, the blood rushing to my head as if I was standing upside down. I swallowed the lump in my throat, working up a shaky smile for Jasper.

"Is everything alright, Miss?"

I nodded, fighting to make my voice as steady as possible. It didn't work, and the result was a confident squeak, a testament to my timid nature.

"Uh, yeah, no problems here."

Jasper did not look convinced, but he let it slide as he started to close the door. "Just let your driver here know when you're ready to come back. Titus will make sure you get anywhere your heart desires. And I've instructed him to take you to all the best places. I'll see you when you return!"

I nodded, clutching my purse to my stomach like a lifeline I was afraid to let go of. I had no idea where we would go tonight, but anywhere was better than this awkward encounter. The door shutting between myself and Jasper was like the last nail in a coffin, and my claustrophobia started acting up immediately. Titus, the big burly driver in the front seat, looked over his shoulder at me with a cheesy smile on his face.

"Oi, I'm Titus; nice to meet you, miss. Anywhere you've got in mind tonight, or should I start you out with some 'o my favorites?" His smile seemed genuine, and he seemed more natural, unlike the unnatural feeling I got from the two vampires.

"You lead the way, Titus. I'll chime in as we go."

He turned to his wheel, leaving the divider open between us as he pulled the car out of the drive and onto a cleanly paved road. We toured the countryside as he told me tales of growing up not far from here, in Scotland. His father had been an artist, and when his mother had died suddenly after a car accident, he'd gone to live with the insufferable man for a summer. While there, he'd met Lucien in a pub and helped him fight his way out the back after a drunk swung a fist at him.

Lucien had responded to his kindness by offering him a legitimate job—personal driver and bodyguard. Of course, tired of his life with his father, Titus had jumped on the idea, and he'd been working at Master Sabatini's and Mr. Trudeau's orders ever since. It was good pay and not too intense, and he was even given a small cottage on the property to live in. Titus hadn't even seen that level of compassion from his own family, and he'd been quick to agree to the terms.

He'd never once complained about the strange hours his boss kept, and he'd always made sure to be on his best behavior around the Master especially. He seemed to disapprove of his harsh accent and manner of speaking, so Titus had worked hard at toning down what he'd picked up in the highlands. He turned his eyes to the rearview mirror, watching her expression as he talked about the places they visited.

"So the villa is actually right up against *Monte Pellegrino*, and it boasts some of the best views in the country. Over there to your left is the Gulf of Mondello; it's the port and beach scene over there. The mountain butts up against the Tyrrhenian Sea, and it's a big tourist attraction. We're actually headed into the city of Palermo now, where I'll show you some of my favorite haunts."

He paused for a moment, eyeing me through the mirror. I assumed he was waiting for a response, so I scrambled for some small talk, still struggling with the car's claustrophobic atmosphere.

"So, the beach? Are the sands really white here?"

His burly laugh filled the car's interior, the atmosphere lightening with his outburst. "Ah, I think ya mean the beaches of Spain. Ours are pale, sure, but not white. They're a modest beige, I reckon, but they don't disappoint." He cleared his throat, looking back at the road. His calm demeanor helped ease my frantic mind, and I sat back and tried to calm my racing heart. I reached into my purse, pulling out the familiar bottle of Xanax and passing it up for a pre-rolled joint I'd thought to stash in my bag.

I had run low and hadn't wanted to bring a huge supply over on the plane with me, so I took a chance, knowing it was either that or be an anxious mess the whole time. "Hey, um, Titus?" His eyes slowly slid up to meet mine in the mirror, and I took a deep breath, steeling myself for my next words. "Uh, so you get around a bit in the city, right?"

"Aye, I do." His eyes went back to the road, navigating smoothly around sharp turns in the beautiful landscape.

"You wouldn't know where to find certain *things*, would you?"

Titus chuckled in the front seat under his breath. "You mean drugs? I mean, there's plenty of clubs with plenty of people-"

"No, I mean *herb*, Titus. I take it for medication, and I'm honestly a wreck without it. It was too sketchy to bring it on the plane, so I left mine at home."

Understanding shown in his eyes, and he nodded in the front seat, pulling a phone out from the center console. "I've got some friends I can get a hold of."

After we'd discussed the specifics, he'd placed a call and set up a meet. Since we had time to kill, he'd pulled over to discuss the options I had for sightseeing at night.

"So the museum is closed, but there's the beach. It's a nice place to go at night. The stars are so bright, and they reflect off the water, so you can't even tell it's nighttime. Or you could hit up one of the local pubs with me, have a local wine while we take a stroll on the pier. And then there's the Piazza Pretoria, an open fountain that lights up beautifully at night. It's not too late to take a peek at the opera house, but it's probably too late to get a ticket. The botanical gardens do night viewings, and then there are the mountain viewpoints we could drive to."

I was amazed at how much there was to do at night. Coming from the US, where everything shuts down after a certain time, being here was like having a nighttime escape. It was still very warm and comfortable weather, even though the sun had set, and I struggled to decide what I wanted to do first.

"How about the wine and then the beach?" I suggested keeping it simple for now. Played it safe; wine and the beach would be a great relaxer, and the openness would help my anxiety.

"How about I do ya one betta'; there's a little spot on the pier that sells bottles, and we could take a nice walk in the sand with a bottle in hand."

"Two for one, I like it." I found it slightly easier to make typical small talk, now that my mind knew we would be free of the cramped car shortly. Or maybe it was because I knew I was talking to someone *human.*

Titus opened his door, stepping out and pulling open my door for me. He was sweet, the complete opposite of the people he worked for. And he was human, so there was that.

Why couldn't I find a guy like Titus who was interested in me? No, I had to be out here kissing vampires as if I had a death wish. Of course. I stepped out, grabbing my purse as my feet hit the hard ground outside. Titus closed the doors, locking up the car behind us.

The keys swung lazily from his finger in a slight arch as he motioned for me to follow him.

"The pier is just down this street and around the corner. Everything is pretty easy to get to around here, but if you want to look at other parts of Sicily, we may have to make a day of it. Mountain travel is time-consuming, and traffic is always horrible."

I nodded, knowing he couldn't see me. I didn't feel like chatting right now, concentrating on the route we were taking from the car in case we were separated. It was a habit I'd developed over time; being anxious tended to make you paranoid and led to overthinking every situation. I always planned for the worst, and some days it was exhausting that my mind immediately went to its darkest corners no matter the situation.

"Oh, you know, I think ye'd like the Cappella Palatina. It's some absolutely stunning architecture. It's pretty religious, being a chapel and all, but it's really worth the view. You should check it out while you're here in Sicily."

We rounded the corner and my feet found purchase on cobblestone streets, the feeling aesthetically pleasing. I had always admired good brickwork roads, and the biggest travesty of our time was watching them be paved over instead of repaired and maintained. Italy's culture and respect for its history were refreshing compared to the states, where we preferred to shove most of our seedy history under the rugs. Titus led me down the street until the cobblestones turned into wooden planks.

We'd finally arrived at the pier.

The line to the single kiosk on the long walkway was thankfully short, and I followed Titus closely as he joined the rest of the people waiting to be served. He turned to me, a quizzical expression on his face.

"Do ya like white wine or a hearty red'en?"

His brogue was thicker the longer we were away from the villa, and I found it oddly endearing. "I'm not picky. I do like a good red wine, but Moscato is also nice."

"I've got just the thing," he chimed as he stepped up to the counter. The man behind the kiosk looked like he was ready to call it a night, the weary lines etched permanently into his weathered face. Still, he pasted a smile on for each customer and did his best to appear friendly.

"What'll it be for the *signora* and her beau?"

I blushed but didn't bother to correct him. Titus spoke as if he'd been here before, calling the vendor by name.

"Oi, Mario, let's have that *Cerasuolo di Vittoria* you keep hyping up, *yea?*"

Mario's lips broke out in a wide grin as he reached under the counter and pulled out a beautiful bottle of wine, the entire label hand-drawn. The artwork looked stunning, and it was not mass-produced, but drawn for each bottle with care and affection. When Titus handed the bottle over to me to examine, I needed only a second to decide.

"Yes. This is perfect."

Mario laughed, a robust sound among the dim echoing conversations of the pier. "*Signora*, you haven't even tried it yet."

"I don't need to. If it's worthy of a hand-drawn label this ornate and well-done, it's got to be a damn good wine." Wine might not be my forte, but I knew a good drink when I saw one. You wouldn't catch a cheap company commissioning artwork like that for their bottles. This was a labor of love, and one I appreciated.

I handed over my card as Titus fumbled with his wallet, smiling in earnest at the vendor as he charged me for the wonderful bottle in my arms. He handed my card back, along with two plastic wine glasses and a wink.

"Enjoy that wine; it's the best Sicily makes."

Titus was still protesting the fact that I'd paid as we made our way over to the nearby table filled with wine corkscrews. I popped the cork like a pro, one fluid movement pulling the soft stopper from the neck of the bottle. Pouring two glasses, I replaced the cork and swirled the wine in my glass as I leaned down to inhale the sweet aroma.

The wine was aromatic, and I closed my eyes as I savored the heady scent of beautifully aged grapes mixed with the slightest hint of strawberries. Intrigued, I lifted the rim of the glass to my lips, sipping slowly. The flavor burst against the inside of my mouth, lighting my taste buds up in enjoyment. My hat went off to whoever managed to create this splendidly balanced flavor. It truly was a beautiful wine.

A little moan of pleasure slipped out from between my lips as I licked the lingering flavor from my mouth. I froze when I heard a familiar voice in the darkness.

"I see Titus has shown you Sicily's best wine. If you like it that much, I'd love to show you the vineyard someday."

My eyes snapped open, searching the beach for the source of the voice. They focused on a dark figure leaning against a lifeguard stand, his face obscured by the shadows. The figure stepped forward into the moonlight, and my breath caught in my throat.

Lucien.

CHAPTER 11

~IZZY~

I froze, my eyes blinking rapidly to erase him from the landscape. It was a feeble attempt, but I couldn't keep myself from trying. Lucien turned up his lips in a sexy smile, and I felt my limbs melting under those smoldering crimson eyes, his piercing gaze feeling like it could read the words written on my soul.

Since when was I a poet? Barf.

Being in Italy must have brought the romantic out in me. I reached over for the bottle, tipping it up to yank the cork out with my teeth. Lucien looked over to Titus sitting next to me, his eyes narrowing threateningly. Titus jumped up from the ground, his eyes nervous. He looked back at me, confusion marring his sweet features. He mouthed *I'll grab that for you* to me before heading over towards his boss, dusting the sand off of his pants awkwardly.

"Aye, bossman, I was just showing the lady around on Mr. Trudeau's orders. I was about to show her the beach."

Lucien's lips twitched just barely, as if it pained him to lift them in a smile. "I will be more than happy to show her around the town. Would you be so kind as to stay with the car? I will call for you when you're needed."

Knowing when he was dismissed, Titus tipped his hat to me and headed off, abandoning me to the care of a vampire. I chuckled, the sound feeling slightly hysterical as I assessed my situation. I had no idea where I was, I had forgotten how to make it back to the car, and I was alone. Well, not completely alone.

There was Lucien.

I steeled myself for whatever was about to happen, the memory of how I'd last seen him fresh in my mind. I could feel the warmth of my embarrassment climbing up my neck as I struggled to meet his eyes. I found them staring right back at me, two perfectly symmetrical orbs that seemed to study me curiously. I watched as something else clouded his vision, and he ran his fingers through his hair, pulled back once more.

Was he embarrassed too? Or ashamed? Lucien cleared his throat, and I held my breath, waiting for him to speak.

"Ah, do you like the wine, Miss Stanton?" His voice sounded strained as he struggled to make small talk to avoid the elephant in the room. Two could play that game, so I took the bait.

"It's nice. Wine isn't usually my thing, but this has a nice flavor. The vendor said it was local?" I looked back down at the bottle, running my fingers over the detail in the artwork on the label. He didn't speak, so I continued my observations. "This artwork is a custom job. It's absolutely stunning. Do you think the artist is local?"

Lucien sat down in the soft sand beside me, his eyes distant as he glanced out at the beach. He almost appeared wistful. "Each bottle's artwork is unique, and we commission quite a few local artists to do these labels." He reached out, turning the bottle in my grasp until the art was facing him. Pointing to the bottom corner of the label, he continued. "This one was done by Trissania, one of our older artists. She's in her seventies, but she'd got the steady hands of youth. Her bottles are some of the most precious ones in the collection because she only does one a week."

"Y-you…you?" I sputtered the words out, trying to make sense of what he had said. "You mean this is *your* winery?" I stared down at the valuable bottle in my hands, tipping it up to the rim of my glass to fill the plastic vessel. I would need all the assistance I could get to calm down and function around this man.

He nodded, a small smile pulling at the sides of his lips. *Lips that had felt so good against mine.* "Yes. My neighbor and I are equal partners in the winery that sits just behind my home. Perhaps I could take you to meet the artists sometime if you would like?"

His eyes had turned away from the shore, and they focused down on me, pinning me to the spot. I was paralyzed, my body a traitor to my wishes. Thankfully, my lips still moved, and I prayed my brain could make them communicate properly.

"That would be nice. I think I would like to meet this Trissania. Her pictures are so *vivid.*"

Lucien leaned in towards me, his hand finding purchase right next to mine in the pale sand. "Not as vivid as your eyes are, *cara mia.*"

I gasped as I choked on my own surprise. "These eyes? Ha, haha. They're nothing special—"

"Nonsense," he declared, his free hand reaching up to reach for the wine bottle I held like a lifeline. I released it instinctively, letting him move it to the side as I stared into his stunning eyes. I was mesmerized, and for some reason, I couldn't look away. His pupils seemed to dilate as I watched them. I blinked, but when I looked back, his eyes had returned to normal. I doubted what I'd seen, but my brain wouldn't make a connection with the red flags waving frantically in front of me.

"I don't see what's so special about them. My mother used to say they were creepy."

He brought his hand to mine, cradling my grip on the wine glass. He brought it to my lips, tipping it back as I swallowed the offered drink. I felt so scandalous, sitting here on a beach with practically a stranger, letting him feed me wine and kiss me senseless. I'd never been this *uninhibited* before, and it felt so…*freeing.*

"They aren't creepy to me. When I look into your eyes, it's like a window to your beautiful soul. I could drown in those golden pools until the sun comes up."

Before I could put the mental brakes on, the words escaped my lips, making me cringe as I watched his expression with apprehension. "Wouldn't want you to burn up in the morning sun, would we?" I slapped my hands across my mouth, the moment ruined with my dumb comment.

Curse my stupid mouth.

He rolled his eyes, muttering under his breath as he chuckled to himself. "Fucking *Bram.*"

I just sat there, hiding my face behind my hands, my embarrassment warm on my skin, as he grumbled for a moment. I felt his hands against mine, pulling them away from my face. I flushed an even brighter red as he revealed my expression.

"Perhaps you've mistaken me for Dracula. Let's just say that Bram was a bit too heavy on the fictional aspects of his own kind. He wasn't as concerned with accuracy as he was with shock value."

I must have looked like a gaping goldfish, my mouth opening and closing like a moron as I fought to process what he'd just said. I finally forced myself to vocalize, the sound coming out so faint it was almost imperceptible.

"Y-you're telling me he was a vampire?"

Lucien rolled his eyes again, and I feared he would get them stuck there before the end of the night. "First off, *stellina,* it's pronounced [vam-PIER], spelled v-a-m-p-y-r. Second, *yes.*"

"*Vampyr,*" I said, rolling the pronunciation around on my tongue like I was savoring the first bite of dessert. Lucien observed me, his eyes traveling to the glass in my hand. In a flash, he had grabbed the bottle to refill my glass for me, and I couldn't seem to say *no,* even though I knew I should. "What else have I gotten wrong all these years?"

"Oh, *cara mia,* you have no idea. But no worries—we have all the time in the world for me to teach you."

His eyes glinted dangerously, and I felt heat pool low in my stomach. My chest felt lighter, and I was more relaxed than I had a right to be. I handed him a cork for the wine bottle, and he secured it without breaking eye contact with me. I felt light, free, uninhibited, and it wasn't unpleasant. I hadn't felt this comfortable in a long while, and it concerned me that I found this level of calm with a complete stranger.

"Why don't you tell me about yourself? All I know about you is your name. And your…um…" I gestured vaguely at him, intending to indicate his vampyr affliction. "You know, your need to drink blood and whatnot."

"Ah, my *immortality?*" He reached for my glass, and I let him take it, watching him spin it to lay his lips where mine had been seconds before. The sight of him licking his lips after tasting the wine set off a slow burning fire inside me, and I wanted nothing more than to taste the sweet wine from his lips. I felt energized, emboldened by the alcohol and the secluded atmosphere of the beach.

I tipped back the glass and downed what was left of my third glass, feeling a strong buzz pulse through my body. I ignored the alarms that told me not to behave out of character, to tell him goodnight and have Titus take me home, and instead, I leaned in, the plastic wine glass falling from the tips of my fingers as our mouths collided. I grabbed his shirt, pulling him towards me with such force that I toppled backward, Lucien falling over me. Somehow, our lips stayed together, moving against each other like two starving lovers.

I didn't understand this primal attraction to Lucien. I couldn't wrap my head around my behavior towards him, and I wondered if I truly had become so disconnected from other people that I'd literally fallen for the first man to swoop in with chivalry and sex appeal. His hands were braced on either side of my head, and I felt the sexual tension building, nearly giving into it before realizing we were still on a public beach. I gasped, somehow managing to shrink back into the sand beneath me.

Lucien pulled back, still hovering above as he stared at me, his eyebrows practically touching his hairline. "Well…that was…" He blinked, unable to find the words to explain what had just happened. I was secretly pleased by his reaction because it meant he was just as affected by me as I was by him. He sat straight up, pulling me up to a sitting position beside him.

"Why don't we go for a walk? I can tell you whatever you want to know about me. I'll try to answer any questions you might have."

I agreed if only to prolong our inevitable return to the villa. I enjoyed my time with Lucien, and I hadn't dissolved into a fit of panic since his arrival, which was a vast improvement.

"Sure." *Boy, was I a great conversationalist.*

Lucien offered his hand to help me up from the ground. I took it eagerly, pulling myself off the sand. He led the way, wine bottle and glasses in hand, walking down the length of the beach with confident strides. He didn't wait to see if I was keeping up, and I felt compelled to keep pace as we walked along the shore. His free hand grazed mine occasionally as we moved leisurely, the skin-to-skin contact sending a little thrill down my spine every time.

"Well, did you have questions that you wanted to ask me?" He stared straight ahead, but I sensed the ire in his voice. I wanted to get this right, so I took a deep breath and started with the obvious.

"So what about the sunlight burning you to dust thing? Fake?"

He nodded. "Very untrue, especially for an Elite."

My eyes were round as saucers, intrigued by even his dismissive answers. "An Elite? What does that mean?"

"Elites are vampyrs who have been alive for a very long time. Their enhanced senses and peak powers are amplified and superior to younger vampyrs."

"There are *others?*" I knew my expression must have been a sight. This was the biggest shock of my life, and I couldn't learn enough. "What about the whole bat thing?" I saw his expression darken to absolute horror and laughed. "That's a no. Hmmm. How about you? Tell me about yourself."

He sighed, rolling his eyes in frustration. "All the questions you could ask about my kind right now, and you'd rather know *my history as a human.*"

"Well, yeah. You're still a human, Lucien; you're just an immortal one now. That doesn't mean you've turned into something inhuman. You're still you, right?"

~Lucien~

I contemplated that question, honestly unsure of the truth to the base of it. Was I still me?

"I'm . . .I'm not sure. I haven't felt human in a very long time. But," I sighed, looking over at the wide-eyed wonder written all over her face, "*you make me feel human again.*"

She blinked rapidly, something I noticed she did whenever she was having a hard time believing something. "Me?" she squeaked, pointing to herself jerkily.

"You." I felt my lips curl up in a smile, this one feeling more natural than the forced ones I'd become used to dishing out when necessary. "You have made me feel something different from the minute I saw your picture. It's part of why I offered the villa up as a vacation for you. I'm glad you accepted, but I am sorry my cousin didn't warn you it was also my primary residence. I can't imagine you were expecting to be sharing it with anyone."

"It's fine. I really appreciate the offer to stay, as I've never been able to afford to leave the states for a vacation before. My parents were always jet-setting with friends, but they preferred to leave the baggage at home."

"Such a shame they didn't appreciate you the way you deserved. I am sorry you had to suffer like that."

She chuckled, trying to cover the tears she was barely keeping at bay. I'd noticed them shimmering in the corner of her eyes but assumed she wouldn't want to be caught in a moment of weakness. I could allow her this one moment without embarrassment.

"You're deflecting to me to try and avoid the question. Didn't you say you'd answer any question I had?"

She had me there. "You're right. Let us start with who I was, and then you can draw your own conclusions on who I've *become.*" I took a deep breath, slowing my pace even more as I spilled my history to her. "I was born in 1803, or thereabouts, the illegitimate son of an Italian architect and a back alley barmaid. My brother was your boss's great great great grandfather. I grew up in the back of opera houses and brothels, and I became a wild, uncontrollable youth. At sixteen, my mother fell very ill, and in just a few days, she had passed. I became a street urchin, doing what I could, where I could for some food and coin for a room. I thieved, conned, and tricked my way to a comfortable existence, and I would have been content to step on the backs of others to get where I wanted to be, had it not been for my untimely death and subsequent Turning."

"Who turned you?" Her eyes showed no hint of fear, and I wondered why this beautiful human had been sent to me by fate. *Was this a trick? Would she truly be the first to accept what I was? Or would she eventually run too?*

"My creator was none other than a young Edgar Allen Poe."

CHAPTER 12

~IZZY~

"You're kidding. You *have* to be. How is that even possible?"

In some sick way, it all sort of did make sense, and of all people on the planet, I guess it made sense that I could appreciate the irony. Two of the best gothic writers of literary history, and they were creatures that haunted their own printed word. Poe, a vampyr. And Bram Stoker. How crazy, and yet, oddly fitting.

"Yes, it is odd, isn't it?" He chuckled under his breath. "Not everyone knew the *real* Poe, but I did. He was a nasty man, and he thought I would be so grateful for him 'saving' me— after taking a sizable chunk out of my neck and killing me himself—that I would become his eternal companion. I had no desire to prostrate myself to a child molester, and I left after learning what I could about what I was."

I gasped, covering my mouth with my free hand. It was shocking to hear that a man who produced such striking poetry and prose could be so vile in real life. I was disappointed to hear one of my literary idols trashed, but since I hadn't had the chance to meet him in life, I only had his historical recollections to go on, and to be honest, they were pretty damning as well.

"What happened to him? Did he hunt you down?"

"He tried. But I was good at hiding and willing to travel further. He ended up killing himself, ashamed at what he was, or distraught at being rejected, who knows. I went to his funeral. He'd doused himself in lamp oil and lit himself on fire. It wasn't pretty, but I had no sympathy for the man by then. I'd always resented him for making me into what I am today."

I frowned, stopping in my tracks. "I don't resent him Turning you. Who knows where I'd be now if I hadn't met you at the gala." *The truth, what I'd really meant to say, was 'if not for him turning you, I'd have never met you.'* I swallowed my secret passion, trying to rein myself in.

Lucien smiled at me, and I genuinely felt he meant it this time. I was getting good already at telling when his smiles were sincere and when they were fake. As someone who avoided social interactions, I'd grown to be a skilled people-watcher.

"I am glad to have been at your service that night. I can't believe it's only been two days. I feel like I've waited for you for my whole life."

I couldn't tell if he really meant that line or if I just misunderstood him. I could feel the drink slurring my speech, slowing my reactions. I was sober enough to know that I shouldn't take another drink and drunk enough to know what would happen if I didn't sober up soon. I closed my eyes, trying to calm my breathing, I paced it to the slow rhythm of the waves against the shore, and I felt my feet carry me slowly to the white foam left behind by the waves that beat upon the sand. As the first wave kissed the tips of my toes, I took my shoes off, abandoning them as I felt the sand squish up between my toes satisfyingly.

I let the water lap over my feet, the cold sending a shiver down my spine as I walked along the surf, poking at the incoming waves with my toes playfully. I was too far gone to care how I looked or who might be watching me. I was having *fun,* and it had been forever and a day since I'd felt this *free.* I never wanted this feeling to stop, and I twirled around in the moonlight, dancing to the beat of a song that drifted from a nearby restaurant terrace. It was old 50's music, and the words to *Volare* by Domenico Modugno echoed out over the water. I swayed in the light breeze, and I didn't tense up when I felt Lucien behind me, swaying with me in the crashing surf, his loafers discarded next to my own footwear.

"You know, we could come back out soon, have a night on the town. You'd be surprised how much there is to do in Palermo at night, and all of Sicily has a secret nightlife that you only have to look around to see. It is why I've been able to stay so well hidden for so long. It's perfectly normal to be a nocturnal Sicilian."

His arms wrapped around my shoulders, holding my arms in a gentle embrace as he swayed with me to the next slow song that played softly in the distance. He sang softly along to the words, probably from memory, as I couldn't hear them clearly from so far away. I closed my eyes as I let his body guide me, swaying slower and slower until I felt us stopping. His hands turned me around, and I knew I was wearing a goofy smile, but I couldn't bring myself to care. *Thank you, vino.*

I opened my eyes, still smiling sloppily at this gorgeous, well-kempt man in front of me. If he could look at this drunken, loose-as-a-goose woman in front of him and still see something special, then I would give in, and *que sera sera,* as the French would say.

"Whatever will be, will be..." I muttered, focusing on the crimson swirls in his sexy eyes that reflected my own golden gaze. Lucien arched an eyebrow, a smile teasing the side of his lips.

"What's that, *il tesoro?*"

"I wish I knew what all these lovely Italian words meant, Lucien."

He was silent as I gasped, realizing it was the first time I'd called him by only his first name. The whole thing sounded so informal, so *scandalous,* and I shuddered as I wondered if he'd finished what he'd started when I left the villa. I suddenly had the urge to reach out and touch this man. Being disconnected from my usually-rational brain, my body acted on its own, my fingers brushing against his shoulder gently, surveying the sharp, defined lines of his blazer. He stilled, one hand still around my waist, our bodies inches from each other as I trailed my fingertips down his jacket sleeve, rubbing the silk of his shirt where it met the edge of his blazer cuffs.

His eyes felt like they were burning a hole in the top of my head as I stared down at his hands, my nails trailing slowly along his long fingers, taking my time to drag them agonizingly slowly back up his arm and to the collar of his jacket. I brought a second hand up to meet the first and pulled gently at the knot in his tie.

It had been forever since I'd undone a man's tie, but it was like riding a bike—once you learn, you never really forget. I untied the knot, slipping it free of his collar. I let the expensive fabric slip from my hands, watching it fall to the sand beneath my feet. I swallowed the slight panic that flared in my mind, pushing myself to keep going. Smart me wanted to stop right here. Buzzed me said I might as well enjoy it while I could. Even dreams have to end sometimes.

"Well," he muttered as I began working on the buttons of his blazer, "*il tesoro* means my sweet. *Cara mia* is my darling, *stelina* is little star. Everything I call you is a term of endearment, rest assured, *signora.*" Two more buttons popped free, one after the other in quick succession. I pushed my hands inside his jacket, splaying my hands out over his heart, reveling in the feel of the steady rhythm beneath my hands.

"Your heart still beats," I observed very matter-of-factly.

"Did you think it would not?"

I shrugged, honestly not sure what I thought. All of this was so confusing and so unbelievable. "I don't know what to expect with you."

He shrugged off his jacket, letting the crisp fabric fall behind him, the spray of the surf turning the edges of the fabric a darker grey. I sighed at the idea of a dry cleaning bill for such an expensive jacket but paid it no more mind as I felt Lucien's nipples pebble beneath my fingers. I could feel his breathing grow rapid and shallow, his nostrils flaring as I absently flicked the hard nubs through his shirt. The friction of the fabric on his sensitive spots drew a moan from his lips, and he closed his eyes, throwing his head back as I explored his body.

I had no idea what I was doing or why; all I knew was that my body was reacting to his in ways it had never reacted to any other man, and I ached to feel his skin against mine, his lips on *my* tender spots. I felt the familiar lust settle in my core, and I arched into him, feeling his arousal against my thigh. My lips were inches away from his neck, and I thought to myself, *what the hell.*

I moved my lips against the pulse in his throat, and I bit down on his skin, my hands gripping his shirt as if it were my anchor.

The last thing I felt was an overwhelming pleasure, sending waves of intense shock through my body, and then everything faded to black.

~Lucien~

Fucking Christ, this woman had a death wish. She'd bitten *me,* the vampyr, instead of the other way around. My blood was like the most powerful aphrodisiac, and to a mere human, it was probably overwhelming. I felt her body shudder uncontrollably against mine before feeling her go limp in my arms. I glanced around, making sure there were no witnesses to what had just happened. My hand went to my throat, checking the tiny puncture where she'd broken the skin.

It was already healing, meaning she hadn't got much of my blood, but even a drop was enough. She'd probably blacked out from the intensity. Izzy's forehead was hot to the touch, almost like she was running a fever. I lifted her into my arms, positioning her to look asleep to any passerby, and grabbed our shoes and the bottle of wine. Snagging her purse with my teeth, I dropped the tiny bag on her lap and leaned sideways to get my jacket. I cursed my male brain as I watched the salty sea water drip off the costly fabric. This would be a fortune to clean, but it was but a drop in the bucket to me.

I walked back to the sidewalk like that, the two of us painting quite the image. Many would assume she had too much to drink and pay us no mind, but I hoped we didn't run into any good samaritans who asked too many questions. I needed to get her back to the villa, and fast.

She stirred in my arms, and I moved into a nearby alley, leaning up against the brick building for support as I fished my phone out of my pocket. I dialed up Titus, barking sharp, frenzied orders into the receiver of the cellphone. Within a few minutes, he had pulled the car around to the opening of the alley, a concerned look on his face.

"Is the lassie alrigh', boss?"

"Yes, Titus, just a bit too much to drink. I'll have Jasper ready her room if you would be so kind as to take us back to the villa promptly."

I slid into the car, rearranging everything as we pulled away from the dark alley, putting Palermo behind us as the miles melted away. Izzy's fever was finally fading, and I breathed a sigh of relief that she seemed to be just out cold and not suffering any ill effects from drawing blood. She stirred in her sleep, but she didn't wake, thankfully. Before I realized it, we had arrived back home, and I pulled her from the car, grabbing her purse and the wine before calling out over my shoulder to Titus.

"Grab the jacket and shoes and leave them in the foyer for me, would you? I'll deal with them later."

I didn't wait for a reply, wasting no time in taking Izzy directly up to my bedroom, slamming the door behind me. I laid her on the duvet covering my bed, running my hand across her forehead. She stirred again, this time opening her eyes, her gaze confused.

"What happened? We were just on the beach…" She looked around at her surroundings, recognizing the room from earlier today. A blush crept up her cheeks as she noticed she was in the middle of my bed.

"You bit me. And it was not your finest moment, considering a drop of my blood can be fatal to a human."

She looked down at her hands sitting idle in her lap, and I watched her shiver slightly. "It didn't feel like death. It felt…amazing."

"My blood is a strong aphrodisiac, and it's fatal in large doses." I raised an eyebrow as I watched the facts sink in.

"But I was attracted to you before the bite."

I felt my pants grow tight at her revelation. *She must still be buzzed.* I was not the type of man to take advantage of a woman, and tonight was no different. "If you feel the same way in the morning, we can discuss it then. Maybe, for now, you should get some rest."

I walked over, sitting next to her on the bed. I felt her reach out to lay her hand next to mine, gauging my reaction. I stilled, waiting to see what she would do next. The bed shifted under her weight as she shuffled around, approaching me from behind. Izzy's body leaned up against mine as she reached over my shoulders, running her hands back down my chest as she placed kisses on my earlobe.

My blood was strong, but not this strong. This wasn't a reaction to the bite; this was the true desires of one Izzy Stanton, buried deep beneath her proper, anxious demeanor. And I would be the one to release the lynx from her cage. I sighed as she whispered in my ear, her breath tickling my skin, my pants becoming an uncomfortable prison.

"I need to feel your skin on mine, Lucien. I don't know *why*, but I need you. I feel things about you I've *never* felt for *any man* before. Please, Lucien, just for tonight, let's forget about propriety, forget about rules. *Let's just let whatever happens, happen.*"

I barely recognized the woman behind me, her claws raking up and down my arms as I cut loose, letting my lust rise to the surface as I turned and captured her lips with my own, lowering her back to the bed.

CHAPTER 13

~IZZY~

"Let's just let whatever happens, happen."

I barely recognized myself as the words slipped from my mouth, revealing my deepest desires. My nails raked up and down Lucien's arms as I cut loose, lust rising to the surface as he turned and captured my lips with his own, lowering me back on the bed.

I couldn't seem to find the word *stop*, and I realized I didn't *want* to stop. This was the real me, and I had *needs*. My anxiety had gotten in the way for so long, I'd forgotten what it felt like to be myself and feel confident in a situation. I wasn't sure what had caused this drastic transformation, but I embraced it, locking my hands around his neck as he kissed me senseless. Lucien's tongue tangled with mine in a desperate dance, both of us hungry for the other. But then, he pulled away suddenly, a frown marring his classical features.

"We can't do this. You've been drinking. It's…*not right.*"

Oh great, a vampyr with a conscience. How convenient. And just my luck, too.

I frowned as he sat up, pulling farther away from me just as I managed to overcome my anxiety and break free of my tethers. I knew I must be pouting, but I couldn't bring myself to care, eyeing the half-full bottle of wine sitting nearby on the bureau.

"If you're going to be a prude, then I'm going to finish this wine." I scrambled to the edge of the bed, my bare feet gliding along the smooth wooden floor beneath them as I approached the dresser. I plucked the decorative bottle from its temporary home, doing a little dance as I yanked the cork out with my teeth. Behind me, I heard Lucien mutter under his breath, so I turned to face him, firing the cork off at him from between my lips. It hit him in the center of the forehead with a resounding *thunk*, and he cursed under his breath in outrage. I paid him no mind, preferring instead to survey the room a bit more, now that I was inside it and not…*preoccupied.*

I blushed as the memory of his erection flashed across my mind, teasing me with what I couldn't have. Lust turned into frustration instantly, and it was like I had dumped a bucket of ice water on myself. Now, I was just angry. Angry at the situation, at this frustrating, suddenly *chaste* gentleman who had been delectably nibbling on my neck like I was a snack earlier.

The bottle tipped back again as I heard music come on behind me. I narrowed my eyes at his choice, some crazy classical operetta, and he cracked a slight smile.

"Do you not like the selection?" He held out a remote to the surround sound, and I yanked it from his hands, eyeing the unlabeled buttons that littered the thing before I tossed it on the bed. My hand dipped into my purse, which had been sitting with the bottle, and retrieved my phone. A few clicks later and I'd readied a playlist I used to turn on to unwind at home. I looked expectantly at Lucien, waiting for him to figure out what I wanted to do, but he simply sat there on the edge of his bed, smirking at me as if I was the funniest thing in the world.

"Does this thing have Bluetooth or an aux cord?"

"Um," he said, glancing over at the wall-mounted head unit, "I guess, maybe *both*?"

Rolling my eyes, I made my way over to the stereo, grabbing the aux cord and shoving it into the headphones jack on the base of my phone. My impatience was bleeding into every action I performed, and Lucien took that moment to laugh at my fumbling movements as I missed the hole several times.

"Your aim is terrible, isn't it?" It was honestly frustrating that he found a perverted pleasure in my Freudian slips, considering he had no interest in taking this further. *Tip the bottle up again,* my mind screamed at me, and so I did, not caring that I was fast becoming a bit too buzzed again.

"No, my aim is *right on target.*" As soon as the words were out of my mouth, the speakers blasted Bruno Mars' *Versace on the Floor,* a very *pointed jab* at the man on the edge of the bed. *And sip.* Another swill of wine later, there was a moment of clarity where I realized I was digging myself a hole, but I was too drunk to care. I danced around to the beat, holding the bottle of wine like a lover pressed tightly against my breasts. I swayed seductively, my back to the bed, eyes closed as the sounds swirled around me.

I felt his hand reach around me to grab the wine bottle, and for a split second, I tightened my hold on it, not wanting to share it with him. But he tugged the bottle free, lifting it to his own lips, a sexy smile on his face as he downed all but a sip of the wine. He handed the bottle back to me sheepishly as I frowned at the tiny amount left in the bottom. My moan of displeasure was audible, and I leaned back, lifting the bottle to the sky as I opened my mouth, intending to fountain the wine from bottle to throat, but I listed sideways, bumping into Lucien. The dark red wine splashed out, staining his stark white silk button-up, to my abject horror.

Now I'd ruined his shirt.

~Lucien~

She set the bottle down on the bureau, rushing back over to inspect the damage she'd done to my beautiful shirt. The *expensive* shirt that I'd had since 1908. I cringed at the blossoming stain across the front, sighing my frustration.

Well, she wanted you naked, it seems she found a way to get what she wanted.

I knew she hadn't done it on purpose but the irony was inescapable. I had turned down a gift, all wrapped up neatly in an eager little bow, and fate had paid me back by forcing my hand, trying to encourage the inevitable to happen. I'd taken the bottle and downed a quarter of it; I'd been so mesmerized by the way her body moved in that cute little dress that I was willing to do anything to distract myself. Her long, lithe legs dancing around in my bedroom, the skirt of her dress just barely decent, it all drove me wild, and I found myself attracted to every part of her at that moment.

The wine was already working its way through my system, and I couldn't keep my eyes off her. I knew this had been a terrible idea from the start. I knew better than to drink that wine when I was already struggling to keep my hands to myself. But the sight of her tipping that bottle back while she teased me with these sensual songs drove me absolutely wild. I needed her like the desert needs rain, and I was a thirsty man stumbling in the sand.

Or I had been until she'd spilled the wine on me.

She'd hurried back across the room, her hands flying across the buttons of my shirt as I undid the cuffs of the slick fabric, tenderly pulling the buttons from the hand-stitched holes that secured them. I tugged my arms out of the sleeves as Izzy freed the last button on the front, still muttering apologies.

"I'm so so so sorry, this shirt looks so expensive, Lucien I didn't mean—"

"It's fine, really. I'll have it cleaned." *That was gonna be a hell of a bill.* "You don't need to panic. Accidents happen."

"I'm not normally this clumsy, though." She eyed my chest as I pulled the shirt off my back, a thin sheen on my chest from the wine that had soaked through the silk. Her gaze burned a trail across my pecks, sinking lower to eye the abs that I worked hard to maintain. I puffed up with pride, the alcohol buzz melting away the years of apprehension and disinterest towards humans that I'd built up. I felt loose…*wild.*

Izzy reached out her hand, placing it gently against my shoulder. It laid there, unmoving as we both stared down at it. My mind was swirling, the wine blurring the line between sophisticated, gentlemanly me and uninhibited, free me. If I didn't get control of this situation, it would end up exactly where I had tried to avoid taking it, and we would both regret it in the morning.

"Izzy…maybe we should call it a night."

The only sounds from her lips were an affirmative hum, but neither of us moved an inch. Her fingers flexed against my cool skin, and I reached up to capture her wrists with my left hand. I dropped my favorite shirt to the floor behind me, and something inside me clicked, like flipping a switch.

There's no going back if she doesn't stop this train from derailing.

If she told me no, I would listen. If she turned to leave, I wouldn't stop her. But I was unable to stop what we'd set in motion, and I feared she had no desire to either. Her eyes met mine, and she leaned forward, her tongue darting out to lick the swell of her bottom lip. I held my breath, suddenly unsure of myself. Was it truly right to let this happen when we were both inebriated?

"Lucien?"

Hearing her whisper my name like it was the most secret of sins had my inner monster clawing at the inside of my mind, eager to be free. I swallowed my trepidation, not daring to look up from her hand sitting on my shoulder.

I managed to whisper a response, my body on edge. *"Si, amore?"*

She finally let her hand trail down my chest, coming to rest over my heart. My hand stayed around her wrist, moving with her hand as she felt my heartbeat under her slender fingers.

"Do you always have to be so serious? Can't you just cut loose for a night?"

"I'm always serious, *amore,* I can't change what I am."

"It's not healthy to always be serious all the time. All work and no play makes Lucien a dull boy."

Her eyes rose to find mine, and I saw a swirl of mischievousness in her beautiful amber eyes. My lips twisted up in an honest smile, amused by her words. "I'm not all work and no play. And I am certainly no *boy*."

As soon as the words were out of my mouth, I knew I was toast. There couldn't have been a more provocative word choice, especially in this moment. Izzy's eyes narrowed, and she bit her bottom lip playfully, plotting her next words carefully.

"You know, this wine really sets the *mood*. " She leaned forward until her lips were brushing mine, dangerously close to sparking a raging fire between us. "Maybe you could show me how a *man* handles the job?"

I groaned, shoving her away with the last bit of control I had left. "I won't take advantage of you while you're drunk, Lizzania Stanton. I might be a monster, but I am not a *reprobate*." I stormed over to the chair in the corner, throwing myself into it as I hung my head in my hands, ashamed. I'd let this go too far, and a sick part of me wanted this. I wanted to take her, right here in my bed, and not regret it the next morning.

I'd done worse with women before. Women who were on far more than wine. But with Izzy, it was…different. I didn't want to hurt her, and it pained me to imagine her rejecting me in the morning. But my brain was shutting down, and I could feel the thirst rising. It wasn't blood I craved, however. It was *her*, this beautiful woman before me that set me on fire and made me salivate with longing. I wanted every part of her, and I strained against my own self-restraint to keep her safe.

From between the cracks in my fingers, I saw two bare feet appear before me, and I groaned in agony. "You don't understand." I shook my head, still buried in my hands, wanting to fall through the floor. Here I was, an elite, showing weakness in front of a human. *Deplorable. A disgrace.*

She reached out, pulling my hands away from my face

gently as she kneeled between my legs. I met her gaze with my own tortured crimson one, and I knew she could see the pain written on my face. But she didn't recoil, and she didn't shrink away.

"Lucien," she breathed, her eyes searching my own, "let me have tonight. We can worry about tomorrow in the morning." She stretched up to crush her lips against mine, hungry and starved. Her tongue sought entrance at the crease of my own lips, and I parted them to allow her access, her sweet taste mingling with my own. I devoured her, taking all she had to offer as she wound her arms around my neck, leaning into my body. I wrapped my arms around her waist, pulling her up to a standing position with me. I broke the kiss, knowing there was no going back, but needing to hear her say the words before I gave into this burning desire I had for her.

"Are you sure, *cara mia?*"

She pulled me back in, her lips pecking at mine before trailing to my earlobe. She nibbled it hungrily, and I was putty in her hands as she whispered in my ear.

"I've never wanted anything in my life as much as I want this."

With those words bouncing around in my brain, I felt the last string tying me back snap, and I cursed the wine and the music as I let myself *feel* for the first time in what felt like forever.

CHAPTER 14

~LUCIEN~

Our lips found each other again, the need more obvious now as I felt her thigh pressed against mine, and I knew she felt how eager I already was. My arousal wasn't subtle, and I had the decency to blush as she dropped to her knees, working on my jean buttons with a speed I hadn't known she possessed. *Where had the timid, anxious little wren from earlier gone?*

Not that I minded the switch up. This fiery vixen knew what she wanted, and she went for it without apology. When her hand brushed against the swell of my cock straining against my boxers, I bucked like a randy teen, her purposeful caress eliciting a moan from deep within me. If she kept touching me like that, I'd surely make a fool of myself.

"Aren't you moving this a little *fast, cara mia?*"

She looked up to meet my eyes, and the sight of her on her knees below me had me weak again. She licked her lips like she was about to devour me, and I leaned down, dragging her to her feet. I wasn't about to let her control the pace. She'd asked for a demonstration, and she'd get a good one.

I picked her up by the waist, and her legs instinctively wrapped around my hips as I walked her over to the edge of my bed. I could feel the warmth of her hot core against the opening in my trousers, and I throbbed with the desire to ram myself deep into her. I set her on the edge of the bed, unwrapping her legs from my torso gently before taking one of her ankles in my hands, turning her leg outward to expose the soft inner skin of her calf. She gasped, leaning back on her elbows as I trailed kisses from her ankle to the inside of her knee, and still further, until my lips met with the hem of her dress, sitting at mid-thigh.

Izzy let her head fall back, and her blonde waves brushed against my comforter as she enjoyed my ministrations. I nibbled at the inside of her thigh, just below her dress, and she moaned seductively in response, not shy about making her pleasure known.

Oh, I might regret this in the morning, but I was going to enjoy tonight…

~Izzy~

He planted tiny, gentle kisses along the inside of my leg, and my skin tingled every time I felt his lips getting closer to his end goal. I practically died on the spot when he stopped at the hem of my dress, and I had to restrain myself from yanking it up to afford him more access. I leaned my head back, closing my eyes as I savored his tiny nibbles on my sensitive inner thigh. He knew how to mix the best of pleasure and pain, and I silently thanked the gods for his skill. He turned my insides to mush, and I felt like a puddle of desire and want, my every pore aching for him to take me completely.

I hadn't felt like this before *ever*, and I tried not to dwell too much on my intense attraction to Lucien, languishing in the feel of his lips on my skin instead. I felt his hand snake under my skirt, trailing up the outside of my thighs until his fingers ran into the lace fabric of my panties. With a single deft movement, he was snaking them down my legs, and I blushed as I realized I was *dripping* for him already.

His hands had disappeared with my black thong, and I shivered when one of them crept back up under my dress, his fingers trailing along my skin agonizingly slow. I held my breath, afraid to open my eyes as I felt a single digit slide down my slick, wet folds, coating him in my juices.

The moan that escaped my throat was scandalous, but I couldn't help myself as his finger trailed up and down my slit, teasing my body to a near-frenzy as I squirmed under his hand. Lucien pulled away his finger, and I was so out of it, I leaned up to look at him in displeasure, but I caught sight of his blood-red eyes instead as he shoved my dress up around my waist and replaced his finger with his tongue, flicking the tip across my clit as I struggled to breathe.

I couldn't look away as he kissed my most sensitive spot, drawing illicit moans and cries from a place in me I'd never seen before. His hands cupped my ass as he lifted my hips to afford himself better access, and I screamed out in pleasure as his tongue slid inside my hot core, fucking me with his mouth as he lapped up every last drop of my juices. When his fingers slid inside me to join his tongue, he curled them *just so* and hit a spot no man had ever touched. My hips jerked heavenward as he thrust his digits in and out of me, his tongue drawing my clit to a hard nub as he drove me over the edge of ecstasy, and I felt the first orgasm crash over me like the waves of the ocean.

What had this man done to me?

~Lucien~

I lapped her up as she shuddered in the throes of an orgasm; not the only one I had planned to give her tonight. I lifted my mouth from her hot, tight center, reaching down to free my cock from these confining pants I still wore.

I could feel the moist beads of pleasure on the tip of my shaft, and I couldn't resist stroking it a few times as Izzy watched, biting that adorable lower lip of hers. The single act was so sexy it made my dick throb in eagerness. I jerked my hand up and down as she watched me touch myself, my eyes widening in surprise as she reached a hand down to touch herself in time to the pumping of my hand. When she slipped a single finger inside herself, I couldn't hold back any longer, pulling her hands out of my way as I settled between her legs. I gently urged her backward on the bed, and I crawled between her thighs on my hands and knees, kicking off my pants and boxers at the base of the bed.

I puffed up as I watched her eye me appreciatively, reaching out a hand to touch me. I closed my eyes, stilling myself as I felt her hand wrap around my cock, testing out its size. She slid her fingers up and down, dragging moans from the very depths of my soul, and I leaned into her touch, needing her as much as she needed me.

I'd had no idea until right now how badly I'd missed the touch of another. But somehow, I just knew it wouldn't be the same with any other woman. Her touch shook me to my core, making me do things I'd never wanted to do before. Her hand sped up, and I felt my balls tighten as I grew close to losing it in her palm. A second later, I'd brought the head of my shaft against her tight opening, pressing insistently against her as she moaned in eager approval.

"Lucien, please…"

I leaned in until my lips were against her earlobe, careful not to slip inside her slick folds. I wanted her to beg me; I needed to hear her plead for sweet release. I had what she needed, and I would not give it to her until she pleaded for mercy, no matter how badly I wanted it, too. "What do you want, Izzy? Tell me what it is you desire…"

She shivered at the feel of my breath against her skin, and I trailed kisses slowly down to her breasts, taking one pert nipple in my mouth, rolling the hard nub between my lips as I teased her with the tip of my tongue. She arched her back, shoving her breasts against my mouth as my free hand rolled the other nipple between my thumb and forefinger. I basked in the whimpers coming from my sweet little minx, and I brought a hand down to her dripping folds, slipping a finger inside as she bucked against my hand. Finding her wet and ready, I wasted no more time in slipping the head of my cock deep inside her, burying myself to the base in her tight little pussy. She screamed out my name, riding another peak as she came around my cock.

"Lucian, oh *fuck, please*—"

"Yes, amore, say my name. Beg me."

I hadn't expected my little minx to be so responsive to my demands, but the next words out of her mouth had me practically blowing my load right then and there.

"Lucien, please," she begged, weaving her hands in my hair as she pulled my ribbon loose, *"I need you."* She tangled her fingers in my hair and yanked it hard, bringing our faces nose to nose. I gasped at the pain, my cock twitching inside her throbbing core. Her lips brushed against mine as I looked deep into her eyes. Her next words were barely audible as she pulled my hair back, the sweet pain setting me off. *"Fuck me, Lucien. Give me what I need."*

Her words were like lighting a brush pile with a spark in a drought, and I slid my cock out, thrusting into her over and over while she babbled my name incoherently, grasping at my shoulders as she took my sizeable cock like a champ, her hips meeting me thrust for thrust. The headboard of the bed rocked against the wall, the repetitive banging sure to erase all doubt what we were up to, but I paid it no attention as I stroked Izzy from the inside out, my tongue crashing against hers as we swallowed each other's moans of pleasure. My pace increased, over and over slamming into her with such force I thought I would break her, but she clawed at my back, begging me for more with every part of her body. She wrapped her legs around my waist, and I slipped deeper than I thought possible into her hot core, the tight wet cavern clamping down around me as her walls convulsed around my cock. Her orgasm rocked her as I continued to thrust in and out of her, the friction driving her insane as she shuddered beneath me. But I wasn't done with her, and I flipped her over on her stomach, slipping a hand under her to prop her firm ass up in front of me. My cock was dripping with her juices, and it jerked in front of me, my head resting against her soaked slit from the back.

I leaned over her from behind, hearing her whimper as my cock pressed against her asscheeks, the slick cum coating her bare ass. I ran my fingers through her hair, wrapping my hands around the ends of her blonde curls as I gave her a second's warning.

"I'm going to fuck you so hard that you beg me to stop."

She moaned into the mattress as I yanked on her hair, slamming my cock deep into her swollen folds, her back arching as she screamed to the rafters above in ecstasy. With each thrust I pounded my dick deep inside her, ramming her unforgivingly as she moaned my name, pleading with me.

"Fuck, Lucien, please fucking PLEASE, I need to feel you cum in me."

She slammed her ass back against my hips, and I arched my spine, feeling my cock twitch deep inside her tight pussy as she came with me, milking me for all of my hot seed. I panted from the immense pleasure, leaning over her as I throbbed inside her, still filling her with my juices as I shuddered in absolute pleasure. I felt myself go limp, and I collapsed next to Izzy, pulling her into the crook of my arm. I held this beautiful angel close to my heart, amazed at how close to her I felt.

Her breathing was rapid and shallow against my chest, her body still trying to catch up to the marathon we'd just run. I closed my eyes as she snuggled against me, her hair tickling my nostrils lightly. My hand cradled the back of her head, pressing her against me as if I could absorb this feeling of contentment into my own body just by being closer to her. I brushed my lips against her temple, and I could feel the last of the buzz wearing off.

Before we drifted off to sleep, I whispered in her ear,

unsure if she could still hear me or not. Perhaps it would be better if she couldn't hear me; I didn't want to chase her off.

"Sleep well, *anima mia.*"

My eyes drifted closed, and I fell asleep cradling my saving grace in the crook of my arm.

CHAPTER 15

~IZZY~

The first thing I noticed when I woke was that I wasn't alone. And that concerned me because my brain was screaming *you sleep alone*, but my body wasn't reacting. I felt sluggish, weak, and my head was pounding. The body next to me stirred, and I tried hard not to breathe. *In, out, in, out...deep breaths.* I knew what to do to prevent the oncoming panic attack, but sometimes my body didn't cooperate. I kept my eyes closed until I heard a door open and close, followed by some running water. Finally alone, I took a moment to survey the room as I caught my breath.

This was *definitely* not my guest room. I groaned, holding my head as pieces of last night came back to me in a rush. The memories were fragmented and out of order, but now I could tell I'd probably had too much wine—my memory never worked smoothly when I'd been drinking to excess. The sheets on the bed were a black satin, so soft and smooth against my skin that I had to refrain from rubbing all over them. There were spots of white on the expensive fabric, and my clothes were scattered around the room, which meant only one thing, considering there was a second outfit on the floor with mine. *I got laid. And it must have been good for me to stick around afterward.* And then it hit me.

Lucien. Shit.

Just as I whispered his name, the bathroom door swung open, revealing a dripping wet Lucien, a white terry cloth towel draped low around his hips, the knot so loose it threatened to come undone at any moment. His eyes were cast at the floor as he rubbed his hair with a second towel, his abs rippling as he stretched his arms over his head. I couldn't help but admire his toned physique as he toweled dry; after all, *I was only human.*

As if he could feel my eyes on him, he looked up, wearing the sexiest smirk I'd ever seen. His eyebrows lifted at the sight of me; the only thing separating my body from his gaze was the dark fabric clutched desperately between my fingers. I swallowed my unease and offered a shaky smile back as I tried to focus on breathing. His body took my breath away.

Dios mio, is it legal for one man to have a body that show-stopping?

I felt my fingers twitch around the sheet, my heart rate increasing as I watched him take a step towards me. Suddenly, I was filled with an unexplainable dread, and panic took over as my body flung itself off the side of the bed and onto the floor in one ungrateful jerking motion. My brain screamed *run*, but my body couldn't follow the orders yet, and I landed on my bare ass on the hardwood floor.

"Ow, dammit," I muttered as I rubbed my hip, surveying the damage. Lucien was beside me in a flash, his body shaking uncontrollably. I thought he was angry, which only fueled my panic more as I struggled to cover myself again. Lucien's fingers curled around my wrist, moving my hand out of the way so he could inspect for himself.

"Did you get hurt? That was a hell of a fall."

I looked up at the teasing in his voice, realizing he was shaking from repressed laughter.

"Do you f-find something funny about my i-injury?" I groaned as he poked a tender spot on my thigh—

Wait, when had he exposed my thigh?

"It's gonna bruise. You *humans* are all so sensitive and delicate; you really should be more careful. I'm not going to *eat* you, Lizzania. Well, only if you ask me to."

My eyes jerked up to meet his at the sound of my full name. "H-how did you know my whole name?"

Lucien rolled his eyes at me as if I should know this. "You introduced yourself at the gala, remember?"

Oh yeah. "Most people don't say it correctly the first time," I whispered. "It's not a very common name variant."

Lucien rolled his eyes, looking at the ceiling pointedly. He sighed heavily, his chest rising and falling with his deep breath. I clenched my thighs together as I felt myself reacting to his closeness. Lucien's nostrils flared as I tried to scoot away from him, my panic attack climbing up my throat. I couldn't think straight, the wine had left me with this raging headache that beat against the insides of my skull, and I was hurt—a fine way to start the morning after a night of amazing sex.

Sex. I'd almost forgot we had sex. Cue intense panic.

It had been a while since I'd hyperventilated, but I found myself putting my head between my raised knees, no longer caring if the sheet slipped to reveal a little bit of skin. I couldn't stop my racing heart and shallow breathing, and I could see the little black spots on the corners of my peripheral. Lucien's hand stretched out to rest lightly on my shoulder, and I shivered at the coldness of his skin.

He pulled back suddenly, a frown revealing the only emotion on his face as he retreated across the room, grabbing my purse off the bureau by the door. As he reached inside it, I tried to protest, but my body wouldn't respond, and all that came out was a whimper. When his hand emerged, my inhaler and a pill bottle were in his grip. I breathed a sigh of relief as I realized he had recognized what was going on and had thought to grab my medication.

I eagerly took the inhaler from his outstretched hands, my hands shaking as I brought it to my lips, taking two quick puffs deep into my overreacting lungs. I held my breath for a moment, an unimaginably difficult task while in the midst of a panic attack, and I felt my breathing slow as the albuterol did its work. My throat felt less constricted, and I hummed my thanks as my eyes drifted closed, enjoying the feeling of calm that began to wash over me. I felt the pill bottle's cool plastic against my upper arm, followed by a slight rattle of the few pills in the bottom.

"Do you need these too? I wasn't sure what you needed, so I brought both." Lucien's voice sounded strained, but I couldn't focus on that, instead choosing to stare across the room at the wall.

"I think I'm fine. I just need a minute." I glanced around, testing out my mental state. The spots were gone, and my shakes had mostly dissipated, leaving me slightly relaxed and moderately functional. *Yeah, I just needed a minute.*

Lucien stood, and his towel chose that moment to fall to the floor from his salacious hips, putting me at just below eye level with his *impressive* manhood. Even at rest, it was sizable, and I couldn't help but blush as he caught me staring, his cock twitching in eagerness. My brain short-circuited, and I watched myself reach out to wrap it in my hand, squeezing the shaft gently as I looked up to meet his eyes.

~Lucien~

This vixen would be the death of me. Her fingers encircled my already stiff dick, stroking my shaft as I looked down at her in wonder. She'd gone from anxious mess to erotic plaything in about thirty seconds, and although I wasn't one to refuse a good hand job, I reached down to pull her to her feet, staring into her lovely amber eyes. She left her hand wrapped around my shaft, and I wasn't eager to remove it, so I let it remain.

"I thought you needed a minute," I panted as her grip pulsed around me. I was getting harder by the second, and if she kept that up, we would only end up back in that bed she'd fallen from minutes ago.

Her blush was adorable, and she leaned down to pick up

the abandoned black sheet, covering herself in an attempt to salvage her modesty. *Or at least I thought she did.*

She didn't come back up from the floor, and I felt her hand disappear from my manhood, only to be replaced by her hot, wet mouth. Her lips encircled my head, and I moaned low when she took the length of me deep into her throat, not even flinching as she swallowed me whole. It was so hot, I had to fight not to blow my load against the back of her throat immediately.

Maybe it had been **too long** *since I'd let myself enjoy pleasure.*

My eyes rolled back in my head as she worked her magic on me with her mouth, the carnal sounds she made only fueling my lust. I glanced down to peek at her, and I found her touching herself on her knees, a hand between her legs as she fucked herself with her fingers.

Jesus fucking Christ, what did I do to deserve such an amazing gift?

"Oh, *fuck* Izzy, get up off the floor, please. I can't take much more of whatever it is you're doing to me."

She smiled coyly as she rose from her knees, but she left her hand in its' place as she captured my lips with her own. I could taste myself on her, her sweet lips moving against mine eagerly as I backed us over to the bed. When the sheets tickled the back of my knees, I sat back on the soft mattress, and to my amazement, Izzy climbed atop me, her hands against my shoulders to steady herself as she rubbed her soft, wet folds against my raging hard-on. She dragged moans of ecstasy from my throat as I leaned back, enjoying the teasing motions she made with her hips.

When she lifted herself, I almost didn't notice, and she slammed herself down on the top of my stiff cock, impaling herself with my shaft as I groaned, my member throbbing inside her tightness. I grabbed her hips, unable to control myself as I rammed into her, lifting her off me only to pound myself into her over and over again. I felt her shatter around me as she screamed my name to the rafters, but I didn't stop. I couldn't stop until I'd found my release, buried in this fiery woman atop me.

~Izzy~

"Lucien, fuck yes, please—"

I had lost all rational thought when I'd reached out for his cock, and every bit of brain function had been put on hold when I'd decided to take him into my mouth. And then I'd been so turned on by the feel of him stroking the back of my throat, I'd reached down to thrust two eager fingers inside my tight, throbbing core. I whimpered around his dick as I finger-fucked myself on my knees in front of a man I'd known for a few days.

What are you doing, you idiot? He's gonna think you're loose, and that's all you'll be good for is a fuck.

My brain made some logical points, but I couldn't stop. I was so close to the edge, but I needed to feel him inside me again. Last night hadn't been enough, and my body reacted to his in ways I'd responded to no man before. I was alight with a fiery need, and only he could satisfy it.

He'd pulled me to my feet, but I hadn't waited for him to speak. I leaned in and kissed him, my tongue needing to be inside his mouth, letting him taste himself on my lips. His cock twitched in eager anticipation, and I knew we were heading down this road at breakneck speed when he sat back on his bed. But I had no brakes, and I had no desire to find any, either. I climbed atop him, taking his pulsing hard-on all the way inside me as I crouched above him, riding him like the prize pony at the fair. My pussy drenched him with my desire, the slick juices coating him as I made sounds with my body that would make a whore blush.

Lucien grabbed my hips, and I knew I was about to get exactly what I'd been looking for. His cock rammed into me so hard it hurt, but the pain soon gave way to pleasure, and soon he had me cumming atop him as he pumped into me over and over, seeking his own release. When I felt his hot seed fill me, his cock twitching against my tight walls, I knew he'd reached his peak.

"Lucien," I whispered as I leaned against his chest, spent and sated, his cock still buried between my thighs. At the mention of his name, I felt it twitch inside me. *Was he already ready for another round?*

"Mmmm?" he mused, his arms going around me to wrap me in an embrace. "Can I do something for you, *stellina?*"

The irony of his word choice was not lost on me, and I giggled as my hand shot up to cover my lips. I felt him stiffen inside me, and my laughter turned to gasps as he took that moment to flip me onto my back, his tender, slow movements a complete 180 from his animalistic need only minutes ago.

"Let me show your body the same appreciation you showed mine, my sweet." His head dipped down as he backed away from me, and I gasped as his tongue began cleaning the evidence of our fast fucking from my swollen, sweet hole.

"Mmmm, Lucien, whatever you're doing down there feels amazing."

He looked up from between my thighs, my juices dripping from his lips. I moaned at the erotic sight, feeling myself getting wetter with every breath he blew against my abs.

"I'm happy to be of service, ma'am. Just relax and let me take care of you." His head dipped back down, and the heavenly man ate me out for nearly an hour. I came so close to the edge every time, only for him to stop and tease me away from a release. By the time he'd decided he was finished with me, I was a whimpering mess, begging to be fucked.

I was a hot mess for this man, but I couldn't bring myself to care. Something about him woke things in me I hadn't known I'd been hiding, and the satisfaction from finally having my sexual needs met was on another level entirely.

"Tell me what you want, *cara mia.* Speak your desires to me, tell me what you want me to do to you."

I blushed at his brashness, but I did as I was told, moaning as he slid a finger up the inside of my slit. "I want you inside me...please...*please, Lucien.*" I squirmed against his hand as he slid a finger inside me from behind, dragging me to the edge of the bed and flipping me onto my stomach, so that my legs hung over the side. My feet touched the floor, and I gasped when he entered me slowly from behind, my legs spreading to accommodate his stiff cock.

I realized I was literally about to greet the sunrise with his cock between my legs, and suddenly there was no other way I wanted to start a day. If I only had this for a week, I would take it every day willingly and go home a changed woman.

~Lucien~

I rammed into her from behind, her perky tits bouncing as I rocked her with my thrusts. She took all of me and begged for more as if she'd never been properly fucked in all her life.

"Oh Jesus, *Luc, yes! Yes! Oh...*"

A smirk played across my lips at her erotic moans. She was cutting loose, and her pussy begged for sweet release as it throbbed around my shaft. I groaned with each thrust, knowing I was close to release. I reached around her waist, my deft fingers finding her swollen clit. I moved my fingers in time to the rhythm of my thrusts, and I stiffened inside her as we found our release together, her pussy clenching as I spurted my hot cum deep inside her.

Thank god I was sterile. Or at least, I assumed I was, as I'd never had a woman come back with a child in tow in all my 200-ish years.

"Fuuuuuckk," I growled as I slammed into her one last time, feeling myself go limp inside her tight walls. I slid out of her, falling face-first on the bed beside her. She collapsed flat on her stomach, a soft moan escaping her lips. I reached out to caress her cheek, my fingertips brushing lightly against her soft skin.

"Stay with me? Stay here in my bed a little while longer, *cara mia.* Humor me."

Wordlessly, she snuggled against my embrace, and I decided then and there to enjoy every moment I got with this beautiful angel before she went home to her regular life.

But maybe she didn't have to…

CHAPTER 16

~LUCIEN~

When I finally felt Izzy fall asleep, I carefully snuck from the bed, taking care to sneak my pillow under her arm to stand in my place. I could hear the faint melody of the organ piano coming from the parlor, and I pulled on a pair of sweats, not bothering with a shirt or underwear as I slipped out of the room, the door closing with a quiet *click* behind me.

Jasper must have something on his mind. That's the only time he ever plays Bach's Toccata and Fugue in D Minor.

Sure enough, I found him in the expansive room at the front of the house, sitting not at the piano but the synthetic organ in the corner by the window. His arms moved so fluidly as he chased his fingers across the keys, energetic and morose at the same time. No matter what Jasper played, it was always excellent, as he'd had much time to practice in the two hundred years we'd been alive together. While I'd turned to business ventures and boats, Jasper preferred art forms, ranging from cooking to music and everything in between.

I fought the temptation to interrupt his depressing and haunting rendition of Bach's most intricately gothic piece to date, deciding instead to sit on the piano bench while I watched his back. The music imbibed him with a purpose, and his whole body was involved in the song as he poured out his soul to the audience of one. He knew I was here; he'd be a fool not to have sensed my arrival.

There was so much about my friend I didn't understand, and until now, I hadn't been driven to inquire. But for some reason, waking up before dawn next to such an amazing lover had put me in a mood of lightness that I hadn't felt in a lifetime or longer. I decided to ride it out, realizing a change in my demeanor couldn't be that bad.

Glancing at the far wall, my eyes grazed over the bookshelf where I'd kept my oldest novels, my favorite series, the long-forgotten first editions I hadn't lifted in a decade. My fingers itched to skim their textured covers, and I found myself in front of the collection before I even realized I was standing. There was not a single speck of dust on a single book, and I realized my butler must have been taking care of them for me in my severe disinterest.

I pulled a single book from the shelf, a book that had been my favorite for years: Dante Alighieri's *Divine Comedy,* first edition. The title simply said *Comedia* on my copy because I'd gotten my hands on one of the original production copies at a boat show one year. I ran my fingers over the worn leather cover the previous owner had commissioned for the book's exterior. He, too, had appreciated the value in the work he'd acquired and wanted to ensure its safety and longevity.

As the last haunting notes of the song rang out across the room, I heard Jasper's familiar voice turned condescendingly on me, not for the first time.

"You know, you should probably act like a human more often. It does wonders for your mood, young master."

"So, what you're saying is, I need to get laid more often?"

I watched as Jasper shook his head at me disapprovingly, as if he were speaking to a child who wouldn't listen. "No, sir, what I'm saying is, you—never mind…" he trailed off, seeing my brow raised in intrigue. I was daring him to correct me, and he knew it. He also knew it was wise to be silent, as I rarely listened to advice about myself that came from other people. Cockiness was one of my many flaws and one of the few I'd brought over from my time as a human. "How is Miss Stanton this morning?" He quipped, crossing his arms over his chest defiantly.

My bluster evaporated as I vividly recalled the night—and early morning—we had shared. I cleared my throat, throwing my brain anywhere but on the lovely woman in my bed.

"I'm sure she's fine, but I will need you to get Titus on call. I plan to take her out today, on the town."

Jasper's jaw dropped to the floor, and he struggled to pick it up. "But it's midday," he said, gesturing to the window where the natural light filtered in. "It's going to sting, even with high-level sunscreen, and your age."

My eyes turned towards the bright natural light, and I stretched out a hand, letting the direct rays of the sun fall on my skin. I didn't burst into flames like Bram had led everyone to believe was a part of this lifestyle, but it did cause me discomfort, and I twisted my arm as my skin began to tingle. I'd have a sunburn today in a few hours if I weren't careful, but luckily this wasn't my first rodeo.

Yanking my hand back, I absently rubbed my wrist, turning back to Jasper with a smug look on my face. "You forget who you're talking to, old friend Sunlight is the least of my worries."

Jasper grumbled as he trudged off to find Titus. The driver liked to hang out in the garage, tinkering on his old car when he had a free minute. I had invited him to bring his collector's car into the main garage for a better atmosphere for restoration. And if I was honest, the car definitely was a beauty. I enjoyed watching it come together.

I appreciated all the finer things. I was a connoisseur of wheels, wine, and waves. I made a mental note to ask Izzy if she could swim, as I finally had an excuse to take *The Raven* out on the water after her long slumber. That classic sailboat deserved better, and I felt ashamed that she'd sat so long. All because I'd locked myself up to hide from *emotions*. I'd felt human, and I desperately tried to ignore that part of me.

No more.

My mind made up, I decided to head back up the stairs to find some clothes for the day and relax with a book until my new companion woke up.

~Izzy~

Everything hurt. My whole body was sore and swollen, and for the first time since last night, I was finally clear-headed. I still had a headache, but at least my thoughts were clear. I groaned, stretching out in the huge bed as I tested each limb for functionality. Finding myself mostly intact, I pulled my arms back in around myself, feeling a cool breeze against my sun-kissed skin. The curtain had been pulled back to let in the natural light, and it had made its way across the bed, bathing me in a spotlight of sorts.

I need a shower. And a handful of aspirin.

My legs felt like Jell-O as I dangled them over the edge of the bed, preparing myself to stand and seek out my clothes. My dress had been discarded on the floor, and I yanked it over my head quickly, searching for my shoes. *There, across the room beside the door.* Once I had the strappy sandals in my hands, I grabbed my small purse on the floor beside the bed, where I vaguely remember falling last night.

If he sees me like this, I swear I'll die. I'm a hot mess. This is embarrassing.

I could feel my nerves on fire as I searched around for my undergarments, finding my bra draped haphazardly over the back of his chair in the corner. I tucked it into my bag, searching around for my thong. I *knew* it had to be here somewhere, but I couldn't see it, and it was only a matter of time before he came looking for me.

Unless he sleeps in a coffin in the basement during the daytime. Jesus, that sounded cheesy. I gave up on the thong, heading to the door just as I heard footsteps start up the stairs. It was now or never, and my feet flew gracefully across the floor as I silently sprinted for the door to my own room. My hand reached the doorknob before the person climbing the stairs reached the floor I was on, and I had never yanked a door open as hard as I yanked mine right then, closing the door quietly just as the footsteps stopped. I leaned my back against the inside of my door, deciding I needed a shower before I broke down into a puddle of anxiety.

The repercussions of last night came rushing back to me as I sat against the door, biting back tears. I'd gotten sloshed, something I *never* did, and I'd lost all sense of self-respect, chasing the sexy vampyr man like a bitch in heat. I'd practically forced him to fuck me, and I'd crawled into bed with him eagerly after knowing him for only two days.

I couldn't believe myself. Reduced to a common whore in less than a night by a bottle of wine and a sexy set of eyes. I felt my skin flush as I began calling the images of his hard body against my own to the forefront of my mind. *A cold shower would be fantastic.*

Numbly, I stood and made my way to the attached bathroom, pulling back the curtain to find a surprising variety of shampoos and soaps. I sifted through the choices before deciding on one that had been hidden under the sink cabinet, far in the back. It was a scent I personally used at home, though I couldn't often afford it, and like they said, *when in Rome*, so…

As I stepped out of the shower, the cool air teased my skin, so I made a mad dash to the closet to find something to wear. Settling on a strappy floral dress that stopped at my knees, I turned to the bureau, rifling through my unmentionables. My hand closed around a matching lace set, and I decided to go with it, knowing there was no way anyone was about to be seeing these today.

I had *morals*. Today, I would stick to them. *Hopefully*.

I'd managed to get halfway through applying some basic makeup that I always had stashed in my purse when there was a knock at the door. I quickly pulled my dress over my head, smoothing out the wrinkles as I opened the door without thinking.

Lucien stood in my doorway, a hand braced against the top of the frame as he dangled what appeared to be a small cloth from the fingertips of his other hand. His lips were turned up in a sexy smirk as my brain struggled to connect the dots. To my mortification, the black fabric was none other than my missing thong from last night, and I wordlessly snatched it out of his hand as my face turned a bright shade of red.

"You forgot something in my room, *cara mia.* Tell me, do you have plans for today?"

His eyes were friendly, but there was a hint of lust in them as I watched him look me up and down, licking his lips appreciatively. I had to remind myself—*morals.*

"As it just so happens, I do *not* have plans for today, Mr. Sabatini." I crossed my arms, tossing my thong onto the bed as I smiled up at this dangerously sexy man. "Did you have anything in mind?"

He lowered his hand from the doorway, stepping inside my room to get closer to me. My claustrophobia tingled at the back of my mind, but I managed to tamp it down, ignoring the tight feeling in my throat.

His lips curled into an even wider smile; gone was his morose demeanor. It was as if a new version of this man stood in front of me. "Well, I have some suggestions. We could explore the city, or I could take you out on my boat. But we should really save the boat for a cloudy day, so we don't burn that beautiful skin of yours."

I laughed at his dry humor—if anyone should be worried about the sun, it wasn't me. "You just don't want me to see you go up in a cloud of dust when you burn up, isn't that it?"

He groaned as he hung his head, chuckling to himself. "I told you last night; I can't combust in the sun, *stellina.* It's merely uncomfortable to deal with." He reached forward, twisting a lock of my hair around a finger as he stared deep into my eyes. "How about I take you around Palermo today? My treat. I'll even let you pick the car."

My eyes went round as the implications in his words hit home. "You have more than one car?"

"I have many modes of transportation, *amore.* If you would like to meet me downstairs with some sensible shoes, I will show you. We will be doing a lot of walking today."

I stood there, waiting for him to close the distance between us and kiss me stupid like he had the night before, but Lucien simply chuckled as he detangled his finger from my hair, his hand brushing against my cheek as he pulled away. I stood still as a stone as he turned to leave. *Find your voice!*

"I didn't accept your offer yet!" I called after him as he walked down the hall. He stopped, throwing a rakish grin over his shoulder at me.

"But you will, Miss Stanton."

My knees went weak at his brazen confidence. He was absolutely right—I had no intention of turning him down. I was on *vacation,* and I was determined to enjoy myself. I laced up my favorite pair of Converse and bounded down the stairs, barely remembering to grab my purse on the way out.

Today was going to be a good day.

CHAPTER 17

~IZZY~

The garage was jam-packed with car after car, from sporty and brand-new to classic muscle and everything in between. I couldn't believe the amount of money that was stored in this one garage, on wheels. There were so many choices, I didn't think I could ever pick just *one*, but I strolled up and down the row of sweet rides, weighing the pros vs. cons.

"Do you have a favorite?" Lucien called out to me from the corner of the garage, where he leaned against the doorframe, his arms folded across his chest.

I shook my head as I continued up the rows. Some of these, I could identify thanks to some trivial knowledge I'd absorbed on collectibles. In the far corner sat a cherry red Ford GT, racing stripes down the middle of the hood. To the left of that one was a baby blue Mercedes Benz with a drop-top. Further along, was an Oldsmobile Toronado, and clear at the end sat a Lexus. There were some SUVs along one wall, and another section of the garage housed bikes and scooters of all types. My eyes lit upon an old Vespa, and I knew right then and there that I'd made my decision.

"This one," I said, pointing to the corner with the bikes. Lucien's brows rose in surprise, but he simply smiled at me as he wandered over to the place I'd pointed. His hand came to rest on a bigger street bike, and he turned to me, a questioning look in his eyes.

"This beast? I don't know—"

"No, *this one!*" I stood beside the classic scooter, running a hand along its sleek frame. The thing looked like it strolled out of a 1950's classic black and white film, and I could see myself zipping around on the back of it, my dress skirt flapping behind me like a banner in the wind. Lucien's hand wrapped around mine where I had grasped onto the handlebar, and I looked up at him, feeling slightly jittery and nervous.

"Well, I wouldn't have expected you to pick the Vespa, but it *is* a good day for a ride. What the hell." He swung a long, muscled leg over the side of the scooter, straddling it between his powerful thighs. He grabbed a helmet off the handlebars, handing it to me before reaching for a second. I put it on as he watched to make sure my chin strap was secure. "Do you want to drive or ride behind me?"

I eyed the scooter apprehensively, knowing I didn't have much experience driving one, but my excitement won out.

"Are they hard to drive? I've never ridden on one before."

He moved back on the seat for me, gesturing for me to take the seat before him, his arms easily reaching the handlebars even from the back of the saddle. I slipped under one of his toned arms, trying to readjust my skirt so it wouldn't ride up too high. As I settled in at the front of the bike, I felt one of Lucien's arms wrap around my waist as his other hand flipped a few switches on the other side of the bike's gauge dash.

When he rocked the bike to the side, I nearly fell off, but he quickly kick-started it and rolled us forward towards the garage door. My feet settled on the frame's running boards as he reached around me and revved the gas. When the little scooter lurched forward, I let out a squeal, reaching out to grasp the handlebars in my shaking, sweaty palms. When Lucien leaned against my back, I felt his hot thighs straddling my hips, and a little thrill ran through me. His proximity did things to my head that I didn't quite understand, and I wasn't sure if I liked it or hated it.

The miles flew by in a flash as the Vespa screamed down the roadway at a speed I wouldn't have imagined possible out of such a small machine. Still, my mind wasn't on the road like it should be. It was on a one-track path to the feeling of his growing stiffness pressing into my back.

Was this increased libido a vampyr thing? I made a mental note to ask him when I was less embarrassed about it. I shifted as we went around a turn, and I heard him moan behind me, his hips angling slightly to press insistently against my ass through the fabric of my sundress.

I tortured him like this the whole ride into town, smiling like a loon until I pulled off the roadway and onto a little side street in Palermo. I followed Lucien's pointed directions until we arrived at a fancy restaurant on the waters' edge. The smell of marinara, baked bread, and fine meats wafted from the interior of the building, intensifying a hunger I didn't know I was blocking out.

Lucien's leg nudged a kickstand out from beneath the Vespa as it came to a stop, and I felt his hand brush against my ass for just a second as he untangled his arm from my waist, swinging his leg over the seat of the bike. Once he'd dismounted so elegantly, he offered me his hand, and I placed mine in his waiting grasp, letting him lead me to the *maitre'd* who stood by a tall podium. Lucien spoke in fluent Italian to the well-dressed man, and a young woman led us to a booth in the corner of the covered patio seating. We sat down as she handed us menus, Lucien taking the seat facing the entrance to the patio. That left me with the seat opposite his, facing the ocean.

"So, the menu is in Italian, but they include a nice collection of pictures. If there's anything you want to know about I can translate for you."

I glanced down at the menu, finding the pictures a helpful navigational tool for the menu. I thumbed through the pages of the menu, my eyes drawn to a picture of a stunning pasta dish, one I recognized.

"Is it cliché to eat pasta in Italy?"

He leaned over, peering at my page until he saw the carbonara. His grin widened, reaching his eyes this time. "The Carbonara here is done in the classical style of Rome, and it's the best carbonara dish you'll have anywhere in the world. Promise."

I closed my menu, satisfied with my choice. "Then the carbonara it is."

The young woman came back around to the table, batting her eyelashes at Lucien as she leaned over to greet us. "I'm Fanny, and I'll be your waitress today. Would you like to start with some drinks and appetizers?"

Lucien looked back over to me, his eyes studying me as he ordered some wine and fresh-baked bread. As the waitress bounced off to put in our order, I surveyed the scene, watching a couple move around on the empty dance floor nearby. They swayed to the musical talents of Andrea Bocelli's "Cuando Me Enamoro", and I suddenly had the urge to get up and sway to the music.

I glanced over to Lucien, who was back to scowling as the song's last notes died out. As Bella Bella Signorina played out across the stereo, I tapped my feet to the beat playfully, wishing I'd get asked to dance. From the looks of it, Lucien wasn't the public dancing type.

~Lucien~

I'd seen that look in plenty of women's eyes before. Izzy wanted to dance, and her tapping toes were hint enough that she was waiting for me to ask her. But I was not too fond of dancing and for good reason. When the second song died out, Izzy tried her hardest not to stare pointedly at me. Thankfully, the waitress quickly arrived with our bread and wine, and I smiled as I ripped off a piece of the loaf and offered it to Izzy.

She took the bread, setting it down on her side plate as she lifted the wine to her lips, taking a huge swallow of the beautiful white chardonnay I'd ordered her. La Vie En Rose played next, and the Italian old soul inside me wouldn't let me deny her any longer. I stood, rolling my eyes at myself and my weakness for this human.

"Would you like to dance, Izzy?"

She looked up at me as if she'd never been asked to dance in her life, so I took her hand and pulled her from her seat, moving slowly in time to the music as the beautiful love song played around us. I felt her lean into my chest, practically purring as she wound her arms around my neck. I swayed back and forth, spinning her once or twice for good measure, our feet moving in sync with each other as if we'd danced the same dance thousands of times.

As the last notes died out, I leaned back to stare down at this beautiful creature in my arms, the woman who had singlehandedly managed to bring me out of an emotionless slumber and revive my feelings. She'd made me care for something other than myself for the first time in a long time. It wasn't an unpleasant feeling, but it was *new*. I wasn't used to taking others into consideration. Appreciation danced across her features as I drowned in her joyful gaze; yet another thing I wasn't used to quite yet.

"Come; let's head back to the table. I'm sure our lunch will be ready soon."

~Izzy~

The food arrived at the table right after we did, and the pasta was unlike any I'd ever eaten before. I stared wordlessly down at my plate, amazed at the rich flavor and immense dedication to the culinary craft evident in the creamy sauce. The chicken was grilled to perfection, and the herbs and seasonings were fragrant and fresh, as they should be.

Was *everything* better in Italy? I eyed the man across from me, who was tearing into a particularly rare and juicy steak with wild abandon.

Yes, things were definitely better in Italy.

"So, I didn't think you guys would eat normal food…what with the blood-drinking and all."

Lucien sighed, setting his fork down as he rolled his eyes. "This again? Fucking *Bram* and all his bullshit. I *knew* I should have hit that fucker harder."

"*Language,* Lucien. There are other people around."

"I'm two hundred years old, *cara mia; I* do not care what other people think of me anymore."

It was my turn to roll my eyes at him now, pouting as I tried to keep my attention off the delicious food before me. "Well, you should. You should care what I think of you, at the very least."

He sighed, the sound heavy from years of frustration, leaking from his lips like air from a bad tire. "Listen, it's not my fault you have so many misconceptions about vampyrs. Hell, Bram didn't even spell the damn term right."

"You have an unhealthy obsession with Mister Stroker—"

He burst into laughter at my comment, and I stared at him in confusion, his mirth shaking his whole frame. "Oh, Bram would have loved the Freudian intonations in that one, *stellina.*"

I tried to ignore him, but it was a losing battle, and I searched around in my head for anything to say. Finding nothing particularly witty, I opted for the obvious. "So what else do you have planned for us this afternoon?"

Lucien took a sip of his chardonnay, checking his watch carefully. "Well, I think we have time for an art museum, and maybe a cathedral. The typical tourist things. Unless you had something else in mind?"

"I like typical tourist things," I quickly interjected, afraid he would decide to take us home early if I objected to the sightseeing he had planned.

He offered me a smile as he reached for the tab at the edge of the table. I tried to protest, but I knew which one of us was in a better position to pay this lunch bill, and it wasn't me. We evened up with the waitress, and Lucien led me out of the restaurant area, leading me past the Vespa and down a side road. I glanced back at the scooter, confused.

"Are we leaving the Vespa behind?"

"Yeah. Where we're going, we won't be far. So we can walk from here and come back for it later."

I followed Lucien as he weaved between people packed in the narrow alleys, his grip on my hand gentle but secure. If we were to get separated now, I would surely get lost. A tall man on my right fell sideways into me, and I felt my hand get ripped from Lucien's as the man fell over on me. He didn't reek of booze, so he wasn't likely drunk. The man didn't bother with an apology, huffing disdainfully at me as he turned to walk away before a familiar figure stopped him in his tracks.

"Where do you think you're running off to with the lady's wallet, friend?"

The man went pale as he looked up at Lucien, who stood wearing an angry scowl as he held the would-be thief in place.

"U-uh, here, take it! I-I meant no harm, sir. Musta been a mistake. *Scusi'*," he muttered, handing me back the black leather wallet he'd lifted from my purse. Lucien shoved him off down the alley, in the opposite direction from us. His hands found mine as he helped me off the ground, eyeing me carefully for injuries.

"Did he hurt you?"

"Nah," I lied, brushing the dirt off the side of my dress where my hip had gone down. "I've been in worse altercations. I should be fine."

Lucien's hand found my chin as he tipped my face up to meet his scrutinizing gaze. "I am sorry you were accosted. I should have been watching better."

I couldn't help but laugh at his concern, his remorse. As silly as it was, this vampyr was worried he'd not taken good enough care of me while walking down the street. I couldn't help but rejoice in the feeling of someone caring for me like he already did.

"You're hardly at fault for a pickpocket, Lucien. I'm fine, really."

He didn't seem convinced, but he shrugged his shoulders, leading me away from the scene of the run-in. "Stay closer this time. I don't want to lose you…*in the crowd.*"

I sighed as he tacked on the last of the sentence. For a moment, I had let myself believe he'd fallen for me as I'd fallen for him. That he didn't want me to go. But at the end of the week, my vacation would end, as all dreams do, and I would go home to my boring life with my asshole parents and my Spanish housekeeper and waste away my life trying to keep my parents afloat until they died.

Life has a funny way of crashing back on you when you're floating high as a bird.

CHAPTER 18

~IZZY~

We'd finally finished touring the last museum for the day and were headed back towards the restaurant where we'd left the Vespa parked. The day had stretched out, and we'd covered so much ground my feet were screaming. But I'd never seen such a vast collection of artwork, nor had I ever seen such beautiful murals as the ones painted on the vaulted ceilings of the chapels. Being with someone who was as old as some of the history himself added to the significance. It was like he shared his life with me through the collected remnants of the past that still struggled to remain.

I thoroughly enjoyed my time with Lucien, and he had a charm to him that men from my time hadn't been raised with. A charm only a woman like myself could appreciate. It was old-fashioned, but it was touching, and I found myself drawn to him like no man before. He was different, unique. *Not of this time. Not like other men.*

He held out his arm for me to take as we prepared to cross the cobblestone street, the foot traffic still populous for late afternoon. Cars honked around the corner and far off in the distance, their varying melodies singing out against the dull roar of the civilians around us. I wrapped my hand around his offered bicep, clinging to him as we dodged people to get back to the Vespa.

But the Vespa wasn't where we'd left it, and I felt a moment of panic. "Didn't we park the Vespa here?"

Lucien chuckled lightly, looking back at me with a smile. "I had Titus bring us a new toy to try out since the evenings are a bit cooler, and I'm not quite done showing you around." He pointed to the space behind where I'd expected the scooter to sit, and my eyes went wide. I couldn't bring myself to pick my jaw back up off the ground, and I knew I looked twenty kinds of fool, but I didn't care.

"You have a Jaguar E-type? I've only ever heard about these. I never expected to see one in person." I chewed on my lower lip, finally beginning to grasp just how much income this man must have amassed in his two hundred years alive.

"Don't do that, *cara mia,*" he whispered, his voice a bit breathless.

I studied his profile, wondering why he wouldn't look at me. "Do *what?*" I chewed my lip again, having developed the habit over the past year.

"That," he said, raising his eyebrows as his eyes finally met mine. "It drives me a bit *batty* when you nibble on that lower lip of yours."

Lucien was all seriousness, but I burst out in uncontrollable, side-splitting laughter at his unintended innuendo. As I gasped for air, he stared at me in confusion, his hands on his hips.

"What is so funny, *stellina?*"

I held a hand up as I clutched my midsection, gasping for air between laughs. "You…you said *batty*. All I could think was you turning into a bat and flapping away in the night. H-hilarious!"

He grumbled at me under his breath, mumbling about *'Fucking Bram'* and shaking his head. If his eyes had rolled any further back in his head, they'd have been stuck there.

~Lucien~

Fucking Bram and his bats. I shook my head, feeling my eyes rolling back into my head. As much as I studied the inside of my eye sockets this way, you'd think I'd have gotten them stuck that way. Still, I pasted a smile on my face, mostly because the joke actually *had* been funny. I just wasn't quite used to laughing at myself.

"Are you ready to take a ride? I want to show you the sands of the Mediterranean at sunset." I'd had years and years to learn the best things about my homeland, and in two hundred years, nothing had come close to the feeling of a sunset on the ocean, the colors reflecting off the waters as prisms of light reflected in all directions. It would take your breath away the first time you witnessed it, and I wanted to share the experience with Izzy. I found myself wanting to show her everything I loved about my home, in the hopes that she might stay—

Hold up, you idiot. Why would you want her to stay here? I loved the solitude, the familiarity of Jasper and I, and no one else. But something about her called out to me, and as her fingers peeled away from my bicep, she tugged away from me, trotting over to the car as she eyed it with appreciation. Izzy appreciated fine, classic things. Things like my car and the villa. The sailboat.

Myself.

I watched her as the wind brushed the hair over her shoulder, exposing her neck. I could hear the beating of her pulse in her throat, just below the surface. I could smell her, the heady mixture of flowers and cinnamon an odd but pleasing combination. I could have her, right now if I wanted, taking the life from her throat and sating this need I felt building deep inside me.

I needed to taste her. To drink from her, absorb the lifeblood that kept her alive. *Be one with her in more than just the bedroom.* If I were a betting man, I'd say that I'd fallen in *love* with this beautiful flaxen-haired maiden, but I knew that couldn't be true.

I had no soul to devote, no heart to love her with, no feelings to share with her. I was an emotionless pit, a soulless immortal doomed to be alone forever. Time had proven that. Time, and a woman. I'd sworn off other women after I'd been betrayed, but somehow Izzy's eyes had pierced me straight to my core, refusing to take no for an answer. I'd been magnetically drawn to her as if a force unstoppable was determined that we should meet.

But I'd never expected to fall head over heels for the anxious human. Because of her run-ins with debaucherous men, men like the one *I* had been as a human, I felt compelled to help her. To protect her. And though my mind had been too stubborn to see it, to admit what was happening, I couldn't ignore it any longer. The easy smile on my face as she looked back for me, her own lips curling up as we locked eyes, was too much to ignore. I couldn't remember when my smiles had stopped feeling forced, but I surmised today had been the tipping point.

She'd been so eager to learn about all the places we'd visited today, and I'd been all too eager to tell her about the places I remembered when they were first created. When they still served their intended purpose. I shared my own history with her, and she drank it up like a little kitten at the cream bowl. She'd been interested in learning about me, and I'd wanted her to know everything. I felt so at ease with Izzy, as if instinctively I knew she would offer no judgment of my character or condition. She seemed to get along with me well enough, and I could finally admit what I was feeling, though confusing and strange after so long, was *love.*

I was smitten. Absolutely lost in her eyes. I think I had been in love with Miss Lizzania Stanton from the first time we met.

She circled my car, her fingers inches away from the brand new restoration paint job, but I didn't scold her like I would have anyone else. I couldn't bring myself to yell at her. She was pure, innocent. *Everything I was not.* But I would keep her as long as I could, enjoying everything about her while I had the chance, because I was a selfish prick.

But I would be *her* selfish prick, as long as she would have me. Who knew how long that would be. I had an eternity. She only had a lifetime.

"Lucien, come on! We're not going to make it on time if you don't hurry up."

Her arms were crossed over her chest, her brows climbing her forehead as she pouted prettily at me. I felt that sensation in my chest intensify, and I stepped towards her, taking her in my arms. I didn't care who was watching, who was walking by. I wanted nothing more than to kiss this woman, and I'd be damned if anyone would stop me but this beautiful angel herself.

"Yes, the sunset. But first," I whispered, leaning down until we were nose to nose, "you look so absolutely delectable standing here. Might I steal a kiss from the fair beauty?"

She laughed, her sprightly laugh carrying across the cobblestones to echo around us. "Since when do you men ask permission to kiss a woman?"

I growled, immediately on the defensive. I abhorred being compared to mortal men, who didn't know their ass from a hole in the ground when it came to women. "Since it's the proper thing to do when courting a lady."

Her eyes went wide, a blush creeping up her cheeks as she looked down at my chest, her fingers splayed out across my shirt. "Is that what we're doing? Courting?"

"Well," I muttered, clearly out of my depth, "not exactly, but I can't think of a word to better describe this…"

"How about we not worry about terms and worry more about getting on the road, so I can see this amazing sunset you talked about."

She had a point. I opened the passenger door for her, helping her inside as I closed the door behind her. I rushed around to the driver's side, getting in the car as quickly as possible. I wanted to be as close to her as humanly possible, as long as I could get away with it. Even being separated from her outside of the car was giving me anxiety. She'd already been attacked and robbed today. I didn't want anything else to happen to her. And if I wasn't next to her, how would I protect her from all the danger around her?

More importantly, who would protect her from *me?*

We drove in silence to the beach, pulling up just as the edge of the sun touched the water's horizon. I helped Izzy out of the car, holding her hand as she reached down to remove her shoes. I followed suit, shoving both pairs on the floorboards of the car before shutting the door. With her hand still in mine, my heart felt light and free. I pulled her behind me, leading the way to the perfect spot to watch the sunset from.

The smooth shore hidden behind the bend was a perfect place to sit and rest in peace, and I sat on a large piece of driftwood, feeling my skin tighten uncomfortably as the sun danced across it. I had pushed myself today with the sunlight, and I would pay for it with discomfort later. For now, I shrugged it off, choosing instead to relish the moment I was in right now. I'd ignored physical pain plenty before. I could do it again, for her sake.

"This is beautiful," she muttered, her eyes cast out over the deep red and purple of the sky, the colors mixing and weaving back and forth like a dye job on the clouds. Her eyes flickered over to the gentle waves breaking against the shore, leaving behind their frothy foam as the water retreated into the sea. The seagulls above us were raucous and annoying, but she didn't seem to mind as she turned her whole body to soak up the tinted light. She was like a sunflower, opening herself to the sun, even as it departed for the evening.

I wanted her to open up for me like that. To expose her innermost self… To feel comfortable with me. But I was nothing if not honest, and I knew her body and her instincts would warn her off me, whether she wanted it or not.

I could enjoy this bloom, but she would never be mine. This was not my garden to pick such a flower from.

"Izzy," I started, searching for the right words to convey how much she'd come to mean to me over the course of a few days. I looked up and met her gaze, my eyes searching her for the courage to continue with the words that were caught in my throat. "I…I—"

Izzy leaned forward, her full attention devoted to me. Before I knew what I was doing, I grabbed her shoulders, pulling her against my chest in a tight embrace. She wiggled across the driftwood bench we sat on, snuggling deeper into my panicked embrace. "You are important to me. I don't understand it, nor will I pretend to. But something about you draws me in. *I need you*, Miss Stanton. I want you to stay with me, here in Italy."

She frowned against my shoulder, her hands balling into fists in my linen shirt. I felt her nails dig in as she shivered slightly, her pulse racing. "I have a life in the states, Mr. Sabatini. I can't abandon my life on a whim. But," she whispered, her voice wavering slightly as she looked up at my face, "we can have the time we've been given. It will be ours that nobody can take from us. We have now, and if now is all we have, I'd be happy to spend it with you."

I had so much admiration for this woman who was wise beyond both of our years. My lips crashed down on hers with a raw need, and she clung to my shirt as I pulled her back against me, not caring that we'd fallen to the sand. I leaned against an elbow as our tongues fought in a battle of desire, and I knew she needed this just as much as I did. She didn't fight for dominance, happy to let me lead the way in this battle of lust.

My hands reached under her skirt, brushing against her hips, over the thin string holding her thong in place. I growled appreciatively at her preferred choice of undergarments. Nothing in my time as a human had been this attractive on a woman. *So sexy. Especially on her.*

"Lucien, should we be doing this on the beach?" Her concern was laden with need, and her protest was feeble, at best. "What if someone sees us?" She sat up suddenly, moving off my lap as she glanced around.

"This is where I go to be alone with my thoughts. Nobody

but me ever comes here. Your virtue is safe with me, milady." She tilted her head back, groaning under her breath as my hand trailed down her neck, to her collarbone, and lower, to the swell of her breasts. "Well, maybe not your *virtue.*" I lifted her back up to sit on my lap, the two of us sprawled out in the sand. My hand trailed down the side of her chest, along her ribcage, and she shuddered beneath my touch.

Her sharp intake of breath was enough to let me know she wanted this as badly as I did, and I lowered my lips to hers again, tenderly this time as I savored the sweet taste of strawberries on her mouth. Her chapstick, most likely, but I didn't mind. Everything about her was so sweet, so decadent; it was like having my own personal dessert cart. I made love to her mouth with my own, nipping her lower lip as she was prone to do to herself. I left marks on her jawline, my hand snaking up to cup one of her perky breasts beneath her dress.

"Lucien, *yes,*" she moaned, her eyes fluttering shut as she writhed beneath my steady hands. As if to mock me, my hands shook as I moved them to the dip of her abdomen, grazing lightly over her stomach in my travels to her panty line. I wanted to feel her, but I wouldn't take her here, on the sand. I just had to feel her at this moment. I ached to know that she needed me as much as I needed her.

"Tell me what you want, *cara mia.* Speak your desires to me."

"Please touch me. I need to feel you. I-I *need you*, Lucien," she begged, her hands clutching my sleeves as desire overwhelmed her. Her face was flushed, and she looked like a goddess there on my lap, begging to be touched by *me.*

Wasting no time, I trailed my finger along the edge of her bikini line, teasing her until I encountered the dampness of her juices on the fabric of her thong. Shoving it aside, I gave no preamble as I rammed two digits inside my beautiful flower's sweet core, working her like a mandolin string as I explored her hot, eager sex with my roving fingers. She writhed atop my hand, bucking with wild abandon as her body sought out its own release.

I gave it to her, never one to be a selfish lover, and I swallowed her cries of ecstasy as she shuddered in orgasmic release, my fingers still buried to the hilt inside her throbbing core. I cleaned her up, carrying my angel back to the car. She didn't protest, her body sated and relaxed from our quick lovemaking on the beach, and I secured the seat belt around her chest, letting my fingers graze her collarbone one last time as I moved away.

She would probably sleep the whole way to the villa, but I…

I was wide awake, stunned by the knowledge that I was in love with this woman.

CHAPTER 19

~LUCIEN~

I made it about three-quarters of the way back home before she stirred in the passenger's seat next to me, stretching like a sleepy cat on the leather seat. My hands tightened on the wheel of the car as her dress slid up higher on her thigh, exposing her tanned, soft thighs. *Eyes on the road, you moron.* I might survive a car accident, but Izzy certainly wouldn't. The little yellow lines moved quickly beneath my tires, rolling down the road in front of my car before disappearing under the bumper, left behind us in the darkness of night.

"Are we almost back to the villa?" She turned to the window, her eyes settling on the mountains in the fading light. "Did I sleep the whole way back?"

I chuckled at her concerned tone. She seemed to think it was offensive to me that she'd taken a nap. "Almost, *stellina.* But it's no problem. I enjoy the quiet—*sometimes.*"

After years and years of existence, I was still amused by the things humans worried about. Such trivial issues in the larger world picture, but human lives were too fleeting for many to focus beyond their own path. I had been given several lifetimes to contemplate the world and my place in it, and yet even with the ability to do more, I didn't; simply satisfied to sit in my high tower in solitude. Human lives didn't interest me.

But this one did.

~*Izzy*~

I woke in the car, feeling stiff and cramped in the leather seat, my knees tucked up against my chest. Feeling like a good stretch would do the trick, I let my limbs reach in opposite directions, extending them to their full length as I shuddered in pure bliss. *Yes, this feels nice. Work those muscles.*

I suddenly felt like there was a flame burning me alive, and I glanced up to see Lucien staring quite pointedly at my very exposed legs. Yanking my limbs back into control, I hastily covered myself, clearing my throat as I assessed the scenery passing by. "Did I sleep the whole way back?"

He chuckled at me, his eyes on the road as we flew past the beginnings of a mountain range. "Almost, *stellina.* But it's no problem. I enjoy the quiet—*sometimes.*"

I smiled at his attempt to make me feel better, but I felt like I'd missed out on so much time. Even though it truly wasn't a lot of lost time, I felt despondent, as if that single solitary hour would break me. "Well, I would hate to waste any of the time I have here in Italy. It's not often that a girl gets a dream vacation with such an *accommodating host.*"

He noticed the bait but refused to bite, acting the gentleman once more. "I do so hope you *enjoy your stay* in my modest Italian villa. Maybe tomorrow I can introduce you to the artist of that wine bottle art you so admired."

My face lit up like the sky on the Fourth of July, dazzled and excited. "Really? That would be so *spectacular!*" I knew I must look like a child in a candy store, but I couldn't bring myself to care. I was truly excited to meet such a talented artist and see how she worked.

I watched Lucien's hand reach out towards the radio dial, flipping between stations until hearing a song he liked. I cringed, recognizing the terrible catchy tune. "I wouldn't have pegged you for a Taylor Swift fan."

He shrugged sheepishly, glancing in my direction. "I'm not. I assumed all you women liked this stuff, though."

I bent over to twist the metal knob between my fingers, snickering at his terrible assumption. "No, I most certainly am *not* a Taylor fan." That woman's music felt like Stevie Nicks watered way, way down, and I had no respect for her. I twisted the dial until I recognized some middle-ground reggae. Bob Marley was a classic, and I'd never encountered someone who didn't appreciate his music on one level or another. "This is much better," I muttered, swaying to the beat.

I sang to the music, unashamed of how terrible my voice must sound. The music took over me, and I closed my eyes, leaning my forehead against the cool glass of the passenger window. Recognizing the vineyard in the dark hillside, I smiled, knowing that meant we were close to the villa. I wanted to climb between the sheets of my bed and drift off to sleep until noon tomorrow. Maybe tan on the beach, go for a swim. Who knows? I was in Italy, after all, and *When in Rome*...

"Would you like to go out on my boat tomorrow? It's supposed to be cloudy but warm. The perfect day for a vampyr to stay in the sun all day—on a day it hides its face behind the heavy clouds."

His voice cut through my rendition of Buffalo Soldier, grabbing my attention quickly. "Did you say go out on your boat?"

He nodded, a slow smile spreading across his lips at my visible excitement. "The Raven, my sailboat in the boathouse. We can take it out for the day or longer. It has a full-sized Captain's Cabin below deck." He shrugged, pulling into the long driveway of his home. I felt a sense of welcome here, as if I belonged in this strange world, so far apart from my own, but I shook off the feeling, knowing it was simply a longing for a change of scenery.

But I was responsible, so I would go back to my job and my

life in the states, only because I knew nothing else. It was inevitable this dream would end in a few short days, and I would probably never see this handsome vampyr again. I was, however, content to be his personal plaything for the duration of the trip if he would have me. I knew better than to catch feelings for a man so far out of my league. *Out of my species, for that matter.*

"I think that's a great idea, Lucien. I'd love to go sailing with you tomorrow."

His joy danced in his crimson eyes, and I was pleased that my acceptance had brought him happiness. When I'd first met him, all he'd done was scowl the whole night. *Now look at him. Two days in, and he's breaking out of his shell. And I'm not normally a people person.*

The car pulled up to the main loop, stopping in front of the villa entrance. Lucien stepped out on his side, hurrying around to my door before I could put my hands on the handle to open it myself. He swung it wide, gesturing for me to exit the car as he offered me a hand up. "Milady?"

The night was dark by now, and I couldn't clearly see the villa, but I knew it was the same one we'd just left this morning. "Thanks, Lucien," I said, taking his hand to step out. I wobbled a bit as I stood, my legs still weak. Thankfully, Lucien had noticed, and he supported me until they would cooperate, never once indicating he'd noticed my weak knees.

Such a gentleman.

When we walked in the villa's doors, Titus was waiting for us in the foyer with Jasper, and Lucien tossed him the keys wordlessly. Jasper held up a finger, his glance worried and anxious.

"Young Master, I don't mean to be a bother, but there's an urgent letter for you on your desk in the study—"

Lucien's hand shot up, waving Jasper off with a flick of his wrist. "I'll be sure to check it out later, Jasper. If you would be so kind as to send us up some refreshments, I think Izzy and I will retire to the second-floor commons to relax, maybe watch a movie…"

He looked down at me, studying me intently. I think he

was waiting for me to object, but I had no desire to. Watching a movie was a relaxing way to spend the night, and I was more than happy to *Netflix-and-chill* while on vacation.

"I'm up for whatever."

His megawatt smile spread even further across his face until it seemed like it must hurt in its intensity. "Fantastic. Shall we?"

I cast one last glance over my shoulder at Jasper, whose face was frozen in what looked like fear. "Are you sure you shouldn't check that letter—"

"The letter can wait. My time is best spent elsewhere right now." As if on cue, I felt his gaze travel down my body, lighting a path as he undressed me with his eyes. I shivered as a

thrill ran down my spine, the tiny hairs on my arms raised as my body created its own static field. I was a vibrating ball of electricity, and if Lucien touched me right now, I'd probably shock him dead.

I followed him up the stairs, mouthing *'sorry'* over my shoulder as Jasper watched us go. Lucien opened a large set of double french doors at the top of the stairs that I hadn't noticed before. Swinging them wide with a flourish befitting a vampyr, he stepped inside, swinging his arms around himself as he turned. I silently took it all in, enjoying his excitement at sharing this new part of his home with me.

"I rarely come here anymore, but this was my personal commons, or sitting room. I had the Baby Grand installed in here when we first built this add-on, and only my own hands have coaxed the music from her keys." He walked over to the piano, his fingers gently caressing the solid wood as he dragged them from one end to the other. The entire room was in spectacular shape for a room he hadn't used in a while, and I suspected Jasper must have been taking care of it in his master's neglect.

I saw the longing in his eyes as he studied the keys, his finger striking out a single, solitary note that somehow seemed to speak for his entire soul. It sounded lost, out of place in the large, quiet room, and I found myself feeling like I *was* the note, drifting in a strange, empty world, trying to find my place outside of my personal song.

I watched his fingers twitch just above the keys, saddened by his struggle to refrain from placing his hands back on it, bringing out the melodies from his past. I suddenly wanted to hear every musical piece he'd ever played; I wanted to know what it felt like to listen to him draw out the stories behind intense sonatas. I wanted to see the picture he painted with his songs, and before I could stop myself, the words were out of my mouth.

"Why don't you play something for me?"

~Lucien~

I stared at Izzy, speechless for the first time in as long as I could remember. I had plenty of women ask me to play the piano for them, but I'd never before been so eager to acquiesce to their request. Something about the innocent way she asked me, as if she could feel my emotional connection to this instrument, made me melt inside.

I hadn't played for anyone since I was a new vampyr. My past had ruined it for me, and I'd abandoned this beautiful piano in this room, locking the door behind me. For over a century, it sat idle behind these heavy oak doors, and Jasper had snuck in while I was away to tidy up the room, but he had honored my wishes never to play this piano. It was the reason we'd had a second piano and an organ installed on the ground floor, as he also liked to play.

I knew I was a hard person to live with, so who was I to deny my only friend his passions in life? Jasper had been my first victim as a new vampyr, and I had panicked, taking him to my creator to fix him. He'd forced me to turn my butler, and I'd stumbled through the procedure, hurting him more than was necessary. He struggled through the change, but when he came through on the other end, he didn't run from me. He had been the one constant in my life, though I'd hurt him not once, but twice.

I'd been much more practiced by the time Florentine came along.

"Earth to Lucien?" She snapped her fingers at me, waking me from my deep inner thoughts.

"Ah, right. You know, I actually would like to play for you. Do you have a request?"

She shook her head, biting her lower lip again while she moved around me to sit in the window seat. When Izzy had made herself comfortable, I turned to the piano, my second oldest and dearest friend. The one I had neglected for too long. I inhaled deeply, taking in the familiar scent of lavender that wafted around the room. My hands ached to be atop the keys as I wracked my brain for a meaningful piece to play for her. Something that was the perfect pace, but also the perfect balance of light and dark.

The harmony of Yin and Yang, like she was to me.

Cracking my knuckles, I laid my fingertips against the ivory keys, my eyes drifting shut as I went through the opening notes to Yann Tiersen's *La valse d'Amelie.* One more deep breath and I released the beast within, knowing the only way to truly soothe that side of myself was with music.

The music flowed from my fingers freely, as if it had been but a day or two since I'd last played, and I took a small sense of pride in that fact as I let the music flow from my hands.

~Izzy~

His shoulders were squared, his muscles flexing as his hands glided up and down the long set of keys, his fingers deftly picking out each individual note clearly. I noticed his eyes were closed, and I smiled as I realized I had expected him to take out sheet music and play from the piece itself. *But of course, if you've had two hundred years to play, you're bound to memorize your favorites along the way.*

I watched, transfixed as his fingers flew across one another, hands overlapping at times to hit every note. It was like the piano was an extension of himself, his hands intimately connected to him in a wordless understanding. I could feel the raw emotion in his choice of music, and the lines on his face melted away as his expression relaxed, letting go of all that negative as the notes rang out in the large room. A solitary tear slid down my cheek as I felt the music call out to me, touching a part of my soul locked away since I was a little girl. I felt light, almost as if I could fly away, floating in the summer breeze like a loose feather. His notes painted a picture in my mind, and as I embraced the imagery, I realized I'd been swaying to the music. Lucien watched me, an amused expression on his face, but I paid him no mind, rising to my feet. The commons was a large room with a lot of open space, and I felt like I should *move*. The music spoke to me, and I was powerless to obey it.

Lucien seemed unfazed by my sudden movement, and he simply watched me as I floated around the room, spinning in slow circles with my arms stretched wide. I let the solemn notes carry my spirit, feeling like I was a part of the song itself. I felt silly to have such a response to a song, but I couldn't bring myself to sit back down. It was an almost frightening compulsion, as if my body had a mind of its own. As the music slowed some, I moved to join Lucien on the bench, and he shifted slightly to the side, allowing me space.

He offered a genuine smile and nothing more, seemingly pleased with my decision to sit with him. His body twisted and weaved back and forth as he played on, the notes lighter now than they had been earlier. I was unable to look away, transfixed on his hands as he plucked the keys with the skill of a master. I knew what those fingers could do to me, but I had no idea they could be so enthralling on a piano.

His tongue darted out once or twice to lick his lips, and I wanted nothing more than to reach up and touch that beautiful smile he wore. It was harder than I had expected to resist, and I looked down, wondering where my senses had gone.

I leaned my head against his shoulder as the last notes bled from his fingertips, drifting away in the breeze. If time could stand still, I would admire this man while he played piano forever, watching his fingers create musical masterpieces that spoke to my soul.

CHAPTER 20

~IZZY~

We sat like that for a few minutes after the last note rang out, each of us afraid to move first. I couldn't bring myself to break the odd spell that fallen over us. But as par for the course of life, there was a knock at the doorway, and Jasper cleared his throat, wheeling in a cart with food and drinks on it.

"Sorry to interrupt, but your refreshments, sir. Also, about the letter—"

Lucien waved him off, his eyes narrowed dangerously as he sent a silent message to Jasper: *get out, or else.* Jasper sighed, closing the doors behind himself as he left the room. Lucien smiled as he wrapped an arm around my shoulder tenderly. My skin tingled where he touched my skin, and I felt suddenly hot, as if the temperature in the room had risen twenty degrees. Fanning myself lightly, my eyes wandered to the dishes on the cart, my mouth salivating at the sight of what looked like chicken alfredo. *Pasta in Italy. Just what the doctor ordered.*

Lucien's eyes met mine, glancing down at me with a slight frown on his lips. "Come, let's enjoy the food and drink Jasper has brought us." He swung around on the bench, releasing his grasp on me as he stood to make his way to the cart. The minute his arm left my side, I felt lost, adrift. I actually had to choke back a sob as he walked further away from me.

What the fuck is wrong with me?

"What's on the menu tonight?" I laughed as I tacked on the rest of my joke, hoping he would appreciate my quick wit. "Am I the appetizer or the entree? Table for two, dinner for one..."

The joke fell flat as Lucien turned to me, a tortured expression on his face. "Neither. I don't eat my guests, Lizzania." His eyes pierced my soul, and I was nervous in light of the poor joke I'd made. I knew I was in trouble when my parents broke my whole name out; I could only imagine what that meant when a vampyr drew it out.

"That's a shame," I muttered flippantly, watching Lucien do something I didn't think was possible.

He *blushed.*

"Jasper has sent up alfredo chicken and some garlic bread. I also see some red wine here, which will be nice, although I'd have preferred a white." He poured one glass from each of the two bottles on the cart, setting the first one down in front of me. "If you make yourself comfortable on the couch, I'll bring the food over."

As he busied himself with the dishes, I grabbed both glasses and made myself at home. I really was a low-maintenance girl, but it was going to be hard to go back to my normal life after experiencing this level of decadence. *A girl could get used to this lifestyle.*

When he set the bowl on the coffee table before me, the scent hit my nostrils, and I inhaled the rich scent of parsley, oregano, and cayenne pepper. *Spicy, just how I like my alfredo.* I twirled the linguine around the fork, lifting a dainty portion to my lips in an attempt to seem civilized. I couldn't keep myself from slurping up the last of the dangling noodle at the end of my fork, and I heard Lucien moan from beside me on the couch.

"I *know,* this food is *amazing,* isn't it?" I hummed my approval as I took another bite, realizing Jasper was truly a king of his domain in the kitchen. His food was decadent but balanced perfectly, with just enough of everything to draw out all the flavor and richness in each bite. *It was really a shame that we didn't have a cook like him at home. I'd be wider than a house.*

~Lucien~

She'd mistaken my moan as enthusiasm over the food, and while Jasper's food was delicious, it wasn't as decadent as the sight of her slurping that noodle between her full lips. I felt my Thirst intensify, not just for her body but now for her blood. Jasper had been smart to send up some blood in a wine bottle so that I could stave off the hunger a while longer. I reached for my glass, smiling when the pleasing aroma hit my nostrils.

Wait.

I sniffed a second time, confirming my own screw-up. I glanced over to Izzy, the glass of what she assumed was wine heading right for her lips. *Fuck.*

"Don't drink that!" I hadn't meant for it to come out so aggressive, but in my haste to prevent her from swallowing my liquid diet, I reached out, shoving the glass from her hand in a panic. The blood wouldn't harm her, but some sick part of me was terrified to let her know I fed from a glass. That she'd almost drank blood meant for me.

That plan backfired terribly.

The glass of wine jerked from her hand as she flinched away from my aggressive advance, spilling the contents all over her brightly colored dress. I'd been holding the rest of the bottle in my hands, and when I'd instinctively reached out to stop her, I'd also thrown half the contents of it on her, as well. Head to toe, she was dripping wet. Her surprised 'oh!' turned into a horrified gasp as she realized what she was actually covered in, and I felt my eyes changing, shifting nearly to black as the Thirst rose to the surface, my prey literally drenched in a drizzle of decadent sauce that only a vampyr could appreciate. I could enjoy licking every ounce of that wasted blood off her body and then feed straight from the source itself.

Get the fuck ahold of yourself, you twit. She's a guest.

And I was no animal. "Izzy, I think we should take you to get cleaned up—"

"Am I covered in *blood*, Lucien?" She stared down at herself, unable to comprehend the situation she found herself in. I nodded, unable to find the words to smooth out the situation.

"Ah, yes. Yes, you are. That was my glass, not yours."

She cringed as she stood, her arms dripping blood down them as she tried not to spill it on the leather couch. A bit too late, but still an admirable trait. Consideration.

"So I'm wearing somebody's blood on myself?" I half expected her to go white as a sheet, and she *did* look about half there. I could hear her heartbeat racing, and I could smell the panic on her as her hormones ran wild.

"Yeah. From a blood bank, Izzy."

She propped her hands on her hips, ignoring the blood now dripping from her hair to her cheek, blazing a path between her breasts. I bit back a moan, wishing more than anything to be able to follow that blood down with my tongue, licking it all up until there wasn't a drop left. I felt my fangs protrude, and my hand shot up to cover my lips, hiding the evidence.

Why the hell was I hiding from her? She knew what I was.

As if reading my mind, I felt her hand tugging mine down, exposing my lips to her line of sight. "Why are you covering your mouth? Are you laughing at me?"

"No! Never," I protested, but my outburst exposed my fangs to her, and her gasp was audible. I watched her recoil in fear from the sharp teeth protruding from my canines. This was it, the moment she ran from the monster, just like all the others. I closed my eyes, not wanting to see her as she walked away from me.

Imagine my surprise when I felt the pad of her thumbs rub along my bottom lip, pulling my jaw down to angle the view better. I tried to talk around the hand on my mouth, but it came out a bit strangled.

"Haaay-whaa ahr yuu doingh-"

"I want to see them, Lucien."

I froze, my whole body on high alert. On the one hand, I wanted her to see the real me, to know who she laid next to at night. On the other hand, I had a deep-rooted shame for what I was, especially when I hadn't chosen this life for myself. I wanted her to see the me that I was before I was a vampyr—before half of me viewed her as a snack.

The *human side* of me. The side I'd buried for a century or more.

She pulled my lip down, her finger grazing the tip of my fangs. She pricked her finger on their sharpness, jerking back slightly, and I couldn't help but lick the tip of my fang where her blood lingered. She tasted so sweet, and I felt my whole body light up, wanting more. Just when I thought I'd gotten myself under control, she looked up at me, a sly smile on her lips.

"Do I taste good?"

Fuck. She'd be the death of me if I weren't already a member of the undead. I couldn't bring myself to answer her, so I just stood there, staring blankly at her.

Truth was, she definitely was the best thing I'd tasted in forever. Blood or…otherwise.

"Why are you staring at me like that? Is it because I'm covered in blood?" She looked down at her dress, which was nearly ruined. Thankfully, Jasper had experience with getting blood out of white linen. She smoothed her dress down the sides, smearing the blood into the thin fabric. It was starting to stick to her skin, painting her like a warrior in the middle of the battlefield.

I couldn't help but lick my lips. She really did look delectable, standing there covered in my dinner. "Well, you're wearing most of my meal now. But if you don't get that dress off soon, you'll never get it back to the normal color."

She looked down at the dress, then back to me, her face incredulous. "You think you could salvage it *now?*"

I nervously chuckled at her incredulous declaration. "Why, yes, Jasper hasn't met a bloodstain yet he couldn't defeat." I inhaled the air in the room like a suffocating man, taking in her scent, and the comforting smell of iron-tinged blood, still fresh. She looked into my eyes, her own betraying the anxiety and sheer terror that flowed through her body. It was a natural reaction that I really couldn't fault her for.

I steeled myself for the words that I knew would eventually come out of her mouth, leaving me for the night to wallow in my own stupidity. It's no less than I deserved for trying to hide what I was. But secretly, a part of me hoped she'd prove me wrong. That just once, someone would stay, unafraid to face their fears.

Izzy stepped back from me, moving to the other side of the coffee table. I fell back onto the couch, my body slouched in defeat. I was ready to prostrate myself at her feet to beg her to stay, and she was putting space between us—a barrier. My head dropped to my hands, my shame and agony rising to the surface as I fought to keep control of myself until she left the room. She hadn't said a word, but I needed none. I had played this scenario over in my head and in real life with countless other women. I'd prepared myself for this from the moment of her arrival.

I waited for what felt like forever until I heard the distinct sound of wet fabric hitting the floor with a slick *smack* against the wood. For the first time in my life, I was actually afraid to look up, but my curiosity got the better of me, and I peered out from between cracked fingers. I could have fainted at the sight before me.

Izzy stood before me in nothing but her undergarments, the lace sticking to her like a second, moist, red skin. I swallowed thickly, feeling myself react to her almost immediately. I was morbidly curious as to what she was doing, and my mind was powerless to stop my mouth as it opened, my hands falling from my face to cover the growing bulge in the front of my pants.

"What are you, ah, what are you doing, Izzy?"

She bent over to pick up her dress, her long legs covered in thin trails of blood that were making their way to her ankles. I licked my lips, both disgusted at myself and aroused by the appetizing mixture of horror and sensuality that was displayed before me, wrapped in tiny triangles of fabric. She walked over towards the door, setting the dress on the bottom shelf of the cart before returning to stand just feet from me.

"I couldn't stay in that thing all night, and you said Jasper could get the stains out. Since it's my favorite dress, maybe you could take care of it, and we can *hang out* while it washes."

My tongue was slow to form words, as if my language skills had flown out the window. "Ah…yes, I can handle that. But maybe you'd like to go get changed into some new…clothes?"

She shrugged, stepping a foot closer. If she closed the last foot between herself and the couch, she'd be between my legs, and I wasn't sure how well I would handle being that close to her right now, with the Thirst in full swing. What I needed right now was to feed and fuck. I couldn't unleash that on her, not this soon.

"Or you could let me shower in your room, and I could put on one of your button-downs?"

My neck ached from the force with which my head snapped around, my eyes focused on the cute little blush that was wandering up her cheeks. *So her bravery shocked her as well, it appeared.* I had to do something to scare her off, or I might just kill her tonight, completely by accident.

"No, *cara mia,* you need to put that dress back on." I zipped over to the door, picking the dress up off the floor, and just as quickly, I was back before her, pulling the damned thing over her head. Never before had I redressed a woman so eager for sex, just to send her away, but I guess there's a first time for everything. She squirmed beneath my hands as she let me put that damned dress back on her body, and her beautiful lips were drawn down in a pout as she looked back up at me.

"You know, if you didn't like the sex, you could have just said so, Luc." She watched as I sputtered for a response, my dick jumping in my pants as a testament that I had enjoyed our drunken night together just as much as she must have.

Fuck all, but it's gonna be a long night. Long and frustrating. I put on my best bad guy smirk, standing to my full height. I puffed up, straightening my spine to seem more imposing, my chest swelling as I tried everything I could do to appear dangerous. My eyes narrowed, and I let the transformation take over, praying this worked. If she didn't leave this room right now, I'd surely spend the rest of the night digging a grave for myself, and for her.

"You. Need. To. Leave." I leaned over her, baring my fangs just slightly, my grin becoming a fierce and frightening visage as I let the beast out to play. My eyes swirled, so dark they were almost black, and I let a low growl escape my throat. "I won't be responsible for the harm you might come to if you stay here, standing before me, covered in blood."

My eyes watched hers like a hawk, but I knew I couldn't possibly hurt her. I'd fling myself from the damned window before I raised a pinky to her. I…

I think I was *falling in love with her.*

I watched as she flinched as if breaking from a spell. Her eyes roamed my face, eyes wide as she took in the nightmare fuel I'd become in front of her very eyes. This was it. This was the moment she leaves.

But she didn't. Her hand reached up to cup my jaw, her breathing shallow as she straightened her shoulders, squaring off with me. Her eyes held mine in a silent battle as she braved this new, scary thing before her. The monster beneath the facade of a human.

The Vampyr.

CHAPTER 21

~IZZY~

"I won't be responsible for the harm you might come to if you stay here, standing before me, covered in blood."

I stood there, staring this man down, holding his face in my bloodstained hands. I left smears of red on his lightly tanned skin, but I paid it no mind, staring deep into his eyes as I mustered every ounce of courage I could find in my body.

I was familiar with the look in his tortured eyes, for I, too, was a frequent visitor of the deep chasm he stood at the edge of. The sadness, the loneliness that swam in his eyes, was heartbreaking on its own, but what really grabbed me by the soul and tore me from myself was the look of defeat that hovered just below the surface, as if he expected me to flee from him like he was some kind of monster.

Though it had only been a few days, I was growing bolder and needier with this man than I'd ever felt with anyone in my entire life. I could feel the pain in his tortured crimson gaze like it was my own, and I ached to take it away, even if he only forgot for a little while. My thumbs brushed against his jawline, and I felt a tear slide down my cheek as a bit of red flashed back into his eyes. His warm breath brushed against my face as he watched that single droplet burn a trail down my cheek.

"Lucien…" I began, but he cut me off, putting his hands on my shoulders to push me away. It wouldn't have taken much to overpower me, but it didn't seem like he was trying, and I wasn't about to give up. Something about this man made me want to fight for him. I couldn't let him drown as others had always let me.

"Please, *cara mia,* I can't—"

"I'm not going to run away, Luc. I'm not afraid of you—"

"But you *should be!"* His voice echoed against the walls of the sitting room, the booming shout reverberating in my very soul. "I am a *monster,* Izzy. I lose control sometimes—"

Wrong terminology, Cassanova.

My eyes darkened with lust as I shoved him back against the couch, climbing atop his waist in all my decadent, blood-soaked glory. My legs spread across his lap as I straddled him, my hands around his neck as I leaned in to nuzzle the soft skin there. My hot breath tickled the tender skin below his earlobe, and he moaned as I nibbled at him as if he was the snack, and I, the vampyr.

I growled out a response against his neck, grinding my hips seductively against him to emphasize every word. *"Lose control with me, Lucien."*

His eyes were cloudy with need and desire as he looked at me, busy with my careful ministrations. I met his gaze with my own firey one; the words out of my mouth couldn't have been more erotic, or more perfect, had he put them there himself.

"If you're not going to take me to your room to shower, maybe you could put that tongue of yours to good use and clean me up."

Holy hell. Did the temperature just climb to the boiling point? I was sweating bullets, and his cock was stiff as a rod of rebar, pressing against the inside of his pants. I needed this man, and I needed him *bad,* but could I do this? Did I really want this? To be his dinner?

Did I know what I was asking?

"Izzy, I—"

I arched back, baring my chest to him in a sensual pose

that curved my spine, thrusting my hips into his. I knew he could feel my arousal through those thin slips of fabric I called a thong, but I wanted to feel more. I needed to feel all of him. Taste him. Touch him.

Devour him, like he would be devouring me.

"Luc..."

His breathing was rapid and shallow as he lifted us off of the couch, my legs wrapped around his muscled torso as his hands found my ass, pulling me against his erection. He strode out of the room and down the hallway, making a beeline for his room.

I couldn't breathe, couldn't think, couldn't speak as we neared the door, his foot slamming it open and then kicking it closed behind us. He shoved my back against the wall, burying his nose in my neck. I felt his tongue dart out, leaving little spots of saliva on my skin that cooled quickly in the night air, dragging a shiver up my spine.

I couldn't help but moan as his tongue trailed down the spot below my ear to just above my collarbone. A small whimper escaped my throat when he gently nipped the tender skin of my neck. "It's not pleasant, you know," he muttered against my neck. I could barely hear him, so I leaned back, strangely curious.

"What's not pleasant?"

He signed, his face falling once again. "Being on the dinner menu for a vampyr. It's painful in the beginning, and uncomfortable. It's like having a fire in your veins for a brief moment, and then you begin to feel weaker and weaker. If I can't stop myself, I could kill you."

I pondered that revelation. It wouldn't be erotic; it would *suck. Literally.* Was I ready for such a step? Was that a commitment I wanted to make to a man who I would probably never see after this week?

Yes. If not now, then when? How often does one get to say a vampyr has bitten them?

"I'll never again get this life experience offered to me. It would be an insult to fate not to offer myself as dinner."

Who the fuck was I all of a sudden? Agatha Christie? Anne Rice?

As luck would have it, Lucien did not find my quippy response as humorous as I did. "O-*Offer yourself as dinner?* What in the literal *hell* are you thinking? You could *die!*" He lifted his gaze to meet mine, and his words became a self-fulfilling prophecy.

If he didn't put his mouth back on me, I would expire. I was hot, *too hot*, and all I wanted was for this man to take me as a meal and take me to bed. Instead, here he was, trying to talk me out of it.

"Tell me, Mister Sabatini, do you often spend your nights trying to talk your dinner out of being eaten? Or is it just because I'm on the menu?"

His face paled, and I could practically cut the awkward tension with a knife. I was painfully aware of my legs still wrapped tightly around his waist, and I squirmed in his grasp, trying to redirect his thought process. For just a moment, it seemed to work, and I felt his chest vibrate with a growl. *It's now or never, bitch. Get your big girl panties off and get to it.*

"Luc, I'd hate to see all this blood go to waste, you know." I drug my finger down a nearly dry trail, picking up a drop at the base of my neck with the tip of my finger. I grinned seductively as I studied the drop of blood on the tip of my finger, and I saw his eyes dart to that perfectly round, crimson droplet. His lips parted to reveal those sharp, deadly fangs, and I swallowed thickly, rousing my courage as I put my finger on his lip, pushing it past to rest on his tongue. The act felt so erotic I was *melting*, and for a brief second, he didn't react, causing me to fear the worst.

But the feel of his tongue licking the sticky liquid from my finger, sliding around my digit in his mouth, sent ripples through my stomach. My legs clenched around him involuntarily as I closed my eyes, moaning at the sensation. *Jesus, what kind of a horrorcore whore had I become?*

Lucien's body came alive as I pulled my finger from his mouth, letting the tip of my finger rest on his lips. When I tried to pull it away, his hand snapped up to capture mine, refusing to let go. I peeked out from under my lashes to see him reaching for my other hand, trapping both of them above my head against the wall. His rakish smile and those nearly night-black eyes roamed over my body, following the trails of blood. He leaned forward, his tongue finding my neck as he cleaned the blood from my skin. When the skin ran into the top of my dress, he growled low, ripping it in half as he lapped up the little pool of blood that had formed between the swell of my breasts.

If it were possible to turn into a human puddle, I would be one soon for sure, with a tongue like that. I just hoped he had plans to use it on the rest of my body. *Everywhere.*

~Lucien~

I have never been so broken and so set free at the same time as I was in this very moment. Lizzania Stanton was doing things to me that another soul on this earth had never done. She was bringing me back to life. Making me *feel.* She embraced my dark side as much as my human side, and her eager trick with the blood has turned on a raging inferno in a once-frozen body. If I didn't bury my dick deep inside this woman—and *fast*—I would combust into a pile of ash.

I let my tongue trail down between her perky breasts, catching the little puddle of blood those beautiful tits had captured for me in their soft valley. I had ripped her dress in my chase of the blood, and I could feel the beast winning out over the human side of me, quickly gaining speed. If I didn't do something soon, I would lose myself to the Thirst, and the experience would be hard and painful for Izzy.

I wanted her to enjoy this as much as possible, with as little pain as I could manage. Such a beautiful gift should be treasured, *and treasure her I would, indeed.*

"Let's get you out of this dress, shall we?" I eyed it carefully, watching her face fall as she registered the tear down the center.

"We won't have to worry about the stain anymore, I guess."

Before she could be sad about her dress I was moving her away from the wall, walking us over to the bed. I threw her on her back against the satin black sheets, my tongue tingling with anticipation as I eyed the meal before me.

"Let's not worry about that for now. Why don't you just relax and let me worry about everything." I kicked off my shoes, leaving the expensive Italian leather laying haphazardly at the foot of the bed. On my knees, I crawled towards her, moving up between her legs purposefully.

"What are you doing down there, Lucien? My neck is up here."

I choked back laughter at her impatience. I was no longer afraid of the action of feeding on her, and the Thirst made my inhibitions and moral lines fade to nothing. I knew when the time came, I would have no problem sticking my fangs deep into her tender neck and sucking the very life from her body. I would penetrate her body and soul, taking the most intimate parts of her for myself.

And I wouldn't feel a bit of guilt. No shame. No regret.

"In due time, *cara mia.* Right now, I want you to bend those delectable legs at the knees so I can slide this dress off of you."

~Izzy~

I was so eager to comply with his demands that I forgot he was between my legs on his hands and knees, and I bent my legs, giving him a full view of the lacy thong underneath my dress. His eyes zeroed in on my core, burning me alive as he devoured the view before him. I could feel the wetness of my arousal soaking those panties, and I squirmed deliciously as his hands came up to grab the top of my sundress, sliding it down my torso.

When my breasts sprang free from the dress, still encased in my lacy bra, Lucien gasped, his hands leaving the dress to cup the soft mounds. I arched my back, and he followed my lead, slipping his hands behind my back to quickly release the clasps. He ripped the thin fabric from my arms, throwing it unceremoniously from the bed.

"Wouldn't want that to get in the way, would we?"

He put his hands around my bare breasts, cupping them as his thumbs rubbed roughly over my pert nipples, the hard peaks achingly sensitive to his touch. I moaned as his tongue replaced those fingers, swirling around first one, then the other, nibbling gently as white-hot heat shot straight between my legs. I needed him, *and bad.* He wasn't moving fast enough, and I wanted to feel him, *all of him.*

"Oh *sweet Jesus,* that feels so good," I moaned, biting my lower lip as one of his hands left my chest to keep tugging that dress down my waist. At this point, I just wanted the damn thing off of me and out of the way, so I lifted my hips eagerly, begging for him to drag it off my body and discard it like he had my bra. *And my dignity.*

His tongue slid up and down the blood trails, cleaning off any undried blood. The roughness of his taste buds rubbed against my smooth skin, giving me goosebumps. My fingers wove through his chestnut mane, and I swiftly untied the ribbon at the base of his neck. When his hair was loose, the strands tickled my stomach as he swirled his tongue around my navel, and I tried desperately to urge him lower with my hands, but he would have none of it.

His head pulled back from my waist, a devilish grin painted across his blood-red lips. I held my breath, afraid he'd changed his mind. *Would he send me away now?*

His voice was low and gravelly as he sat up, pulling me suddenly up with him. "Go wash this watered-down mess off of you, and let me feast on the real thing, unsullied and untainted. If I'm to dine on you tonight, I want to taste *only* you. *All of you.*"

My nipples strained towards his body in the cool air, and I whimpered at the lost contact with his tongue, his hands. *I needed to feel him.*

"But Luc—"

He slid to the side of the bed, pulling me with him as his feet—and mine—hit the floor. I only had a moment to gather my wits before he spun me around, pulled my dress up a bit for me, and gave me a little shove towards his private bathroom. As I took the first step, I felt his hand connect with my ass under the dress, stinging where it smacked me smartly on the cheek.

I bit back an *oh* of shock, jumping a little at the unexpected touch. I'd never been spanked before, and it lent a little bit of naughtiness to this whole experience. I let out a low moan to let him know I liked it before trotting obediently away to the bathroom.

Once behind the bathroom door, all that false bravado just sort of melted away, and suddenly I was second-guessing myself and what I was doing here in the bedroom of the most dangerous, otherworldly man I'd ever met.

What the hell had I gotten myself into?

CHAPTER 22

~LUCIEN~

I hadn't ever spanked a woman before in my life, but seeing her ass peeking out beneath the bottom of her ruined dress, that thong exposing her bare cheeks to my gaze, it all drove me wild. Before I knew my hand had shot out, I heard the resounding *smack* echo across the room, and I watched Izzy jump at the contact. But she didn't cry out—she'd *moaned,* so low I second-guessed if I'd actually heard it. When she reached the bathroom door, however, she'd turned around to peek over her shoulder, sending me a heated gaze as she chewed on her bottom lip.

Heavens above, that bottom lip of hers. She did things to me when she bit that damned thing.

I sat down on the edge of the bed when she disappeared behind the door, waiting for the sound of the running water. At first, I'd enjoyed the taste of blood, needing to find something to distract myself from the full force of the thirst, but it was becoming too much. If she didn't wash the stench of stale blood off of herself, this whole sacrifice would be marred. When I tasted this beauty, accepted her offer, I wanted to taste only her, pure and straight like whiskey right from the barrel. I wanted no mixers, no chasers.

I was a purist.

I shifted uncomfortably, my pants too tight against my

growing need for her. I wanted to bend her backward and rough her up while I devoured her life force, but the human side of me knew that was only the Thirst talking. Izzy was a beautiful, sophisticated woman who deserved love and affection; adoration. She deserved to be worshipped from her feet to her head, taking time to lavish every peak and valley until every inch of her had met with the lips of a lover.

I wish we had more time than the week she planned to stay here.

I blinked as I heard the water turning on, a smile on my lips as the sound of the glass door to my shower opening and closing echoed in the large bathroom. The sound was so quiet, even my advanced hearing had a hard time picking it up. I moved awkwardly towards my bedroom door, not knowing how much time I had to zip over, finish off the bottle of blood, and grab her something to sleep in.

Not that she needed clothes to sleep in, but still.

I hurriedly rushed to her room; thankfully, I found a silk nightgown laid at the end of her bed. I grabbed it and rushed over to the commons, where the half-empty bottle of blood sat against the cushions of the couch. I chugged the contents, wincing as the room-temperature liquid sluggishly trailed down the back of my throat. It was like swallowing molasses, it had coagulated so badly, but I needed to do something to take the edge of this thirst off before I put Lizzania's life in my hands—*and my mouth.* I became painfully aware of my audience as a low chuckle sounded from the doorway. The bottle hit the tabletop with a resounding *clink as* I swiped at my mouth messily, turning to Jasper.

He stood there with a smirk on his face, his arms crossed in front of his chest and eyes full of mischief as he privately enjoyed my desperation. "Reduced to drinking the sludge from the bottom of a discarded bottle? I could have just brought you a new one, Young Master."

"I really wish you'd drop the whole *young master* shit, Jasper. Now is *not* the time for it." I turned on him, standing toe to toe with the smug bastard. This was a side of Jasper I hadn't seen since I was a human. This side of Jasper had *spunk*. He had *moxie*.

Jasper snickered at my attitude, but it didn't phase him in the slightest. He'd long ago grown accustomed to my outbursts. "I left a fresh glass in your room while you were busy raiding hers for that nightgown. I mean, seriously, *sir*, couldn't you have picked a sexier piece of lingerie for the woman to wear in your bed?"

"Where the hell has this smug sonofabitch been this whole time? Your rowdy attitude is back, and I must say it's been far too long, friend."

He scoffed at me, looking away before I could see the glint of surprise in his eyes. "Regardless, you don't have much time before she finishes her shower, so I would head back and down that glass. And be careful if you're planning to do what I think you are. You might mess around and hurt someone."

Now it was my turn to be offended at his appraisal of my intelligence. "You think I would hurt a hair on her head?"

Jasper shook his head, sighing deeply. "I don't think you intentionally would, but humans are fragile creatures. We used to be human; never forget that." He closed his eyes as a small shudder ran through his body. "I'm going to head out for the night unless there's something you need from me. I have an appointment with a lovely lady in town—"

"Oh stuff it, Jasper, I've known you're of the male persuasion for a century now, so you can drop the act." I turned my back on him, looking around for the small purse Izzy had set down earlier. Jasper took that moment to make his departure, quickly slipping out of the room and disappearing into the night.

Great, now it's just she and I. Alone in this entire villa. Jasper won't be home until dark tomorrow. Whatever will we do?

A smile curled the edges of my lips as I thought of the various surfaces in my house that I'd never had a woman on before. And then I imagined them with Izzy splayed out like a feast atop them, taking my cock like a champion bull rider, and my smile got even wider.

Oh, I'm sure we can think of plenty to occupy ourselves with.

~Izzy~

I stood under the scalding hot water, letting the droplets beat down on my back like a thousand tiny fists kneading out the stress of the day. Somehow, I had to work up the courage to go back out there after I'd scrubbed all the blood from my body. The water broke up the dried red trails, the color swirling in the whirlpool at my feet before traveling down the holes in the chrome drain plate. Blinking the water from my eyes, I let the water run over me until the red stopped flowing and then reached for the bar of soap on the shelf beside me.

Mmm, it smells like mint. Refreshing.

I inhaled the fresh scent as I lathered up, rubbing down every inch of myself. My skin felt softer with every pass of the bar of soap, and I scrubbed like my life depended on it. Reaching out for the shampoo, I was frustrated when I couldn't locate any. Just as I was about to brave the chilly air to hunt for a bottle, I heard someone clear their throat on the other side of the glass.

"Looking for shampoo?" His voice was low and gravelly, filled with lust as his hand snaked in holding a bottle of mint shampoo. *The man must like his mint,* I mused. He didn't open the door any wider, and I nervously reached out for the bottle in his hand. When the door had slid closed once more, I breathed a sigh of relief.

I wanted the man, and bad, but I'd rather not have him in the shower with me. Sometimes a girl just needed a moment.

"Uh, thanks. I'll be out soon."

His chuckle echoed off the empty walls of the bathroom, sounding like music to my ears. "Sure thing, *Lizzania.*"

I shivered, but not from fear. The way my full name sounded on his tongue was like heaven, and I wanted to hear him say it over and over while that tongue was on various parts of my body. When the door slid closed once more, I quickly shampooed and conditioned my hair, not bothering to let it sit like I usually would. Something told me I'd be showering again very soon.

I stepped out of the shower to towel off, finding he'd brought me my nightgown and a night jacket, which passed for a short robe on me. It fell to mid-thigh, just like the silk nightie, and I briefly debated throwing my thong back on before throwing caution to the wind.

Who needs panties when you're planning to get lucky?

I smelled like I'd rolled in a mint patch, my skin smooth all over from whatever soap Lucien had stocked in his shower. I briefly wondered if he'd like the smell on me, shaking my head at the thought. *Cool your jets, sweetie. One step at a time.* I placed my hand on the doorknob, letting the smooth metal sit in my palm while my brain made one last-ditch effort to talk me out of this crazy idea.

You can still turn back. Most sane people would have already done it.

But I didn't *want* to turn back. This, for once, was what I wanted to do, and I would bloody well see it through. With a shaky breath, I turned the knob, swinging the door open as I stepped into the bedroom of my new Italian lover.

Lucien Sabatini, Vampyr.

~Lucien~

The moment the door to the bathroom swung open, I was toast. Seeing her in my evening jacket was hotter than it had any right to be, and I would bet money she'd look even better in nothing but my white button-down, the cuffs rolled up around her dainty wrists, the bottom hem just covering the swell of her perfect asscheeks. *Fuck, if ever there was a vixen that captivated me like this one, I had never met her.* My Izzy was one of a kind, and I was dying to show her just how amazing she truly was.

Truth be told, I was also eager to sink my fangs into her delicate, pale throat. I wanted to have her blood running through me as I buried myself deep inside her, in more ways than one. The idea sounded ridiculously cheesy, but I needed to feel her inside me as I was inside her. I wanted to connect with her on a level I'd never reached with another woman. I was ready for this.

Or was I?

"Ah, how was your shower, *cara mia?*" All the time in the world to prepare, and yet the best I could come up with was asking her how her shower had been. It was a *shower*. What an embarrassment I was turning out to be.

Izzy stared at the floor, lacking the self-confidence her lust had worked her into moments before. Her voice was barely a murmur as she shuffled her bare feet on the wood floor, anxious and timid again. "I-it was alright, thanks." She looked up at me, a soft smile on her face. Her eyes seemed panicked, and I feared she wouldn't be able to go through with it. As much as that would have been a tragedy, I was a gentleman who appreciated the principle of consent, and I would not force a lady, especially not this one.

"Do you still…want to do this? You don't have to—"

Her eyes rose to meet mine, a fire blazing behind those golden orbs that singed me in its intensity. The temperature in the room shot up, and I found myself slipping a finger around the edge of my collar, uncomfortably warm.

"*No!* I *want* to do this, Lucien. Don't try to talk me out of it." Her long lashes lowered over her beautiful eyes, and I watched her bite that lower lip intentionally, watching my reaction. She was baiting me, and I couldn't keep myself from responding as I watched her gaze drop lower, to my waist. When those eyes flicked back up to mine, I knew I was a goner.

"Unless, of course, you're *scared*, Luc?"

My eyes must have been nearly black with the intense Thirst burning through my body. *Stick a fork in me; I'm done.* "I am no coward, *stellina.* And you have never looked so delicious as you do right now, standing there before me, a willing sacrifice." I licked my lips, my eyes searing a path down her long, tanned legs. I couldn't wait to put my hands on them. "Come to me, *mia dea. Let me hold you.*"

Before I had time to wonder if I'd come on too strong, she walked into my waiting arms, sighing as I wrapped them around her tantalizing form. I nuzzled her neck, whispering into her ear. "You smell so good. I can't wait to take my fill of you."

A shiver of anticipation ran down her spine at my words. Her head was tilted back, her neck exposed, my hands wrapped around her waist, and yet she still managed to surprise me. "And what about after the sex? Will you still accept my offering?"

If this woman wasn't careful with that mouth of hers…

"I plan to take my fill of you in *more ways than one*, Miss Stanton. The real question is, are you up for the challenge? Is this really what you want?"

She squirmed in my grasp, wrapping her arms around my neck as she crushed her lips to mine with no hesitation. Her kiss was searching, hungry, *needy*, and I wanted to give her everything she desired, and more. I was hard as a rock, and this woman was unraveling me with every breath she took. Her lips ravaged mine, and it was all I could do to keep from going up in a puff of smoke as she trailed her hand down to my waistband, slipping a finger inside the elastic around my hips. I moaned, and her tongue dove between my parted lips, looking for more.

Hunting.

"Mmm, baby, what's your hurry? Eager to be on the menu?" I pulled away from those lips, trying to catch my breath as she melted in my arms. It's like she'd flipped a switch, and gone was the Izzy I knew. Gone was the anxiety-riddled, cautious, scared doe-eyed tease, and in her place was a forbidden fruit from the Garden of Eden, ripe for the plucking.

And I was no saint.

"I want you to devour me, Lucien. In so many, many ways." She ran her hands down the length of her body, the erotic display turning the animal on inside me. The beast was ready to play, and I could tell I was slipping away. I didn't have much time left before I would lose my mind and be taken over by my Thirst. *It was now or never.*

"Let me worship you, cara mia. Let me devour you. Be mine."

Her response was a single word, ripped from her throat as the fires of passion burned her from within. It lit my very soul on fire and threw us both over the edge of a cliff we couldn't climb back up.

"Yes."

CHAPTER 23

~IZZY~

I was loose, wild, and free, and I had no idea what had happened to make me like this. It was as if a switch in my brain had been flipped, and suddenly all my fears and tensions and anxiety melted away, leaving behind a woman in search of something unattainable.

Satisfaction.

Lucien's hands roamed my body, exploring as if we hadn't had our hands all over each other already once before. As if we were discovering each other anew for the first time. I thought I knew every inch of his taut muscles, his athletic build, his strong arms…but I was wrong. It felt more intense this time; every hair on my head was standing on end, and I couldn't stop the building need that pooled between my thighs. I gasped for air as his mouth trailed kisses down my neck, turning me around so he could trail those kisses down the back of my spine, sliding his night jacket off my shoulders to expose my back.

A slight draft wound through the room, sending a shiver down my spine as it caressed my too-hot skin. Lucien's finger trailed down after it, stopping just above my waist. He growled against the back of my neck, just below my ear as his fangs grazed my throat, and I closed my eyes, taking in the primal sound of his voice.

"Do you shiver in fear of me, *seduttrice? Do I intimidate you?*"

I threw my head back, laughing wildly at his incorrect assessment of my trembling state. "I don't shiver in fear of you, Luc. I shiver with my *need* for you." My hands wound around the back of his head, drawing his lips against the side of my neck. "Worship me, Lucien. Light the spark with your lips, and then put out the fire inside me. Just don't make me beg."

His low moan was all the affirmation I needed to know he would see to my pleasure like the gentleman he was. "Gods, *cara mia,* you're driving me insane." He walked us back to the bed, sitting down as he pulled me into his lap on the edge. His lips trailed light kisses down each arm as he slid the thin straps of my nightie off my shoulders, slipping my arms out before he dropped the top of the gown, exposing my breasts to the chilly air.

"I love to put these beautiful orbs in my palms; they're the perfect size for my hands to hold, and you purr like a little kitten when I do *this.*" His fingers tweaked the hard, exposed nubs, and I gasped in pleasure at the brief pain that intensified into pure pleasure. If I had been wearing that thong, I'd have been dripping from it by now, with the way this man could undo me with a single touch.

"Oh, yes…what *else* do you love about me?" I leaned my head back in ecstasy as his lips trailed back up the base of my neck. His legs spread slightly open, and I slid between them, my feet finding purchase on the cool floor. His teeth nibbled on the edge of my earlobe, and I couldn't help but notice that his fangs had come out to play, their sharp edge resting against my soft skin.

His voice was low, almost primal as he whispered into my ear, his words sending a bolt of white-hot desire straight to my loins. "I love the way you feel in my arms. Especially when you aren't wearing any clothes."

Fuck. I turned in his arms, shoving him backward on the bed, leaving his legs dangling over the edge. "Do you want to know some of the things I love about you?"

As my hands went to his waistband, my fingers brushing against the silver buckle resting atop his zipper, he stilled, letting a moan slip past his lips. Leaning back on the bed, his carnal response drove me onward as I rode this wave of bravery I had suddenly found. With a single flick of the wrist, I had his belt undone, sliding it slowly out of the loops of his waistband. The feel of the leather sliding around his waist was erotic and sensual, and I licked my lips in anticipation of what I was about to release.

"Tell me, Izzy—what about me attracts you?"

"Well," I mused, undoing the top button on his pants. His stiff manhood pressed eagerly against the tight fabric, but I wasn't ready to release it, quite enjoying this game of cat and mouse myself. "I would have to say," I whispered, a loud *zip* echoing as I slid his zipper down agonizingly slow, "I find your accent to be my biggest weakness." I slid my hand inside his pants, freeing his swollen cock as I beamed at him, my hands wrapped around his thick shaft. "That, and this right here. I can't get enough of *this.*"

He sucked air like a suffocating man, his gasp echoing across the room as I lowered my lips around his tip, swirling my tongue as I worked him, teasing, my own desire building like a raging inferno inside me. Between his ragged breaths, he begged me. *"Shit, Izzy, please don't stop—"*

I didn't plan on stopping, dear Lucien. I let my lips wrap around his thick shaft as I slid my mouth up and down the length of him, taking him all in while my fingers teased the hair on his thighs. His muscles tensed beneath my palms, but I pressed on, wanting to please him. I wanted to show him he wasn't the only one here in control.

I was a wild and free woman.

Lucien's hands wrapped around my face, lifting my head to meet his gaze. My lips were still parted, and I imagined I must look much like a freshly caught fish, unable to do anything but stare. His eyes were black, the irises a swirling void adrift in the whites of his eyes. This wasn't a hallucination; this was his true self. I swallowed down my shock, trying for a seductive smirk. Considering I had no idea what constituted a sexy smirk, I doubt it landed anywhere near the mark. But his tense gaze wasn't what I was expecting.

"If you keep doing that to me, I won't have time to properly prepare you for the pinnacle of this evening." He licked his lips deliciously as he eyed me much like you would a cut of beef at the butcher shop. His eyes were hungry, and I knew only half of that was lustful hunger. The rest was *actual hunger,* and it was my blood he thirsted for.

I smiled at that. For the first time in my life, I was in control of a man, and I was wielding all the advantages, all the power. It felt nice not to be burdened with my usual anxiety and nerves. My body froze as he leaned forward, capturing me in a kiss as he pulled me into his lap, his hands all over my hips as his tongue danced with mine. The pressure was building, and I twisted my hips, moving to straddle his thighs with my own. His cock bobbed deliciously against my ass, the skin-on-skin contact searing me to my very core. I wanted this man inside me, moving within me. The need was so strong it practically *hurt*, but I accounted that to my decision to ignore my own sexual needs for so long. I'd put myself on the back burner to throw myself into work, and I'd grown… restless. I pulled back from our passionate kiss, gasping for air.

"I want you inside me, Lucien. *Please.*" I was disgusted at the sound of my voice, the high-pitched whine sounding nothing like me. I couldn't stop to analyze the thought; I felt like my body was on fire. Everywhere Lucien touched, it felt as if he'd woken every cell in my body, and I'd become a sunflower, and he, the sun. My very being turned to him, seeking him out like the warm rays of light that were his touch. "I can't *stand it;* I need us to be closer. It's like my body is on fire." I stopped for a brief moment, remembering a little experience I'd had in my early college days with party drugs. "Did you drug me?"

His hands froze, his whole face turned down in a disappointed frown. "I would *never* do such a thing. What you're feeling is the Thirst. It radiates off me in waves, and what I feel, you feel, in a way." His hands went back to my ribcage and I closed my eyes, arching my back as his fingers drew lazy circles against my sides. I pressed my hips down against his lap, shamelessly grinding against him in search of the friction that I knew would ease this fire within me. But the feel of his manhood against my bare thighs, against my wed folds, it *wasn't enough.* I felt needier than before, knowing the prize was so close, yet so far away. Feeling disconnected from myself in the heat of the moment, I heard a low whimper escape my lips as Lucien's mouth descended on my collarbone, trailing little kisses down the path between my breasts. I leaned further back, giving him better access, pressing my womanhood against him as if my life depended on it.

For all I knew, it did. If I didn't get more skin-to-skin contact with this man fast, I would melt into a puddle in the center of his lap. *Why was I so hot? So randy? Why was I burning alive in the midst of sexual awakening? Was this all because of him?*

"Cara mia, I want to be inside of you. I need you." Lucien paused before breathing the next sentence in a near-whisper. "Are you sure you're ready for this?"

I yanked the nightie around my waist up and over my head, tossing it to the side before I lifted myself on my knees. I angled my hips to take him in, but before I could *gladly* impale myself on his generous sword, he grabbed my ass, spinning me around to face away from him. I wasn't sure what he had planned, but I desired his touch, I craved his kisses, and I burned alive with the need for this man. I wasn't about to ask questions. I kneeled above his lap as I felt the tip of his shaft graze my throbbing core. I could hardly believe the wild and needy moan that came from my lips was truly my own, but I knew it to be true.

"Jesus, *yes, Lucien, I need you more than I need air."* I wiggled against his tip, hearing his breathy moan behind my left ear as I felt him slide between my slick folds. *"Fuck, Lucien, take me."*

With a strangled cry, he thrust his hips upwards with a quick jerk, sheathing himself inside of me in one fluid movement. He fit so perfectly, it almost felt like I'd been *completed.*

Like I'd found the last part of myself and been made whole. When he slid back out of me, only to ram it in again, it was the sweetest torture, and I couldn't take it any longer. I reached behind myself as he rocked his cock inside me, the friction building the insurmountable mountain of pressure within my core. I wanted to explode, but I couldn't. It was as if I was still missing the tiniest of pieces.

His hips picked up the pace as my hand threaded into his hair, his lips against my neck as they searched for the pulse beneath. He inhaled deeply against my skin, his rhythmic thrusts never ceasing as I moaned out his name, still needing more.

"I want to taste you, *cara mia*, but I want to taste you as your body hums with orgasmic bliss. Let go, Izzy. Feel yourself leap off the edge."

I twisted my fingers in his hair, giving him a little tug. His growl against my skin was almost enough to make me lose it right then, but that wasn't what I craved. *"Fuck me, Lucien. Don't hold back. Fill me."*

As cheesy as it sounded, I couldn't take the words back. I wasn't in control anymore, but I didn't want to be. I was here for the ride, and I didn't care who piloted my body at this point. I needed *release*, and I knew only he could give it to me.

"Happy to oblige you, *my sweet.*" His hips pulled back, his tip dangling just inside me like a tease before he slammed into me with such force I thought I would split in half. Just as I found my voice to cry out his name, he pulled back again, his pace drastically different now. It was as if he chased the same release, fought against the same pressure as he held me above his lap, ramming into me with the speed of a virile predator. Over and over, he filled me up with such force I felt I would burst, and then his hands left my ass to snake around my front. With one toying on my nipple, and the other between my legs, working magic on my swollen nub, I could feel *everything*, and with the next thrust of his hard shaft, I shattered on top of him, his name like a promise, or a curse, on my swollen lips.

"Oh, *Lucien, yes!*" As I felt his cock stiffen inside me, he jerked wildly, his own cries of ecstasy joining my own as he came inside me, throbbing against my inner walls. I'd never felt so complete in my whole life as I did at that moment, and I sighed as I felt his lips against my shoulder, sliding against the sheen of sweat from our fierce fucking. I felt his tongue dance against my skin, and I moaned, unable to bring myself to protest as I swam back to the surface of my orgasm. I still shook with the pleasurable sensations, his cock still stiff inside me.

And then I felt his arms wrap around me, supporting my weak frame before he plunged his sharp fangs deep into my throat, and a sensation much like burning alive raced through my veins. I couldn't cry out against the pain, but as soon as it had come, it was replaced by pleasure so intense that I felt the walls of my core clench around Lucien's manhood in a fresh wave of pleasure. Just as I felt the edges of my vision fading, Lucien moved inside of me again, stoking me back to life as he drained my body of its life force. I arched against him, and neither of us had to search long for our final release as I faded into unconsciousness, riding another orgasm into oblivion.

As I nodded off, I heard the voice of an angel in my ears, whispering to me.

"Dormi bene, amore mio."

Who would have guessed angels were Italian?

CHAPTER 24

~LUCIEN~

While Izzy slept, I had not, choosing instead to pay a visit to the boathouse. I wanted to take Izzy out on the sailboat before it was too late to.

Before it was too late. There was something I thought I'd never have to worry about—Izzy leaving. I had hoped I would be able to convince her to fall in love with me in the span of a week, abandoning everything about her old life to stay with me. I had been a fool to think she wouldn't go. I knew it would happen eventually; I just didn't want it to. I thought I would be able to let her go at the end of the week, let her return to her normal human life, but after tasting her last night, feeding on her life force as we drowned in a united orgasmic bliss, I wasn't so sure anymore. What if I *couldn't* bring myself to let her go at the end of all this?

I vowed to make her time here as memorable as possible. So now, I would ensure the boat had everything we needed on it, and this evening, we would set sail for the middle of the sea, enjoying two days on the water in the comforting atmosphere of my favorite reminder of my past—*The Raven.* Such a fine ship, owned by the late Edgar Allen Poe. A man I wish I'd never met, and a boat I wish I'd never been given. But that was another life, another time.

Checking to see that all the lights and electronics were still functional, I went over the mechanics in my head, running my hand along the smooth wood that ran the length of the hull. It was like riding a bike—once you learned, you could set it down and pick it back up regardless of the time you'd been away. I had missed sailing, but the boat had gone back into the boathouse when *she'd* come along, ruining everything for me. *She* was the reason I'd shut myself off for so long from the rest of the world. Why I'd hidden from my emotions for so long.

Florentine St Clair. Heiress and pain in the ass. A vicious harpy with a dark soul and darker motives. She'd left me for another man when it became clear I had nothing of monetary value to offer her. I'd loved her as a human, but as a vampyr she'd become twisted, addicted to the power. It revealed her true self to be an ugly thing, straight out of the nightmares mothers warn their children about. She became insatiable, having no concern or care for protecting our identity. After I tried and failed for years to help her acclimate to her life, she felt trapped, stifled, and bored, and decided to leave me for a juicier target.

My best friend.

Florentine had hated this boat, and I had devoted so much time to fixing her that I neglected it. She managed to suck my enjoyment of the little things from my body, and when she left, she took my ability to care with her. I walled myself off, and aside from a few contacts, I kept to myself.

I yanked my hand back as a splinter managed to ram itself under my skin, more evidence that I had neglected this beautiful boat. *Not anymore, old friend.* "Today is the day we put you back in the water, where you were made to be." I patted the side of the hull as I spoke to the boat, knowing it could never speak back to me.

"Talking to inanimate objects is *so* Beauty and the Beast of you, young master."

Of all the times for Jasper to sneak up on me, it had to be right now. "Ah, Jasper. How nice of you to join me. I see you're back early from your evening appointment." His eyes were guarded as if he didn't want me to know what was on his mind, but I know he would tell me if I persisted long enough. "Any particular reason for your speedy return?"

He raised an eyebrow at me, crossing his arms as he sighed. "You know why I came back early, sir. I'd rather not have to spell it out for you."

"Ah," I mused as I turned back to the boat, "you're worried about Miss Stanton." Silence radiated from behind me, so I continued on, trying to get a rise from him. "Well, you're a bit late. I've already had my dinner."

"I would hardly refer to Miss Stanton as your evening meal, sir."

I shrugged, already tiring of the back and forth with the man. Right now, my body yearned to be next to hers, in my bed, and every minute I spent away from her was like torture. It gnawed at my stomach, and I wanted nothing more than to leave the boathouse and retreat into my room until tomorrow at sunset when I planned to launch the boat with Izzy and myself on it.

"Whatever you'd prefer to call her, she's fine and resting in my quarters. Would you like to check her pulse, Jasper?"

He cleared his throat, and I could almost see him sticking a finger around his starched white collar, loosening it in the tense moment. "Well, sir, I'd hardly think that necessary. Your word is good enough. About that thing earlier—"

I held up my hand, cutting him off. I was restless, and only one thing would calm me. "Please prep the Raven for a two-day excursion for myself and Izzy. I'll be launching tomorrow at sunset, and I need it to go swimmingly. Can you make it happen, Jasper?"

"I can, young master. But—"

"Thank you, Jasper; I know you'll have everything just so. I must be going; I do apologize for my abrupt departure." I waved farewell as I exited the boathouse, practically sprinting back to the house and up the stairs to my own door. Standing in front of the heavy mahogany double doors, I was suddenly struck with the urge to be silent, taking care not to wake the angel sleeping in the center of my bed. I tried to be as quiet as possible as I inched the door open, cringing when the hinges protested loudly.

I really *should* take better care of this place.

The room was pitch black, save for the moonlight filtering through a window on the far wall. A normal human would have trouble finding the door in this room, but I could see everything quite clearly.

Normal human, I was not.

I glanced over to the bed, where I quickly realized something was very, very wrong. The huge four-poster bed that was the centerpiece of my room was empty. And Izzy was nowhere to be seen. I froze up, fear racing through my veins at the thought that she'd left, or worse-

The sound of running water in the bathroom restarted my heart and brought me back to life as I realized Izzy was washing her hands, from the sound of it. I breathed a sigh of relief as the water shut off, silently laughing at myself. It wasn't like me to panic; I was always level-headed in any situation. When Izzy didn't emerge from the bathroom, I decided to check on her, not bothering to knock.

She stood in front of the sink, one hand holding her hair back while the other prodded my fang holes in her tanned skin. She winced as her finger touched a more sensitive spot, and I cringed, realizing I'd done that to her.

I enjoyed it, too. What kind of sick jerk did that make me?

"Those will heal a lot faster if you let me tend to them, *stellina.*"

She jumped a million miles in the air at the sound of my voice, not realizing until now that she wasn't alone. "Oh! Jesus, don't sneak up on me like that. You're going to give me a heart attack." She swayed side to side, catching herself on the counter before giving me a shaky smile. "I guess I'm still a little woozy. Maybe I should sit down…"

I caught her as she fell, finally getting a good look at her. Her eyes were dull, her skin turning pale beneath her sun-kissed tan. She was shaking and weak.

"I took too much blood from you. I'm so, so sorry…"

I carried her back into the bedroom, setting her on the bed before rushing back to the bathroom for the first aid kit beneath the sink. I yanked some gauze and medical tape out, along with antibiotic ointment and lidocaine, to numb the sensitive skin, and hurried back to her side.

Izzy was still conscious, but barely, and she looked like she'd given three times the allowed amount at a blood bank. I felt my heart constrict, seeing the damage I'd done to someone so special to me.

"Izzy, I'm going to go ahead and clean up the bite. It's gonna sting for a minute, but—"

"Just do it, Lucien," she muttered under her breath as she clenched the bedsheets on either side of herself weakly. I frowned, picking up the alcohol wipes before pressing them gently against her throat. She hissed in pain, but she didn't move, and I silently praised her fortitude and moxie. She was tougher than she looked, and she took the pain like a champ, allowing me to wipe and blot at the two matching puncture marks above her jugular.

I'd never before stayed for the *after* when I'd bitten other live hosts. I'd always left them in the capable hands of Jasper, or dead, as the case may be. But with Izzy, it was different. I realized now how selfish I'd been, leaving others to clean up my sloppy work. Her puncture wounds were mostly clean, neat little holes with minimal stress to surrounding tissue, and I knew that the saliva my fangs were coated in would seal the jugular after the fangs were withdrawn. But beyond that, I had never bothered to pay attention to what Poe had tried to teach me, more concerned with chasing skirts and enjoying the perks of immortality. When the time came that I was on my own, I realized how little I had actually picked up. Thankfully, Jasper had paid more attention, but it still reflected poorly on my character as a man. I was entitled, privileged, and a complete cad of a human.

Who was I now? Could I be someone Izzy deserved?

Izzy winced as I slathered a generous dollop of antibiotic cream on the puncture wounds, wrapping gauze tenderly around her neck as I inhaled her sweet perfume with each pass that brought us closer together. On the last pass, as I secured the gauze with the tape, I brushed a gentle kiss against the wound I'd left behind, trying to show her I appreciated the offering she'd so freely given.

It took a lot of courage to become the meal of a vampyr.

"How do you feel now?" I whispered the words against her cheek, an arm wrapped around her shoulder as I slid onto the bed next to her.

She reached up to touch the gauze, twitching slightly at the pressure. "It's sore, but not terrible. I've had worse."

"Your body's having a hard time recovering, so I'm going to grab you something from the kitchen. Will you be alright alone for a few minutes?"

Izzy nodded, offering a weak smile as I studied her carefully. "Yeah, sure. Go ahead."

I slid from the bed, making my way quickly to the kitchen to raid the fridge for some food. There were fresh grapes from the vineyard in a bowl on the top shelf and I added some strawberries to the container. I grabbed some orange juice, pouring a small glass before grabbing a bottle of water as well. Snagging a bar of chocolate and a piece of home-baked bread, I threw everything together before rushing back up the stairs. I hoped that the food I'd grabbed would be acceptable to her. I hadn't wanted to be away any longer than absolutely necessary.

What was happening to me?

"Izzy, I hope you like fruit because everything in the fridge was fresh. I just grabbed some of everything…"

As I turned inside the room, I realized she'd passed out again, and immediately I heard alarm bells in my head. *What a time for you to send Jasper off on a chore you could have handled yourself.* I chided myself for my foolishness, knowing I'd made a mistake. And once again, I needed someone to help me clean it up. I set down the tray of food, rushing to her side. Leaning in, I could hear she was still breathing, and the beat of her heart was steady, strong.

She's just exhausted. I really needed to stop panicking every time something looked bad. I was starting to crack up. I was none too fond of this feeling as a human, and I'm none too fond of it now.

"Luc?" I whipped around, my eyes meeting hers as I was filled with the greatest relief I'd ever known. I planted a kiss on her lips before rushing over to where I'd left the tray, presenting it to her like a child proud of their first masterpiece.

"I hope you like fruit. It was fresh and just looked so tasty. The grapes are from my vineyard." I knew I was sputtering nonsense, but I couldn't stop myself from talking. I was compelled to talk around her, for some strange reason. Her smile was reward enough as she took the tray from my hands with a slightly steadier grasp than she'd had earlier. Maybe the quick nap had done her some good.

"I love fruit. Thank you, Lucien." She popped a grape into her mouth, closing her eyes as she enjoyed every bite of it. I had to remind myself there was absolutely no way she was in any shape to do any *extracurricular activities* with me, no matter how good her lips looked around those strawberries in her hand right now. As if on cue, she let out a little moan as she bit into the slice of bread, and I had to adjust my position to keep from embarrassing the both of us.

"I'm glad you like it. You should eat as much as you need. I want you well rested and rejuvenated tomorrow for our trip."

Her eyes lit up, and her smile was already steadier, a testament to the willpower she possessed. "A trip? Where are we going?"

I smiled back at her, truly eager to make her happy. "I am going to take you out on *The Raven.* Two days, just me and you and the salty sea air. Jasper is stocking it up now."

"Really?" Izzy looked as if she couldn't believe her ears. My smile grew wider as I nodded, sliding onto the bed next to her. I grabbed a grape off the stem, popping it between my teeth before slipping it inside my mouth, enjoying the rich flavor of the special grapes.

"Really.'"

I wasn't prepared for her to fling herself at me in a wild hug, and it was all I could do to grab the glass of juice and bowl of fruit before she knocked the rest of it to the floor. I sat there, awkward and unbalanced as she wrapped her arms around my waist, snuggling against my chest. My arms were out to either side, and I leaned sideways to set the bowl of fruit on the nightstand beside the bed. Izzy seemed content where she was, mumbling into my shirt.

"Thank you, Lucien. I'm so excited I can barely stand it!"

I leaned back, tugging her chin up. "You're welcome, but I can't have you on the water in this shape. Why don't you have some of this orange juice," I said, handing her the glass. She sucked the whole thing down in one sitting, and I reached out to offer her the bottle of water I'd set on the duvet.

"Thanks, I was *so thirsty.*" She drained half the bottle before I reached out to stop her.

"You should slow down; you'll make yourself sick." She smiled sheepishly as she stared down at the water in her lap, twirling the lid around in one hand.

"Yeah, you're probably right." She glanced around the room, taking in the dark surroundings. "Should we get some sleep? I'm awful tired." Izzy moved to leave the bed, but I stopped her, confusion on my face.

"Where do you think you're going?" I checked her pulse discreetly again, satisfied with the hearty beating in her veins. She stopped moving, still avoiding my gaze.

"I was going to go back to my room, Luc."

"There's no need to leave. I have all this space, and I can certainly share it tonight. After all, there's only one bed on *The Raven,* and we'll be sharing it for two days."

A smile crept across her lips as she bit back a chuckle. "I guess I could stay, in the spirit of *practice* for tomorrow." When her eyes rounded on me, I felt my insides liquefy, becoming putty in this woman's delicate yet capable hands. "On one condition."

"Name your price, Izzy." I'd give her the damned moon if it meant pleasing her.

"I get to be the little spoon."

I laughed at her innocent and amusing demand, knowing it would be a long night ahead of me with her curled up against my chest. "Sure, *stellina,* anything for you."

CHAPTER 25

~IZZY~

Thank God I wasn't susceptible to seasickness, like my mother.

When Lucien told me he wanted to take me out on the boat, I was a bit skeptical at first. I wasn't the strongest of swimmers, and I'd never been on a boat this size with so few people to handle it, but I felt safe with him. He wouldn't let anything bad happen to me; I was sure of it.

We'd spent the first day scoping out a nice spot for a midnight meal, settling for a small island not far from the Sicilian coast. We'd drifted around for a while before Lucien dropped anchor, and there wasn't another boat or piece of land in sight. I slept like a baby the first night after being introduced to the finer side of using the *motion of the literal ocean* for maximum enjoyment. I'd fallen asleep curled in Lucien's arms, and when I woke today, I let myself wonder what it would be like to do this every day. Wake up in his arms, in his bed.

Knock that shit off; forever for him is a whole lot longer than it is for you.

I knew logically it would never work out, but I couldn't bring myself to care. My mind conjured up image after image of Lucien and I together, on the beaches, in the hills and mountains, in town. Anywhere a vehicle would take us. I wanted so badly to be happy, and I didn't even know how his kind worked. What if his bite turns me? What if there's something he's not telling me?

He taught me to dance on the upper deck, playing some old Perry Como music over the surround system on the boat. His moves were smooth, and I fell naturally in with him, no stranger to dancing. I'd remembered the basic steps, and before we knew it, we were in bed again, tearing our clothes off at breakneck speed. We couldn't keep our hands off each other, and the desire was building every day.

When he walked by, I couldn't deny the attraction I felt for the man, constantly having to remind myself there was more to life than just great sex. But that didn't mean I didn't want to have this man, naked and inside me, every minute of the day. The sex wasn't just great, it was *amazing*, and Lucien touched me in a way no man ever had before. But I kept getting this sinking feeling in the pit of my stomach. Something bad would happen soon. It always went that way when things were looking up for me.

I couldn't catch a break.

On the second day, I nearly cried when I woke to see the familiar walls of his boathouse coming into view. The two days on the boat had ended too soon, and I would give anything to buy myself another day, maybe two. I never wanted this time to end. I'd never had so much fun in my life ever before. And whatever this feeling was, I wanted to investigate it here a little more before going home, but I knew I didn't have time. I stretched lazily as I padded over to Lucien, wearing his white button-down shirt and nothing else.

"Morning, you gorgeous example of perfection."

"Bah, hardly. When I'm placed next to your wonderful self, I look like burnished brass to your polished steel."

We'd fallen into a comfortable banter, and I'd caught myself almost blurting out the big L word last night after he'd chased me over the edge of an orgasmic cliff. Thankfully, I'd still possessed a bit of intelligence left in my mind. That was a dangerous word, and I was about to be flying home in the next day or two. I'd probably never see him again.

I padded back to the cabin, where I had a bag with my clothes in it. I snagged the light sundress out of the backpack, strapping up the gladiator sandals I'd brought with me. When I walked back out on the deck, we were docking, Lucien's shoulders flexing as he tied off the rope to the anchors on the deck boards. I tossed my bag ashore, having packed it this morning when I got up, and I watched Lucien finish securing the boat to the dock. His hands were so sure, so steady as he tied those knots, and I thanked whatever god was responsible for the gift that was this man's body.

He had hardly put a shirt on the whole two days, not that I was complaining. It meant I got to wear them instead, which Lucien found sexier than anything else I'd stashed in my bag.

"Hey, daydreamer, let's head up to the house, shall we?"

I smiled at him, taking his hand as he helped me onto the dock. We walked slowly up to the villa, his arm around my shoulders and mine around his waist, both of us content with the contact.

We'd learned so much about each other while we were out there alone. Some of the conversations had been eye-opening for both of us, and I felt like I really understood him now. I thought back to the day before, smiling as I replayed it in my mind.

"So, tell me about yourself, Miss Stanton. I want to know everything."

I laughed as his hand brushed up and down my leg, our bodies stretched out together on the bow of the boat. I lay between him and the sea, against the edge of the rail.

"As close as our bodies have been to each other on multiple occasions, I think you could call me by my first name, Lucien."

He blushed slightly, clearing his throat as he glanced out onto the water that surrounded us. "Pardon my slip up. I grew up in a time much different from this one, and old habits die hard. Izzy, then."

"Yes, Izzy will work just fine." I closed my eyes as I leaned back, stretching out in the skimpy bikini I'd packed when I thought I'd be alone on vacation. From the looks Lucien had given me since I put it on, he

appreciated my choice of swimsuits. A lot. "What do you want to know?"

"How about your life? What's a day in the life of you look like?"

I leaned backward, sighing as the cool surface of the boat met my hot skin. I was glad Lucien had thought to toss some water on the boat to cool off the wood, or I'd have been blistered on the first day. "Well, I live in Florida, so it's always hot. I get up, get dressed, have some breakfast. I go to work at the museum, come home, and go to bed." I cringed as I realized how boring my life sounded.

"No friends that you hang out with?"

I shook my head. "None that aren't busy with their own lives. There are one or two people I stay in touch with, but that's rarely in person. People get tired of hanging around the woman with anxiety. It's not fun for me to attend big events or packed stuff like a nightclub, so I stopped accepting invitations, and they stopped inviting me."

His eyes were dark, narrow slits, but in the tiny fraction of his eyes I could see, I read the pity. I saw the sadness on my behalf, and I hated it. "I'm sorry your friends abandoned you like that. It wasn't very friend-like of them to desert you when you were uncomfortable. Did they ever offer to do things that didn't trigger your anxiety as much?"

I frowned, realizing they had never offered to do something different. They knew all about my condition; they knew the activities I wouldn't enjoy. But they never offered to do something tamer. It was never about the friendship, it had been all about what they wanted, and I was just an outsider pretty enough to be in the club but not cool enough actually to be more than an accessory.

"I guess they were never my actual friends. I was more of an afterthought."

He pulled me up to sit in front of him, his hands cupping my face gently. "People like that don't deserve your company or your consideration. I personally find you fascinating, and I would rather spend time with you than any other being on this earth."

"As sweet as that is, I'm under no delusion of grandeur. I know who I am. And I'm not that interesting by any stretch of the imaginati—"

His lips crushed against mine in a heated fervor, pulling me atop him as his hands roamed across my back beneath the white cover shirt I'd throw around myself. His tongue prodded against the seam of my lips, and I parted them, allowing him unrestricted access to tango with my own. His hands left a fiery trail down my spine and then back up my sides; I was at a loss for words. Every time I doubted myself, this man lit my very soul on fire, as if using his attraction to fight my self-doubt.

Lucien wouldn't hear of any complaints from me in that department. I very much preferred tangling tongues with this long-haired Lothario on his beautiful sailboat in the middle of the Mediterranean Sea to talking about myself.

"I very much like the way you silence me, Lucien Sabatini."

His primal growl was hot enough to melt steel when it vibrated against the base of my neck, and I shivered, already knowing what was coming for me.

"Oh, I bet you do. And I very much like silencing your words. But there are things I'd prefer to hear from you."

I obliged him, letting this charming rogue remove what little clothing I was wearing, worshipping my body with his own beneath the midday sun on the top of a sailboat in plain view of anyone who might pass by. He'd bent me over the rail and rammed me from behind; he'd had me mount him in the captain's chair; we even 69'd on the bow itself.

It. Was. Thrilling. And I'd never felt freer, more alive, in my entire existence. Sometimes I wished this could last forever.

"Earth to Izzy. Where is your mind at, *stellina?*"

I shook myself out of the daydream I'd been having, replaying our antics over and over in my mind. I'd never had so much fun with one person before in my whole life, and everything about it felt natural. I didn't feel anxious, I wasn't stressed, and I slept soundly when I slept next to him. So why were warning bells going off in my head?

I couldn't bring myself to shake the feeling that something was off, and I'd had that feeling since my feet had touched the docks. It only intensified the closer we got to the villa, but that didn't make sense either. I had been comfortable around Jasper before the trip, and I knew he was the only other person to inhabit this residence.

Lucien swung open the front door, planting a kiss against the top of my head as he pulled me inside. I giggled playfully at his antics, feeling slightly calmer with his distractions.

But my heart sank a million miles into the center of the earth when I glanced up to see Lucien look over my shoulder and freeze, his eyes wide and filled with rage and shock. His jaw hung slack, his face resembling a fish out of water as I turned to follow his gaze, my arm still wrapped around him.

"Well, Lucien, it's been a while, hasn't it?"

The strange woman stood, her brown hair laying pin-straight against her head, cascading over her shoulders like a graceful waterfall. That voice was so nasal that it made me cringe. It sounded like an uncontrollable whine on repeat. Her height could easily match Lucien's with the shoes she wore, and her eyes were the same shade of crimson as he and Jasper shared. I gasped, realizing she must be another vampyr. And from the look on Lucien's face, she wasn't one he expected to see. Her bright pink dress was offset by the fact that she was gaunt and looked half-starved. Her hair was brittle, and her smile was more of an evil smirk, her sharp teeth bared in what passed for a greeting.

Lucien cleared his throat, speaking slowly, as if in disbelief. "Florentine…why are you here?"

Jasper jogged over to his master's side, wringing his hands nervously. I'd *never* seen Jasper nervous. "Young Master, I tried to tell you, she sent word a few days ago of her intention—" He glanced over at the snarky figure behind him, turning his nose up as if she was contagious or beneath him.

Lucien was as white as a sheet, but his words seemed to be returning to him. He still hadn't moved, and I briefly wondered if I should move away from him or stay where I was.

"Why are you here, Florentine?" He asked again, his voice icy and dull as if he had no emotions towards this woman at all. I stared between the two of them, more confused than I'd ever been. His arm was still around my waist, and I watched as the woman he called Florentine finally noticed me standing there. Her eyes noticed our embrace, and they narrowed suspiciously.

"Are you playing with humans again, Lucien? Shame, I thought you grew out of that habit."

She took a step forward, and Lucien crushed me against his hard body, growling menacingly at the other vampyr. "You know you're not welcome here, Florentine. I suggest you leave and never come back. Don't you have a husband to go back to?"

Her eyes softened for the briefest of seconds, showing a hint of her humanity before they turned back into the cold, unfeeling things they'd been moments before. "I would, but he's met with an…unfortunate end."

"So you killed him." His response was so nonchalant I had to replay it over in my head to make sure he'd been talking about a man's life. "Why does that not surprise me?"

She eyed Lucien like a piece of meat, ignoring me completely. I was still so confused, but I no longer wanted to know what was going on when she spoke again.

"Why don't you share that little human of yours? I could use a snack, babycakes."

Babycakes? Someone grab me a barf bag; I think I'm going to be sick.

"Sorry, but she's not communal property."

"I wasn't really *asking*, Lucien darling. I want to eat. I need to *feed.* So unless you want to be responsible for my death, hand her over." She held out her hand expectantly as she moved forward, her eyes drilling holes into me.

Lucien shoved me behind his body as he reached out, wrapping his hands around Florentine's throat. "I warned you never to come back here after you absconded with my best friend, and my sentiments have not changed. You are not welcome here in my home, Florentine St. Clair, and you never will be. And my *humans* are not for your enjoyment, so keep your fangs in your mouth around Palermo, or I'll have your head."

She clawed at his hands, but his grip never wavered, shoving her backward towards the door. Jasper rushed over, managing to swing the front door wide open before Lucien flung the skinny woman off the porch and onto the ground below. As she stood, she dusted her dress off, pouting like a child.

"Lucien Sabatini, how *dare* you!"

"How dare *I?* How dare *you,* madam. You left this place of your own accord, and I told you never to come back. I meant every word." He slammed the door on her, his face showing indifference and rage as he turned, scanning the room for something. He stopped when he found Jasper standing in the corner beside me. "Jasper, I want you to check all the windows and locks, make sure that fucking harpy can't get in here. Lock up everything, and set the alarm system. I want no screw-ups. You know how unstable that bitch is."

He grabbed my arm, leading me upstairs to his room so fast it was all I could do to keep my feet moving beneath me. When we got to his room, he yanked the door open, slamming it behind himself. He turned and did something I'd never seen him do before: he locked a deadbolt at the top of the door.

Okay, *now* I was scared, maybe just a little.

"Lucien?" I reached out to touch his shoulder, but he flinched back from my touch, rushing over to the windows to check their locks as well. I'd never seen him so flustered, and it was enough to set me on edge. Whoever that woman was—and I thought I had a pretty good idea—he *feared* her. Enough to lock his home and stand guard at the windows.

Lucien didn't answer me, choosing instead to drag a chair over to the window and flop into it exhaustedly. He watched outside, his eyes dead and emotionless as he watched the psychotic vampyr female stomp around the driveway, kicking the side of the car, punching the siding on the villa. She even stopped to rip up flowers from the dirt, throwing them unceremoniously on the sidewalk. Still, his eyes were dull, lifeless almost.

"Lucien, who is she?"

He murmured something under his breath, not moving an inch. It was getting serious, and I had to do something. I went into the bathroom, filling up a large glass on the side of the sink with the coldest water I could get. Shutting off the tap, I made my way back into the room, standing just a foot or two from Lucien's still form. I tried one more time to get his attention before I resorted to drastic measures.

"Lucien Sabatini, can you say something?"

His eyes were glazed over as if he wasn't checked in. The time for debate had passed; it was now or never. I splashed the cold water in his face, giggling as he sputtered and coughed indignantly. He stood up to his full height, every inch the imposing vampyr once more. His hands went around my shoulders, holding me in place as he stared unamusedly into my eyes.

"What the *fuck* was that for?" Drops of water rolled off the strands of hair in his eyes, making him look like a drowned cat. I couldn't control my laughter, losing it at the sight of him.

"You look like a wet cat right now…" I wheezed, running out of breath at the hilarity of it all. He wasn't as amused as I was, and he pinned me to the spot with the steely look in his narrowed eyes.

"I'm failing to see the humor in all of this, Miss Stanton."

Oh great, we were back to last names again.

"I wasn't laughing at the situation, just at your appearance." I frowned, looking down at his shirt start to stick to his toned abs. *Focus, bitch, it's not horn dog time.* "I was trying to ask you a question, but you were checked out big time."

"What did you want to know?" He snuck a peek back outside, and I had to fight not to clear my throat.

"Who is she, Lucien? Who is the woman who tried to have me for dinner? And how does she know you?"

Lucien's eyes glazed over, but only momentarily. When he turned to me, they were as crimson as the day I met him. They were also sad, as if a heavy weight rested on his shoulders.

Did I really want to know what he was about to say?

CHAPTER 26

~LUCIEN~

"She was my fiance, from before I was a vampyr. Florentine St Clair, heiress and pain in the ass extraordinaire. She was a challenge, and I was a hunter looking for some challenging prey at the time. When I was turned, I became secluded at the instruction of my creator. For three years, I was missing, presumed dead at the hands of a jealous husband or a crazy drunken shootout. But I rejoined society three years later, and she caught wind of me, hunted me down. She insisted I honor the arrangement we'd had before I'd been created. Before I could tell her no, she was shot by a robber over the few replaceable things in her clutch. She wouldn't have made it if I hadn't turned her. I felt like it was my fault. If she'd never gotten mixed in with me, she'd have gone off to marry some rich man in the countryside, and she'd have never been chasing a ghost through the streets of Rome in the middle of the night."

Izzy stared up at me, her eyes holding no judgment. Instead, all I saw was concern and possibly empathy. She nodded at me to continue, and for some reason I did, unable to stop myself from spilling this dirty secret.

If I was going to win this woman over, she ought to know who I used to be. What I used to be.

"I found her dying in the street. I was drawn by the smell

of the blood, of course, and I was stunned to find her bleeding out from a gunshot wound. So I did the only thing I could think of—I turned her into what I had become, so that she could have a chance at life. At the time, I thought I was giving her a gift. But Florentine didn't see it that way. All she saw was a chain leading to me. She was content to blow through my money and feed her way through half the countryside's livestock before I caught her killing our neighbors. I drew the line there and told her I was putting my foot down. Florentine has never been one to take no for an answer, and she absconded with the only other vampyr she knew—my best friend."

I felt Izzy's hand on my chest, caressing my chest before moving to rest on my shoulder. I laid my hand on top of hers, meeting her eyes again. I wanted her to know how much this betrayal had hurt me. I had to hope she wouldn't do the same to me when the time came to make her choice.

"She left me because all she ever wanted from me was the money in my pockets and the title behind my name. I was a plaything to her, and in her immortality, she turned greedy, vicious, and mean. She said she'd be back when she left, but I told her never to step foot here again. We see how well she listens. I devoted my whole immortality to her, gave her everything she could ever want, and the ungrateful witch burnt my whole life down and left me for someone who let her run wild. I was broken. I walled myself off from the world. I forced myself to become emotionless, so I could never experience that betrayal again."

Her hands locked together behind my neck, her eyes downcast as she processed everything I had just told her. I could practically hear the gears turning in her mind, and I was dying a little death, agonizing over her response.

"So…what changed?"

I glanced up, staring deep into her beautiful amber eyes. *Now or never, you big idiot. Either take the plunge and tell her or kiss your chances goodbye.* "I fell in love with a woman I'd never even met."

Her eyebrows flew up into her hairline, her jaw falling

open in unparalleled shock. *Had I overdone it?* I held my breath, wanting to hear her tell me she'd fallen for me, too. I knew that it hadn't been long enough for her, though. I knew better than to expect her to be ready to say those words to me. She'd only known me a week—

"Does this woman know?" I could see the thoughts flying a mile a minute in her eyes, and I picked my way carefully through this minefield of words.

"I haven't told her yet."

"Why not? Don't you think she'd like to know how you felt before she has to go back to her own life?"

So she *did* know what I meant. This was our last night together; might as well go out with a bang. "I was afraid."

"You? The big bad vampyr, afraid of nothing and no one, afraid? What could you possibly fear?"

I cupped her face in my hands, bringing my forehead to rest against hers. I whispered against her lips, craving her like a flower craved the sun. "I was afraid you wouldn't be able to love me back, *cara mia.*"

"Oh, Lucien," she whispered, her eyes filling with unshed tears. "How could I *not* fall in love with you?"

~Izzy~

I pressed my lips to his hungrily, needing him to know just how much I felt for him after such a short time. I couldn't explain when or why or how I'd fallen for this man, but my heart was inexplicably tied to his in a way I didn't pretend to understand. His hands came down to grab my waist, and I jumped up into his waiting arms, wrapping my legs around his waist. If he didn't take the hint at this point, there was no saving the man.

He pulled back to stare deep into my eyes, his breathing ragged and fast. His nearly black eyes bored holes into me everywhere they looked, and right now they searched my soul. "Tell me, *stellina,* I need to hear you say it."

"Lucien Sabatini, I think I've fallen in love with you."

He nuzzled my neck as he moved us towards his bed, growling against the small bumps that were the only evidence left of his bite from the other day. "You *think?*"

I laughed at his playful possessiveness. I knew throwing in that word would have him riled up, and it worked just how I wanted it to. "How's a girl to be sure when she's never loved anyone before?"

"You've never loved anyone else in your life? There's never been another man you've fallen in love with?"

I shook my head, chewing on my bottom lip. "Never one willing to stick around long enough to give a damn about. Most men don't really enjoy waking up to someone who thrashes around in the blankets if they're too constricting, or someone who wakes from nightmares in a cold sweat mid-panic attack. I'm better on my own; it's been that way for as long as I can remember." He had pulled back from my neck to study me with sad eyes. *Here we go with the pity again.* I had to cut him off. "I'd rather not dwell on it, to be honest. It's a bit of a sore subject, and I do have to go home tomorrow."

His whole body tensed up at the unwelcome reminder that this would all be over in less than a day. Honestly, I felt the same way. I'd just started to get comfortable around a single human being other than myself and Rosa, and now I had to go right back to work again, under a new boss and everything. *Talk about anxiety-inducing.*

"Must you truly go back tomorrow? Why don't I call my cousin and arrange for—"

I placed a finger on his lips, silencing his protest. "As much as I'd love to spend more time here with you, I have a home, a job, pets I can't just abandon—"

"Okay, fine, you win. I'll even drive you to the airport myself. What time does your flight leave?"

"Too soon," I breathed, pulling him in for another kiss. "Quit stalling."

~Lucien~

I could love this woman all night into the morning, and it still wouldn't be enough. When she left tomorrow on that plane back to America, I would immediately feel her absence, and it would drive me insane if left unchecked. I wanted to be beside her every second of every day; how the hell was I supposed to do that from a different continent?

We'd made out, fooled around, made out some more, but neither of us was ready to move it forward tonight. The heaviness of the impending separation cast a gloomy spell over the whole room. I wrapped my arms around Izzy as she snuggled closer against me, her eyes on the movie playing across the room.

I'd thrown in a movie from the days of black and white, and I knew the words like the back of my hand. Maybe they held more meaning now that I had someone to love. I whispered them against her hair as I spoke in time with the main character. As if I was a part of the movie.

"Well, Darla, you see it's really quite simple. You live on the east side, and I live on the west side. We're from two different worlds, and tomorrow when you wake up, you'll be back in yours, and I in mine. It is what it is."

From beneath my chin came a faint voice, repeating back the next lines. *"But Hank, what if it were different? What if I just stayed here, and tomorrow we both woke up in your world together? Who's to stop me from staying?"*

"You and I both know you won't really stay. My world and yours are worlds apart, sweet cheeks. There's no room for a high-class lady like yourself in my world. You're too pure, too good for our world. I couldn't let you do that to yourself; throw it all away."

Izzy sat up against my chest, leaning into my shoulder as I wrapped an arm around her. I pressed my lips to her forehead, feeling just as desolate and desperate as the character on the screen. Neither of us spoke, but the characters in the movie did the job for us, saying what we didn't have the heart to say.

"Why's life gotta be so unfair, Hank?"

"I wish I knew, darlin', I wish I knew."

~Izzy~

True to his word, Lucien had driven me to the airport the next day after treating me to breakfast in bed, taking me out to lunch, and visiting a few tourist trap stores on the way there. I was convinced he was trying to stall so I'd miss my flight. But I didn't want his money to be wasted, so I urged him on at every stop, painfully aware of every watch, clock, and digital display we passed. Each minute that passed was another that I'd never get back and one I'd probably treasure for the rest of my life. Our lives were worlds apart, and besides, we'd only known each other a week. It was bad enough I was sleeping with him, now I was *falling for the man*, and I couldn't find the parachute. It would hurt when I finally hit the ground.

Before I'd left the villa, I'd managed to pull Jasper aside and bullied him into agreeing to keep in contact with me. He'd been a wonderful host the whole time I'd stayed in Italy, and I wanted to send him something from home when I got back. Some of Rosa's homemade baked goodies, perhaps. He'd been adamant that I called him when I touched down so that they knew I made it back safe.

I turned to Lucien, who was busy retrieving my bags from the trunk of his costly sports car. I wasn't sure what it was or how old, but it looked expensive. The leather seats were so soft, the wooden dash finish almost tantalizingly smooth, all the digital gauges on the dash hinted at extravagance. It had been a comfortable ride here, and now I'd be plopping down into a slightly lumpy, overused airplane chair for an eleven-hour flight.

"Lucien, thanks again for bringing me today. I had a nice time with you, and I wish it didn't have to end."

He straightened up, holding onto both of my bags with clenched fists. His eyes were narrowed, and his jaw was set; he was reverting to the Lucien I'd met the night of the party—cold, withdrawn, and brooding. He said nothing, refusing to acknowledge the finality of my departure.

I put my hands on my hips, following him as he headed for the hangar he'd parked nearby. Part of my anxiety was coming back, and my fingers absently wandered into my bag to locate my anxiety pills. With any luck, there'd be another tranq left in that bottle, and I could sleep for most of the flight. Lucien stopped at the door to the hangar, checking in with the flight director at the door. After signing a few papers and arguing over flight heading and departure times, he continued to the jet itself, and I realized I wasn't flying coach today.

He'd commissioned his company jet yet again, once again ensuring my complete comfort during the trip. Nobody to bother me, no feet in the back of my chair, no crying babies and panicky older men who had never flown before. I could just lean back, relax, and pass out before my anxiety got the best of me.

Lucien handed off my luggage to a flight attendant who stowed it while I stood at the base of the plane's stairs, refusing to board. Lucien seemed to be content to busy himself with anything he could, and as much as I hated to admit it, it pissed me off. For a guy who was so mopey about me leaving, he sure was doing anything but seeing me off.

"Hey, you gonna do everything yourself, or you gonna let them do their jobs?" *When had I gotten so bossy?*

Lucien turned to look at me, bearing a striking resemblance to a child with his hands in the cookie jar. He shrugged, looking away as he finished checking the pre-flight checklist, handing it off to the pilot who waited patiently to continue his job. Lucien mumbled a low "sorry" to the poor man before turning around to approach me.

"I'm sorry, I have a bit of an issue with control, and having everything *just so*. I want to make sure you're traveling as safely as possible." He glanced down at the ground between us as if our feet were the most interesting thing in the world right now. "I wish you didn't have to leave. I'd prefer it if you stayed here, with…*me.*"

What had gotten into this man? He'd never been this mopey before. Granted, I didn't want to leave either, but duty called. I had a job to get back to and too many loose ends to just jump ship and stay.

I brought my hands up to his jaw, cupping his face gently. His eyes rose to meet mine, and I could see all the sadness and pain and despair as plainly as when I'd first met him. "I'm only eleven hours away, and I promise I'll call as soon as I touch down."

He huffed, glancing over to the side of the plane. "It's not that."

"What is it then, Lucien?"

His fingers wrapped delicately around my wrists, tugging them down to waist level. "I feel as if this is goodbye, not see you later. And that…for the first time in forever, I don't *want* to say goodbye. Not to *you.*"

His eyes swiveled to hold mine with a soulful stare, and I felt tears threatening the corners of my eyes. "Don't say goodbye, then. I promise this isn't the last we will see of each other, *il tesoro.*"

Surprise crossed his features at my use of his native language. "You've been learning, I see." A smile crossed his lips briefly, and I couldn't bear to see it disappear so quickly. I grabbed his tie, wrapping my hand in it as I yanked him down to my level, kissing him as if my life depended on it. He stilled against my advance before finally wrapping his arms around my waist, pulling my hips against his as our tongues explored each other in one last passionate dance. My fingers knotted in his shirt, and I felt the tears roll freely down my cheeks, the wall finally cracking under the finality of the situation.

Did I really want to leave Italy? Leave him?

The short answer was no, but I couldn't just pretend my original life back home didn't exist anymore. Sure, the Italian vampyr playboy was a nice distraction, but this wasn't *me*. This was vacation me, *give-no-fucks* me. Eventually, I had to start acting like my usual self again and being the responsible person I had always been. But just for one more minute, I wanted to forget all about going home and just be *his*. I wanted to memorize every inch of him; I wanted to pack him in my suitcase and take him home with me. But he had a life, too, and I realized the deep, inner me was more selfish than I'd originally thought.

Lucien pulled away from me, his finger coming up to brush away my tears. A frown marred those godly features of his, dragging his brows together as he looked at the offending liquid on his finger.

"Come now; you're leaking from your eyes, *stellina*. There's no reason to cry. I'm only a phone call away, and if you ever get bored, you just say the word, and I'll send the jet after you."

I had to laugh at his absurdity. "That would get expensive, fast."

"I would spend all my money flying you back and forth on a whim if it meant I could spend more time together with you."

The pilot poked his head out of the plane, glancing down at us. "Ah, sorry to interrupt, but if we don't head out soon, sir, the headwinds won't be so nice, and I'd like to avoid the turbulence that comes behind it."

Lucien nodded, a steely frown settling over his features once more. "Right, I won't hold you up much longer. Thank you for the heads up." The pilot nodded, dipping back into the fuselage.

Lucien pulled me tighter against him, petting the back of my head as he breathed in my scent. "I wish I could bottle this smell and keep it with me. You smell so good all the time; it's like a drug. I can't get enough."

"Lucien, I have to go." I wiggled in his embrace, hoping

he'd get the hint. As much as I didn't want this to end, it was time to go.

His forehead came down to meet mine, his lips a hair away from mine for the last time in who knows how long. "Ah, how I wish it weren't so, *cara mia.* I want you to know, my heart goes with you. No matter what you choose to do in life, I want you to be happy. Promise me that you'll take care of yourself, *stellina.*"

"I promise, Lucien." I pressed one more kiss against his lips, managing not to cry this time. I really would miss him, and as much as I didn't want to admit it, I was almost sure I had fallen completely in love with Lucien Sabatini in this short week.

As I climbed the steel stairs to the waiting plane, I waved farewell to him, mouthing the words I couldn't bring myself to speak to him.

I love you.

The door swung closed on my short-lived fantasy life and I took my seat, watching out the window as we taxied onto the runway, Lucien's form becoming a speck in the distance, hand still raised in farewell.

CHAPTER 27

~LUCIEN~

Everywhere I looked reminded me of her. When I returned to the car, her seat was still warm where she'd sat on the ride here. The faint scent of flowers and fruit, her perfume for the day, hung in the air around me. When I finally made it home, Jasper waited for me on the porch, his arms crossed in front of his chest as he paced back and forth. As I pulled into sight, he peered into the car, his face falling when he realized I hadn't brought Izzy home with me.

Gods, how I'd wanted to, though.

I'd done everything I could think of to stall her, from taking her out to lunch to asking her to take one last beachside stroll with me. She rushed me through everything, insisting she needed to make it home to straighten her old life out again. I hadn't wanted to push her, but she seemed determined to go, so I let her. After all, you can't keep a wild bird caged for too long, and Izzy's wings were too beautiful to be clipped.

Jasper didn't wait for me to shut off the car before he was on my side, opening my door for me with a disdainful sigh. "I see the boarding and departure went as expected. Shame you couldn't convince her to stay. She's made the atmosphere here so much lighter with her presence; I shudder to think what it will return to in her absence."

I frowned darkly, shrugging my shoulders as I hoisted

myself from the seat in the car, not even bothering to close the door as I stomped sullenly inside. The foyer where we'd kissed so tenderly this morning suddenly looked so unappetizing that it made me cringe. I trudged up the stairs to my room, finding the bed empty of the one other person I yearned to see in it. Not usually a fan of dramatics, I flung myself across the bed, sighing as my hands balled into fists. I clutched the smooth sheets on my bed, breathing in the faint remnant of her scent. I rolled around in it, closing my eyes to shut out reality. *If I could just concentrate hard enough, maybe it would feel like she was still here.*

"Perhaps if you click your heels together three times, you'll be transported to the states and can greet her when she gets off the plane." Jasper's droll and unamused tone grated on my nerves as his dry humor fell on deaf ears.

"I don't appreciate the intrusion, Jasper. Can I do something for you?" I sat up on the bed, my feet dangling over the side as I tried my best to be imposing and intimidating. I probably failed miserably if his facial expression was any indication.

"Sir, we have to figure out how to deal with Lady Florentine. She came back around this morning, fists in the air, screaming and yelling about *her house* and demanding to be let in. If I hadn't threatened her, she'd have been out there all day."

My eyebrows rose at the mention of *threat*. "*You* threatened someone? With *what?*"

Jasper's eyes found mine, staring daggers at me. "I pulled out the silver bullets and let her see me load them in the revolver."

"But Jasper, silver bullets don't really work like that."

He sighed wistfully, a sad smile on his face. "*If only*...but *she* doesn't know that."

I pondered that for a moment, realizing I could use it to my advantage. "That's interesting. And useful."

Jasper nodded in agreement, his smirk growing. "I will leave you to your musings. But sir, might I make a suggestion?" When I made no move to stop him, he continued, emboldened. "Perhaps you should consider going to the states to bring Izzy back?"

"Bring her back?" I echoed, confused.

"Yes, bring her back. It's obvious you don't want to be without her. And you somehow manage to be very persuasive when the chips are down."

As Jasper exited the room, closing the door behind him, I played around with Jasper's suggestion in my mind. *Could I convince her to come back with me? Would she want to?*

Can I really live without her if she won't?

~Izzy~

Two weeks had come and gone, and Lucien and I had talked every day. He was the first person I spoke to when I woke up and the last voice I heard before I drifted off to sleep. There were quite a few nights I passed out while we were on the phone, and I could only imagine the snores he must have heard through the phone, but he swore he didn't mind.

He was such an angel, that man.

I hadn't wanted to admit it at first, but my body ached for him, my heart yearned for him, and I hadn't felt the same since I'd boarded that plane in Italy. I'd conked out for most of the flight and spoken briefly to Jasper and Lucien when I touched down. Jasper had tried his best to act like his jovial self, but something seemed off, though I couldn't put my finger on it. Lucien had seemed truly pleased I had called him directly, and he'd stayed on the phone until I had walked back in the door of my parents' house. Rosa practically knocked me over with a huge hug in the foyer, and my parents hadn't seemed to notice I was even gone. *Typical.*

Work had been ho-hum, considering there still hadn't been a replacement curator chosen. I'd had to catch up on a week's worth of callbacks and thank yous to every single person who'd attended the gala. Mrs. Daniels had been very accommodating upon my arrival and seemed to be genuinely interested in my trip abroad.

I sat at the curator's desk, sorting through paperwork when she decided to make an appearance. The door swung open with a flourish, admitting the usually calm and quiet woman into the museum's inner sanctum.

"Miss Stanton, welcome back! I'm glad to have you here at the museum again. You simply *must* tell me all about your trip to Italy!" She smiled at me, taking a seat in the chair in front of the desk where I sat. I had intended to move and allow her the seat, but it appeared she didn't want it.

"Oh, it's nice to be back, ma'am. I've been organizing everything that was set to go out when I left. Right now, I'm chasing down the information for our biggest benefactors from the gala night and signing them up to honor their commitments."

She sighed, waving her hand nonchalantly. "Come, come, enough work talk. Was my cousin hospitable while you stayed at the villa? Did he show you the sights, all the best places to see?"

Oh, I saw some sights, alright. Most of the best sights were inside his bedroom… "Oh, yes, I saw some great spots in Sicily. We tasted the local wine, ate the freshest fish I've ever had, and he even took me out on his sailboat! He's quite the avid sportsman, isn't he?"

She sighed, running a hand through her jet-black hair. "Well, to be honest, I haven't known my cousin Luke very long. He *is* quite the charming fellow, though. I'm glad you had a good time, but I'm equally glad he didn't manage to convince you to stay in Italy. I'd have hated to lose you."

"Oh, no worries, ma'am, I would never leave you high and dry. Besides, I believe in the value of training a replacement before abandoning an employer. Especially one as kind and accommodating as you have been with me." I shuffled the papers on the desk, eyeing the headings of the pages as if I was paying any attention to them at all.

"I wouldn't fault you for choosing love over work, Izzy."

Mrs. Daniels rarely ever called me by my first name, so I almost didn't realize she'd addressed the comment to me. "I'm sorry, what?"

"I said, I wouldn't fault you for choosing love over work." She crossed her arms, smiling smugly.

"Who said I was in love?" I couldn't help but reply with the defensive question, sealing my own fate unintentionally.

Mrs. Daniels rolled her eyes, sighing impatiently. "You don't have to *say it*, dear. I can see it in the way you stare off into space when you get off the phone with him. I can see it in the way you spend your entire lunch break talking to him each day. I see it in the way you carry yourself. You've grown as a person, Izzy. Love tends to do that to you."

I reflected on my feelings for Lucien and the two weeks I'd been apart from him. It was true that I'd been preocccupied since returning, but I *did* miss Italy. I missed the villa and the smell of the sea air in the morning. And if I was honest, I missed Lucien the most.

"I'll admit, I miss Italy. It was definitely a place I could see myself living out my life. But I wouldn't say I'm in *love*. I've only known the man for three weeks. Hardly enough time to love a person."

Mrs. Daniels sighed wistfully, gazing out into space with an expression of longing in her eyes. "I knew my husband was the one the first night we met. He *literally* charmed the pants off me, and I was smitten. I was also emotionally damaged, and he helped me rebuild myself after leaving a terrible relationship."

My jaw dropped open as I gasped. I'd never known my boss as anything other than the strong, fierce but quiet woman she'd always appeared to me. To find out she'd started out damaged, just like me, was a bit of a shock. Her weary smile reflected on my own lips as I wondered if Lucien had been the healing I'd needed, too.

"You should know that I have a curator coming over from the Antonio Salinas Regional Archaeology Museum tomorrow. His boss said he could spare him indefinitely, and I think he will be a great fit here. I only hope it turns out to be a good fit for him, as I'm surely unable to run this ship alone."

"But ma'am, you're not alone. With all due respect, you have me here." I couldn't help but protest, even though I'd never had the guts to do so before now. It was as if I had found inner confidence I hadn't known I possessed.

Mrs. Daniels's weary smile turned to a smirk as she eyed me sideways. "Yes, I do have you here to help me…*for now.*"

As she left the office, her perfume echoed faintly in the empty room behind her, lingering like the nagging feeling that there was something I was missing about what she'd muttered as she left.

For now? Was I going to be replaced?

~Lucien~

The annoying ringing of a loud alarm ricocheted around my bedroom, driving home the hammering in my head. I tried shaking off the groggy, painful throb, but that only made it worse. *How long had it been since I'd had an actual hangover? A hundred years? More?* I glanced over at the table, realizing too late that the sound I was hearing was no alarm but a ringtone. By the time I'd slapped my hand down on the screen and yanked the damnable device to my eyes, it had stopped, and a glaring missed call notice mocked me from the notifications.

One missed call. Izzy.

I hadn't heard from her all day, and here she was, calling at what must be a normal time for her, but it was sunrise here. I groaned as the room spun, pleading with my body to rein itself in. Surely I could handle a little alcohol here and there. I was a *vampyr,* not a *human.*

Jasper stumbled into my room, not even bothering to knock as he dragged ass over to my bedside, a smirk on his pale face. Apparently, he'd joined me in my misery last night.

Or he'd found his own bottle to wallow in. I couldn't remember enough about the night before to discern which.

"What do you think you're doing in here, Jasper? Can't you see I'm trying to die?"

His laughter was punctuated by a thick swallow, a hiccup, and a deathly low groan that I felt in the pit of my very soul. His pain was my pain today. "Young Ma-*hic*...master, you must get up. There's a harpy at the door who won't leave on my or...orders. You're gonna have to...*deal* with Florentine, sir."

This was most certainly not how I planned to spend my morning, arguing with a woman who couldn't take no for an answer. Thank the gods Izzy had the common sense that Florentine did not. How had I ever seen anything in this woman? Had there ever been a spark there? Had I really been that stupid and randy back in my youth that I'd overlook the woman's deplorable character to get under her skirts?

The unfortunate answer was yes, and I'd been paying for it ever since.

I rolled from the bed, throwing on my wrinkled and cold blazer before heading towards what would certainly be the death of me one day. *Women.*

CHAPTER 28

~IZZY~

As the new curator got settled in at the museum, I found myself enjoying his refreshing attitude. It was a welcome change from Mr. Chandless's aloof and distanced manner of handling things. As it turned out, I apparently had been handling all the responsibilities of an actual curator, most likely because Mr. Chandless had been content to make someone else do his dirty work. As I prepared the schedule and callback list for the day, Marc walked into my office with a smile on his face and a dahlia daisy in his hand.

"Ah, the beautiful Miss Stanton. How are you today?"

I chuckled at his greeting. Since he'd arrived, he'd been nothing but polite and respectful, his charismatic approach charming everyone around him. "Hi, Marc. I'm fine; thanks for your concern. I hope the meeting with the mayor yesterday went well?" The mayor was one of our bigger donors, and his name was on a specific wing in the gallery. Marc had met with him yesterday to discuss the plaque hanging above the exhibit.

Marc ran his fingers through his hair, sighing frustratedly. "It went about as well as could be expected. He agreed to the plaque the designer presented, and we modified the font for him. Should be ready to go in a week or two." A muffled *ding* echoed from his breast pocket, and he patted his jacket absently, pulling out his phone. "I think I'll take a look at the schedule for today, and I wanted to introduce you to your trainee, Bethany. She's going to learn the ropes under you. I want you to teach her what you know, what you do, and how you do it. Mrs. Daniels has mentioned expanding the museum, and she's planning to stock up on employees early for it."

I nodded, reading between the lines as he spoke. *Training my replacement is what it is. Did I do something wrong?* I replayed the last week or two over in my head, looking for any indication that I may have slipped up and done something I shouldn't. Daydreaming about it got me almost run over twice while walking to lunch. On my way home that day, I briefly wondered how bad training this new girl would turn out to be, considering my poor track record for human interaction with other people. Would I be able to work around my average anxiety to actually *teach* someone?

At the door to the house, I was accosted by Rosa, who seemed a bit…out of it. I couldn't put my finger on it, but something was bothering her. As she ushered me inside, going on about her brother and his kids, I let my mind wander to Lucien.

He hadn't answered when I'd called, and I was starting to get worried. Usually, he answered every single call, but he'd been missing a call or two every day lately, the frequency growing with each day that passed. Sometimes he would forget to text me back, and I wondered if maybe my shiny outer layer was starting to wear off, like a toy you'd played with and then grown tired of. I flipped my phone open, absently chewing on a fingernail as I scrolled through my contacts to 'J'. *There, found it. Jasper.* I opened a text to him, typing a single word before hitting a brick wall.

What did I want to say to this man? Was this going to be one of those things I looked back on and regretted? Or would this be the first time I actually did something I wanted to do, something that made me happy? My fingers flew across the on-screen keyboard as I typed out a short message.

Hey, call me when you can. Serious question for you. Don't tell Luc.

I closed my phone as Rosa called my name from the other side of the room. "Oy, *mija*, what is going on in that mind of yours? You seem miles away, not here in the kitchen. Is it a man?"

I laughed jerkily, my reaction coming off so unnatural that surely it wouldn't fool anyone who'd ever laughed genuinely in their lives. I cringed as I waited for her to call me on my bull-shit, but she didn't, so I did the only thing I could think of. *I lied.*

"Oh, no, Rosa, no man could occupy my brain more successfully than the ones in my historical texts. I've got an unrealistic expectation of what a man should be, and so I've resigned myself to living alone as a spinster my whole life."

She laughed back at my witty comeback, shaking her head as her eyes rolled heavenward. *"Mija,* you are too much. I don't know a single man on earth who could handle your particular personality."

I could think of one, my mind leered at me. I pushed that thought to the back of my mind as an image of Lucien Saba-tini, naked in all his glory, sprawled across his bed, staring at me with that *come hither* look in his eyes ran across my mind. The way his hands would stretch out, offering me a spot beside him. The way his eyes looked when I was inches away from them, and they swirled the darkest crimson I'd ever seen. When his voice rang out, it made me quiver to my very core.

Snap out of it, bitch.

"—*Mija, por favor,* your attention!" Rosa's hands were on her hips, the look in her eyes shooting daggers at me from across the room. I ducked my head, excusing myself before I got sucked into more conversation about a topic I absolutely did *not* want to discuss with Rosa at the moment.

"Sorry, Rosa. I have a lot of things on my plate right now; excuse me…" I shoved away from the counter, rushing up the stairs and down the hall to the sanctum that was my bedroom. In here, I could be alone with my thoughts and with the feeling growing in the pit of my stomach. *I loved Lucien. And it hurt to be away from him; it physically pained me.* I couldn't wait any longer for a response. Hopefully, Jasper would answer the phone. I needed someone to talk to who could understand the sensitive subjects swirling around in my head.

The phone rang once, twice, three times. I held my breath, afraid it would kick me over to voicemail at any minute. Just before I hung up, Jasper's groggy and rough voice came over the receiver.

"Why hello, Miss St-Stanton. How are you tod-today?" His hiccups broke up the usually smooth speech of the butler, and I was filled with a sense of dread I couldn't understand.

"I'm fine, Jasper. I need to talk to you about some serious stuff, though. Do you have a minute? Alone?"

I could hear Jasper shuffling around in the room he stood in, followed by a brief mumble and the scraping of a chair. Finally, he came back to the receiver. "I'm all yours for a few moments, madame. What would you like to chat about?"

I chewed my bottom lip, unsure of how to proceed. "So, I think…I think I might be *in love* with Lucien." I paused, waiting for him to comment before going on.

"Miss Stanton, I could have told you that two weeks ago."

I choked back a gasp, wondering how he'd guessed. Since I'd obviously fooled myself, I'd thought that maybe others had been fooled, too. Apparently, I was wrong. "I'm worried about Lucien, Jasper. He's acting…*odd.*" I held my breath, hoping he would reassure me that everything was fine and I was just overreacting. When I was met with silence on the other end, I foraged on, trying to get the words out before this new sense of dread settled completely over me. "I was wondering if there's something up with him; he seems…*distracted.*"

Jasper's heavy sigh was punctuated with a hiccup as he prepared to answer me. "Well, you know he *has* been acting a little strange since you've left. Perhaps you could come back and visit? I could always send the private jet over to pick you up."

I chewed it over in my head, wondering if I really wanted to do this. I couldn't get my head screwed on straight, and the last thing I needed was a distraction. *Or maybe it was exactly what I needed.* A vacation after my vacation. Like a drink for a hang-over treatment.

"Let me talk to my boss and see if I can get the weekend off, and I'll fly up to see you all over the weekend and fly back Monday for work."

"I'll let the pilot know to be on standby then. You just say the word." He paused for a moment, the silence heavy on the line as I waited for whatever he had to say. I groaned as I heard the *click* on the other end, signaling he'd hung up on me. *But what had he held back?*

I'd talked to my boss that same night, and Mrs. Daniels had not only been understanding, but she'd also practically insisted I get on that plane this Friday. I'd been given the day off so that I could travel early enough to enjoy the evening on Italian soil, so here I was...packing again. The bag was much lighter this time, and I knew I wouldn't be wearing much of what I brought if Lucien had anything to say about it. Jasper had been thrilled to receive my call the same night, asking him to move the plan to permanent mode. The pilot was ready to leave the station in Florida at 5 am, putting me in Italy roughly around 7 pm. If I was lucky, I could surprise Lucien at dinnertime, and we could spend the night catching up again.

Or doing other things that weren't fit for polite society.

I wrung my hands nervously as we drove around the back of the hangars, where the pristine grey jet waited on the tarmac. Lucien had no idea I was coming, and I had packed a few dresses I'd bought on my way home from work. Things I'd normally never have an occasion to wear. I wanted to surprise Lucien and show him I could fit into his sophisticated little *Vampyr High-Society Club*. I knew he'd accepted me as I was before, but maybe he'd realized I was masquerading in a world not my own, pretending to be someone I wasn't at the Gala when he'd met me. Maybe that was why he wasn't answering like he used to, why he seemed distracted.

Quit psyching yourself out ahead of schedule. You do enough of that in person; you might as well enjoy the flight.

I smiled at my inner voice, realizing I needed to try and relax without the aid of my trusty flight Xanax. If I could be calm around a vampyr with the ability to bleed me dry in a second, I could be brave about flying across an ocean. Maybe I could use this time to get dressed up since I hadn't been in the mood to doll myself up pre-flight. I knew that if I slept on the jet, there would be no reason to primp beforehand, but since I wasn't sure who would be waiting for me on the tarmac in Italy, it suddenly seemed like a good idea to make myself more *presentable.* I rummaged around for my suitcase, smiling when I pulled the gorgeous red dress from the bag.

It had cost me almost two days' salary, but I had fallen in love with the extravagant dress. Normally, I wasn't one to wear red, as it attracted a lot of attention, but I wanted to stand out for Lucien. I wanted to make a statement before I asked him if he minded sharing his luxury Italian villa with me again.

Maybe permanently, the little voice in my head whispered. I tamped it down quickly, scared that my brain had even jumped in that direction. It wasn't anywhere near time for me to be jumping into permanence, especially when I wasn't even sure what I was doing on a private jet headed for a foreign country.

Well, I had an idea, but that was beside the point.

I shuffled around in the luggage compartment until I found my shoes, pulling out some extravagant footwear that would make walking a challenge, let alone anything else. The red-bottomed heels had been a gift from my parents three years ago, a pair that my mother had been devastated didn't fit her. Begrudgingly, she'd handed them over to me, going on and on about how generous it was of her to donate such an expensive pair of shoes to her daughter. And she'd insisted I wear them to the Christmas party every year, showing them off and blasting her *horn of generosity* all over the parlor. Sometimes, I wondered if her friends ever got tired of her bullshit, but knowing how many similarities spewed from their mouths,

I figured she was in good company, as long as she could keep up the appearance of a luxurious socialite.

I felt the plane lurch a bit from some typical turbulence, but my brain overreacted, going into full-on panic mode. I clutched the side of my chair as I whimpered from my crouched position on the floor until a smiling flight attendant approached me, offering her hand. I felt the warmth creeping into my cheeks as I looked anywhere but at her eyes, accepting her hand and standing up again. I felt foolish for such a childish display, but I knew it was a risk, flying unmedicated.

"Would you like some help getting dressed, ma'am? I could help zip you up and do your hair while we fly over the rest of the ocean."

I looked up to see a smile on her face, genuine and friendly. Jasper couldn't have picked a better woman to assist me. Not an ounce of judgment shone in her sparkling brown eyes, and I chuckled as I reached down to grab my dress from where I'd dropped it on the floor.

"I'd really like that. Thanks," I breathed, looking around her uniform for a nametag. "I didn't catch your name."

"I'm Maria. It's nice to meet you. Mister Trudeau wasn't kidding when he said you really hated flying."

I cringed as she picked up my shoes from beside her feet. "It's not usually something I do sober. I try to sleep through flights whenever possible. High anxiety and all that jazz."

Maria smiled at me as she led me over to the onboard restroom, one larger than any plane I'd ever been on. Larger even than most home baths, with all the amenities. I smiled as she grabbed my makeup, confident now that I would look my absolute best when I stepped off this plane.

I had to, for *him.*

CHAPTER 29

~IZZY~

We landed in a different location than before, at Jasper's insistence. I'd wanted this to be a complete secret, and it was his job to get Lucien to Taormina, to where I would be waiting. I'd decided that I could use some practice walking in these heels I wobbled atop, so I took a walk along the path that lined the cliff face. The smell of the briny ocean air teased my lungs, reminding me of what I'd missed this whole time I'd been gone. *I could breathe this in forever. The salty sea air, the sweet grapes in summer…the distinct smell of amber, leather, and oud that clung to Lucien's throat…*

I'd been so deep in thought that I'd spaced out, making it nearly to the top of the walk. I'd forgotten I was walking in unfamiliar shoes, my gait becoming more even and practiced, more fluid as I put distance between myself and the bottom of the paved path. The rails here separating tourists from the cliff's edge were feeble, missing in spots, and it was posted from bottom to top with danger and warning signs. Still, many disregarded the signs, edging towards certain death and risking their lives, all for the perfect photo.

Idiots…life is more valuable than the next social media post.

I glanced around, reaching for my phone that I'd tucked into my handbag. My luggage was still on the jet, and the plan was for me to meet with Jasper before he would bring Lucien the rest of the way to me. I wondered how much time I had before the moment of truth, scanning my call log and text inbox for the last message Jasper had sent me.

There. He should arrive at 730. That means he will be here any minute. I glanced around again for Jasper's familiar visage, finally spotting his greying hair in the distance as he climbed the path. I smiled and waved, and his eyes went wide as he finally recognized me, offering a slight wave back. He picked up the pace as he neared me, panting slightly.

Could vampyrs really be out of shape?

"Well, I'll be damned. Lucien won't even recognize you, Miss Stanton! You *do* look absolutely stunning, if I may say so."

My red dress went to my ankles, flowing behind me like a flame in the wind, and the smooth, silken fabric hugged my body like a glove from my shoulders to my hips, where it flared out for dramatic effect. The long sleeves were a bit warm for Italy, but I just had to have it, and I was shocked to see how light the material was as it fluttered in the ocean breeze. I hoped it was elegant enough without making me look like I was trying too hard.

Jasper embraced me, and I let myself relax for once. My arms naturally went around him, embracing him back in what felt like friendship. It had been so long since I'd had a real friend that I wasn't sure what it actually felt like. I let out a sigh as he released me, holding me at arm's length to look me over.

"Do I pass the exam, Mister Trudeau?" I smiled as his eyes looked back up at mine, genuinely impressed.

"I believe so. More than I had expected. If his heart still beats in that chest cavity of his, it's sure to burst from his ribcage with one look at you."

My smile fell for a second as I remembered the real reason for our meeting. "I hope so, Jasper. But I actually had something else I wanted to talk to you about. Something of a more serious nature…" I glanced out over the cliffside at the expansive ocean beyond, the sunlight reflecting sharply off the whitecapped waves below. "If I wanted to become…what *you* are. What would that entail?"

I heard him gasp beside me, but I couldn't bring myself to look at his face. I didn't want to meet his eyes, afraid of what I would find in them. Sadness? Pity? Anger? After a moment, I felt his hand reach for mine. He ran his fingers over my knuckles as we stared out at the water together. Birds dove at their potential dinners in the shallows as their echoing songs clashed in the breeze, reverberating off the stone face of the cliffs. When Jasper spoke, his voice was low, almost a whisper.

"It isn't easy. There is a lot of pain, and you have to be on death's door for the process to work. So many things could go wrong." He paused, his brows drawing together as a frown crossed his lips. "Lucien would never agree to do it. He's hated himself for turning myself, and even more so for turning Florentine. There's no way he would willingly turn *you.*"

My lips were pulled in a hard line as I struggled not to cry. I had hoped for a completely different answer, but I'd known what he would tell me before the words had even left my mouth. "I knew you'd say that. But surely there's another vampyr out there who would be willing to help me out?"

Jasper's eyes narrowed as he tried not to look at me. *He knows someone.* "There are very few of our kind left, and even fewer who would want to spend the time and effort it takes to raise a new vampyr. It's not an easy task, and it can be dangerous if the newbie can't be controlled. People could die. And besides, Lucien would never allow anyone to hurt you bad enough for a transition to take place." He let the weight of his words sink in for a moment, chancing a glance at me out of the corner of his eye. I was careful not to give anything away as I steeled myself against the tears that threatened at the corner of my eye.

"It's not fair that I only get my human existence to spend with him. What will happen to him when I die? I'll have to age, and he will grow tired of the old, feeble woman I will become." My heart started to race, anxiety creeping in like an old friend who most certainly *not* welcome. "He will not love me then like he loves me now. Things change. But not him....only *me.*"

The tears flowed freely as I felt Jasper reach an arm around my shoulder, pulling me into his embrace. It felt like having an older brother must, or at least this is what I imagined it to be since I'd never had any siblings. I was doomed from the moment these two vampyrs decided to show me compassion. Shown me unbiased, non-judgemental empathy. They didn't let my anxiety define me, or my beauty. Jasper truly was worried for me. He was trying to warn me, let me down easy, instead of giving me false hope. It was a shame that I would only get a limited time in my mortal life to get to know him better, as well.

"You know, you're going to mess up all that makeup on your face if you keep on like this. And Lucien should be here any moment." I stiffened as he released his hold on me, pulling a black silk square from his pocket. "Here, dry that nonsense up. There's no point in lamenting the future you can't predict. You must live for the day you're in, for you never know when it may be your last. Now, why don't you worry about today and leave the future to the gods? I bet that you'll forget all about your troubles when you see who you're really here for."

I smiled at the image that crossed my mind from the day I'd left this island. Lucien, standing at the hangar doors as the plane taxied out onto the runway. I stood in the window as his hand raised in a wave, his eyes shining as the distance between us blurred the view. Or maybe that had been due to the tears that collected in my eyes as I left behind the one person in my adult life I had been unable to live without.

"How is he, Jasper? How has he been?"

Jasper coughed, trying to clear his throat as he turned to look down the pathway. "He's been better, and he could use a shave, from the looks of it. Don't turn around yet," he whispered as my whole body twitched with anticipation. *Lucien was here!* "He hasn't seen you yet, I don't believe. I wonder how long it takes him?"

I shivered as I felt eyes on my back, practically burning a hole through the fabric of my red dress. I had to remind myself to take a breath, forcing oxygen in and out of my lungs to keep my heart beating. The seconds stretched out as I stayed facing the ocean, my lips tight, my eyes narrowed. And then I heard it. The most magical sound that had ever graced my ears; so low and rough, yet so smooth, like a cold wind on a warm day.

"Would you like to explain to me why I climbed all the way up here to these cliffs to meet you, Jasper, when I could have met you at the bottom of the hill, by the cars, or, better yet, at the villa?"

I hadn't heard his voice all day, and it had been weeks since I'd heard it in person, and yet it still managed to send shivers down my spine as the words flowed from his lips. *The same lips that spoke soundless words against every inch of my skin.* I tried not to turn into a puddle on the ground beneath my shoes as I heard him step closer. Jasper tensed beside me, but his voice betrayed no emotion as he drew out the inevitable. *He was really enjoying this.*

"Well, young master, it just so happens the view up here is much more preferable when you consider the company." Jasper's hand tapped the corner of my elbow, and I glanced sideways at his face as a grin broke out across his face. He winked at me, his grin growing as I returned the sly smile.

The silence stretched out for what seemed like an eternity as I held my breath, waiting for Lucien to say *anything.* Every nerve ending in my body sang in anticipation when I finally looked into his deliciously sinful crimson eyes once more. When he finally rasped out words, I felt like my heart would give out from the excitement.

"Who might this be beside you, Jasper? Did you bring along a friend? I hope you're not up to your usual games…I'm not really in the mood for company."

Jasper looked over at me and gave a slight nod. I took one last breath in before turning slowly, my eyes drawn to Lucien like a magnet. I felt my palms start to sweat, my heart raced, and suddenly everything clicked into place. When his eyes settled on mine, it was as if my soul had settled after weeks of being adrift, looking for the port in a storm that would keep it safe. I knew that I would never again leave his side willingly, for I needed no other. His arms were a safe harbor, and his love, the pillow I would gladly lay my head on each night for however long forever might last.

I was *home.*

~Lucien~

I couldn't have been more surprised to see Jasper standing on the top of the cliffs with a woman. But when she turned around, my heart stopped. I picked up the faint scent of something familiar before my eyes locked onto those shining amber orbs that I'd been dreaming of for weeks.

Izzy.

Her smile snapped me back to reality as I struggled to remember how to breathe, the air searing my lungs as I took a tentative step towards her. When her lips turned up in a smile, my self-control snapped, and I raced over to stand before her, my mouth crashing down on hers with all the desperation of a dying man. She moved beneath me as her arms snaked around my neck, hanging on for dear life as I eliminated the distance between us, erasing the weeks in a matter of seconds. I'd forgotten how good she felt in my arms, and I couldn't imagine ever letting her go.

I needed to tell her how I felt. Before she left again.

I grudgingly came up for air, the cool breeze amplifying the realization that our lips were no longer connected. *What a shame.* My eyes searched hers as I struggled to form words to say something, *anything.*

"I missed you too, Lucien." She chuckled at my puzzled expression, her smile tilting my whole world on its axis once more.

"Ah, *cara mia,* promise me you're never leaving me again." I felt like a desperate young man again, but I couldn't bring myself to care. She was like water, and I was a stranded man in the desert, in need of my own personal oasis. I had to have her, and even I didn't quite understand how badly, or why.

"I don't think I could leave you again if I tried. But it would help if you shaved," she mused, rubbing her hand along the beard I was sporting.

"What can I say? When you weren't around to look at me, I couldn't have cared less what I looked like. Jasper's seen me worse."

Her laughter rang out as she wove her arm in mine, leading me further up the cliffs where the view was absolutely breathtaking. But to my eyes, the most breathtaking view here was the sight of my whole world, wrapped up in a gorgeous red gown, and balanced precariously on a set of heels.

"Izzy, what's with the extravagant clothing? It's not like you."

Her brows drew together as she frowned, going suddenly silent. "Well…I was hoping to prove to you I could be a part of your fancy lifestyle. That I could…*change*…to be what you deserved."

I slipped a finger beneath her chin, tilting her face up to gaze into her eyes. "You were perfect just the way you were. I don't need a trussed-up version of you to be happy. I should have stopped you before you got on that last plane. I should have told you then I didn't want you to go."

"You dropped hints, but I needed to go back. If I hadn't returned home, I wouldn't have realized how much I didn't want to be there. I wouldn't have come to realize that home, for me, is in your arms." Her eyes betrayed the deep emotion swirling and fighting behind her strong outward appearance, piercing me to my very core.

Home, for her, is in my arms. I'll never let her go again.

"Izzy, why don't we go back to the villa and get you out of those extremely uncomfortable heels and into something more comfortable…."

A sly smile played across her lips as merriment danced behind her eyes. "Like maybe one of your button-up shirts?" Her fingers trailed a hot pathway up my arm, and I felt my eyes darken as the Thirst rose inside me.

"You're in rare form today, Miss Stanton. Wouldn't you like to see the top before I take you home? Because you won't be seeing the sun for a few days once I've got you out of this dress."

She gulped, letting me lead her to the observation platform. I noticed a section taped off with caution tape, marking a missing piece of the railing. Steering off to the side, I looked off into the distant sea as Izzy inched closer to the rail.

"I've never been this close to the ocean and so far away from it at the same time. That's a hell of a drop to the water."

A familiar voice echoed from behind me as I admired Izzy in the setting sun, sending chills down my spine. "I'll be glad to give you the quick tour, you arrogant bitch! You can't have what's mine!"

I froze in horror as a wild and unkempt Florentine raced towards Izzy, murderous intent flashing in her eyes. I reached out to grab her, but she was too fast. She dodged my outstretched hand and zeroed in on Izzy, who had accidentally backed towards the missing rail in her terror. My eyes went wide as the rest of my immortal life flashed before them. Florentine's hand wrapped around Izzy's neck as she shoved her back towards the edge.

"P-please, don't do this, Florentine-"

Florentine let out a sickening cackle as she watched Izzy's heels scrape at the crumbling rock face, panic and sadness wild in her gentle eyes.

Izzy knew she was about to die. I made one last effort to break Florentine's grasp, but as my hands connected with Florentine's upper arms, she released my love, helping her to her death with one last little nudge. Izzy's eyes met mine as she disappeared over the cliff, her own cries of mortality drowned by my own.

"Nooooooooo!"

I fell to my knees at the edge of the cliff, unable to do anything as I watched the love of my life plummet to her death in the cold waters below. Her scream burned across my brain, engraving itself on every surface of my mind as the evil woman beside me cackled with pure hatred and arrogance.

"Izzy, no!" I didn't register Jasper leaping from the cliff after her, probably in vain. A fall like that would kill a human—my whole life, my happiness, all gone. I didn't even realize I had stood until my hands were wrapped around Florentine's throat. She clawed at my hands, her eyes wide in fear just as Izzy's had been as she'd been shoved to her death. "Why, Florentine? Why her?"

She sputtered for air, clawing at my hands in vain as I fought to keep from choking the life from her body until she'd answered me. She managed to rasp out a single sentence before the rage took over me. "Because you're mine, and I couldn't let her have you."

I crushed her windpipe in my iron grasp, shoving her backward with one swift motion. Very rarely did I tap into my elite powers, but I had lost all control. I threw Florentine from those same cliffs as quickly, as callously as she'd done to *mi stellina,* my heart breaking as it set in that my one chance at happiness had been yanked from me, just as fast as it had been given.

What would I do without her?

I felt my mind splintering into a thousand pieces along with my heart, and black spots were beginning to form on the edges of my vision. *What was happening to me?* Maybe this was what it felt like to die when you were immortal. Maybe the shock of hopelessness was too much for my body, and I was shutting down. Maybe I didn't deserve to live since I'd been unable to save *her.*

As the ability to process rational thought started to fail me, I looked skyward, hoping Jasper would find me and take care of my body, hoping Florentine did not survive the fall from those rocky cliffs, hoping I would die, so I didn't have to go on feeling like I had. Despair took over, driving me to my knees as

I felt a tear roll down my cheek. More followed it as I gasped for air, giving up the attempt to dry my face. Who cared if I cried?

I'm so sorry, Izzy…

I pleaded with her spirit to take me, too, as the darkness swallowed me whole, dragging my mind off into blissful unconsciousness.

EPILOGUE

A lone figure wandered up and down the beaches beneath the cliffs, dripping with seawater as he left footprints in the sand in his wake.

I can't leave her body here. I have to find her. Even if I have to fight the undertow for her, it's the least she deserves.

Jasper trudged along, his body tired from fighting the ocean current for so long already. He hadn't seen or heard from Master Lucien, but he couldn't worry about that now. He had to find Izzy's body, so she could be laid to rest properly. She didn't deserve this, and he wouldn't be able to rest until he'd done everything he could to recover her.

Lucien will be beside himself. I hope he doesn't go on a rampage.

In the distance, a shadowed figure lay upon some shallow rocks just outside of the sandbar. Jasper's pace increased, his feet becoming lighter and heavier at the same time. He knew it wasn't possible for her to have survived that fall, but if that body was Izzy, at least he could give her peace in a proper burial. He waded out in the waist-high water, stumbling over unseen rocks that tore at his feet as he approached the floating body. His hands grabbed her shoulders, dragging her to shore as he gazed upon the pale face of the woman he'd led to her death.

Izzy Stanton, dead before thirty. *What a terrible shame.*

When he'd reached the sandbar, he hoisted her onto the sand, the water lapping gently at the bottoms of her feet as Jasper looked her still form over. Her lips were blue, and she'd probably taken on a ton of water. *Death by drowning is a painful way to go.*

His fingers reached out to open the locket at the base of her throat, fingering the pale gold square gently. The pictures inside were of a Latina woman, easily in her fifties, wearing a soft smile and a white top, and a side view of Lucien that she must have snuck in while they were out on the boat. His hair blew in the wind, and he was…smiling?

I've never seen the young master smile. How sad that I probably never will now.

As he closed the locket, laying it on her cold skin, he could swear he saw her eyelids flutter.

No, that's impossible. She couldn't have survived that fall. Jasper reached out to grab her wrist, feeling for a pulse. His whole body jerked suddenly as he realized he hadn't hallucinated. It was faint, barely noticeable, but the heartbeat was there. As rationality set in, his brief hopes were dashed as soon as they'd formed.

She won't survive long enough to get to a hospital. She's going to die.

Jasper lifted Izzy into his arms, walking towards the long path that led up from the beach to the parking lot where his car was parked. He knew what he was debating was dangerous, and if he was caught, he could be killed. He'd never tried to turn someone before, and he wouldn't be able to go to his creator for help. Lucien would never forgive him for even thinking of turning her.

Jasper didn't even know if he would make it somewhere safe before Izzy's heart gave out. If she died, it was final. *No coming back.*

He ran to the car, laying Izzy out on the backseat before he sat behind the wheel and started it. The vehicle peeled from the parking lot, leaving a trail of dust as it raced off into the darkness of night.

ABOUT THE AUTHOR

Remy Cavilich is a West Virginia native with a colorful and diverse upbringing who has dreamed of bringing relatable and transforming stories to life for readers. From her colorful hair to her fiery personality, she stands out in a way few dare to, and so do her stories. Writing across multiple genres, she puts to use her college studies in English/Creative Writing and her real-life experiences to bring readers the narratives that keep them wanting more. Her breakout series, Out For Blood, opens with book one: The Thirst, a Paranormal Vampyr Romance.

Check out her website: www.remycavilich.com

Want a chance to peek inside Remy's Inner Sanctum?

The Inner Sanctum is Remy's hiding hole, her dragon horde, her wolf den, whatever you want to call it, and it produces a bi-weekly (subject to change at any time) newsletter chock full of fun character takeovers, interviews with a very irritable vampyr, and much, much more!

Take a bite out of her particular dry humor and quick wit, and let Remy hand you the keys to your own Inner Sanctum.

Printed in Great Britain
by Amazon

63627236R00138